THE PORTAL OF CHANCE

THE PORTAL OF CHANCE

CHRONICLES OF THE UNWANTED PRINCESS™ BOOK 1

J.L. HENDRICKS

MICHAEL ANDERLE

Copyright © 2020 LMBPN Publishing
Cover by Fantasy Book Design
A Michael Anderle Production

LMBPN Publishing
PMB 196, 2540 South Maryland Pkwy
Las Vegas, NV 89109

First US edition, September 2020
(Previously published as a part of *Chronicles of the Fae Princess*)
eBook ISBN: 978-1-64971-132-8
Print ISBN: 978-1-64971-133-5

THE PORTAL OF CHANCE TEAM

Thanks to our Beta Readers:

Crystal Wren, Nicole Emens, Micky Cocker, Mary Morris, John
Ashmore, Kelly O'Donnell, Larry Omans, Michael Baumann,
Daniel Weigert, Rachel Beckman, Theresa Holmes, Jim Caplan

Thanks to our JIT Team:

Angel LaVey
Dave Hicks
Deb Mader
Debi Sateren
Diane L. Smith
Jackey Hankard-Brodie
Jeff Goode
Kathleen Fettig
Micky Cocker
Misty Roa
Paul Westman
Veronica Stephan-Miller

Editor
SkyHunter Editing Team

DEDICATIONS

Dedicated to all you dreamers out there.
Never stifle your imagination,
and never stop going after your dreams!

— J.L. Hendricks

To Family, Friends and
Those Who Love
To Read.
May We All Enjoy Grace
To Live The Life We Are
Called.

— Michael Anderle

PROLOGUE

Lilliana ducked her head into the biting wind and continued down the sidewalk. Of the many reasons Boston had been the city of choice for her and her husband, the winter weather wasn't one of them. She pulled the collar of her coat close around her neck to keep off some of the chill, then moved nearer to the crowd in front of her.

Warmth radiated off them, but that wasn't what motivated her to get so close she could just about peek over their shoulders and see what their grocery bags had to say about their dinner plans. She was hoping if she crowded them enough, the people swarming the sidewalk and spilling out onto the edges of the street would take the hint and hurry up or allow her to pass.

Either way, she needed to move faster. The hair standing up on the back of her neck and the sensation of eyes scraping down her spine was enough to confirm her suspicions. They'd found her. Which meant they had found her husband and baby daughter as well.

Lilliana had always known this a possibility. She had never pretended—to herself or to James—that they could simply go about their lives like normal people and forget about her past.

Even if those tracking her hadn't ever found them, a part of her would never be able to fully separate herself from who she really was. That reality put her family in danger, and she had done what she could to prepare herself and her husband for it. From early in their relationship, as soon as she had revealed her secret to him, she had taught James how to move around unobserved and remain hidden so they had some chance of staying out of the grasp of her enemies.

They had succeeded for years, but not this time. They'd been too comfortable and stayed in Boston for too long. No home had ever been permanent, no city would ever be the place where Lilliana and James could settle and live out their lives together. Even after their daughter was born, they'd had to keep moving. But the contentment of being a little family had made Boston too much of a temptation. They'd lingered well after they should have moved on. Days had turned to weeks, which had turned to months—months on borrowed time. Now they were paying the price. She had picked up a tail.

A very good one if she had to make an evaluation. Whoever had been sent after her had tracked Lilliana without giving themselves away until only moments ago. She didn't know how long she had been followed or how much they had learned about her life. She couldn't go back home. Her enemies may have been in Boston for long enough to have already identified her home and learned what few routines she and James allowed themselves.

They may know the grocery store he liked to go to or the park they took Ariana to for fresh air. They may know his favorite bakery and the smell of the lemon spritz cookies which lured him there. They may even know that cobbled street she loved and the dips in the old, worn stones she knew so well. They may already know where she and her family lived.

But maybe they didn't. They may have just arrived and had happened to catch her trail early. She might still have a chance to direct them away from her husband and daughter.

But she couldn't go home. Nothing could make her lead them right to the people she loved the most. This was exactly why she had established a safe house in the city, far away from the cozy apartment they'd settled into when they'd moved here.

Finally, the crowd ahead of her dispersed over a wider stretch of sidewalk, some melting into shops or restaurants and others finding their cars. Lilliana rushed forward, weaving between them as fast as she could. The people she pushed past wouldn't have seen anything odd if they looked at her. Nothing stranger than a woman running like hell down the sidewalk occasionally trying to hide behind one of them. She was always careful to make sure her glamours were fully engaged before walking among the human inhabitants of the city. That didn't stop them from expressing some of their famed Boston kindness of spirit, complete with a few creatively woven, expletive-laden sentences hurled her way.

Their attitude didn't matter to Lilliana. She simply had to escape. If she could lose her tail somewhere on the streets, she could buy herself some extra time. She continued to bob and weave her way between people, pushing herself to move as fast as she could without drawing the attention of the police. Not that they could help her. They wouldn't be able to see who was following her. Besides, a wide-eyed woman rambling about mythical creatures and lands which don't exist probably wouldn't do much to help her.

At least the run was warming her up.

Lilliana hazarded a glance over her shoulder, but no one was behind her. Which didn't mean they were gone. She could still feel them watching her, and she had the distinct sensation of not being alone. Out of the corner of her eye, she caught a shimmer in the glass storefront of a nearby boutique. They were there. They'd managed to conceal themselves, even from her.

She ducked down a tight alley and out onto another street, where she turned and headed back in the other direction for several blocks. Returning to the first street, she retraced her steps. The detour delayed some of her progress through the city but would confuse the trail she left. She ran for several more minutes before she felt confident enough to pause at the stop for the bus that would bring her close to her safe house.

The wait was only a matter of a few moments, but it felt like she was standing there for hours. When the bus finally arrived, Lilliana allowed herself to be caught in the crush of people trying to enter and exit at the same time. Eventually, she was shoved inside, where she landed on the only seat left. She had ignored the little old lady behind her and she didn't even care.

Her hand shook as she fished her phone from her pocket, flipped it open, and dialed James. With every ring, she tried to regain her composure. He didn't answer. Then the beep of the voicemail sliced through her. This might have been her last chance to speak to him for a long time, and she wouldn't even get to say goodbye. But she couldn't dwell on her pain. What she had to tell him was too important.

"James." Her voice was husky as she tried to speak loud enough for him to hear her, but not so loud that everyone around her could. "I need you to listen to me very carefully. First, know that I love you and Ariana very, very much. I always will."

She drew in a breath and let it out slowly.

"I've been discovered. Someone has been tracking me. I don't know for how long or if they know anything about you and Ariana yet. You have to get out. Now. As fast as you can. There's a loose floorboard in the bedroom closet. There's a space under there where I've stashed some things just in case this happened. You'll find cash and the documents you'll need. Take all of it. I won't be going back to the house."

Emotion tightened her throat painfully and tears formed in the corners of her eyes, burning as she tried to bring herself to give the next instructions. They were so final. It had to be done, but Lilliana felt like as soon as she said it, she would be tearing herself away from her family completely.

"You need to make sure Ariana has everything she could need. Pack as much as you possibly can. You'll need at least a few days' worth of baby food and formula, diapers, and wipes. And a few changes of clothes. You don't know when you're going to be able to stop or buy new things, so you're going to have to take as much as you'll be able to carry with you. And don't forget Oscar."

The image of the blue stuffed bunny—well-loved even in the brief time he had belonged to her baby daughter—was all the encouragement her tears needed to spill over and sear their way down her cheeks. The other people on the bus could see her, but it didn't matter. None of them knew her. They didn't know what she was facing or what it felt like to leave this message.

"Please take care of yourself and of our daughter. She has to be your focus now. Think only about the two of you and getting as far away as you possibly can. Stay safe. You're not going to be able to contact me anymore. Just know how much I love you. I will think of you every moment we're apart and wish I was there with you. Kiss Ariana for me and don't let her forget me. Sing our song to her and tell her every day how precious she is to me. I love you, James. More than I'll ever be able to tell you. Now, run."

Lilliana closed the phone and shoved it back into her pocket. The bus was close to her stop, and the anxious feeling was building in the pit of her stomach again. As soon as the bus stopped, she stood and joined the stampede to the exit. She hurried down two blocks, turned a corner, and rushed into a seedy, stained, and battered neighborhood. Stopping beside a green metal trashcan which had spilled the contents of the bag forced inside by some dissatisfied, jaded city worker, she retrieved her phone and stared at it for a few seconds. James might call her back. If he did, she wanted to hear his voice and say goodbye.

The phone stayed silent. She drew another breath, snapped it in half, and dumped the useless pieces into the trashcan. The sensation of being watched returned as she kept walking. But there were people staring at her from their apartment windows and watching her progress from their stoops. A group of men took a few steps after her but hung back when she didn't slow down.

Her safe house was on the next block. If she could get inside, she would be out of danger—at least for the moment. She spotted her shortcut up ahead, a dark alley between two apartment buildings. As usual, the alley smelled of heat pumped through an exhaust fan and of trash in the dumpsters pushed up against the brick walls of the buildings. Littered with garbage and detritus from daily downtrodden life, it was hardly a lovely stroll. But it would get her to the safe house faster.

Lilliana was halfway there, slipping between two tightly positioned dumpsters. The end of the alley was so close she saw an opaque puff of breath from someone strolling by on the sidewalk. That was the last image she saw before an explosion tore through the air and ripped the concrete out from under her feet.

CHAPTER ONE

Phillipsburg, Montana – Halfling Fae Academy
Early June

"If you just focus a little harder, you can figure it out," said the halfling fae teenager. Her long, silver braid shimmered in the sunlight as she turned to address the girl standing across from her.

"Oh, because you're doing it *so* perfectly, right?" the other girl spat.

Several inches shorter, and with hair so inky black it had a blue sheen, she was a stark contrast to her fellow fae. Their appearances marked each of their differences, creating a visual of the distance between them.

As with the two boys who stood several yards away, they were from opposing Courts. Court rivalry was the reason they weren't getting along as they paired off to train in the field behind their academy, perfecting their abilities. But it was also why they'd been forced together.

As the most powerful and promising halfling fae of the Elmhurst Academiae Superiorum, the four young fae were required to train together by the headmaster. They were supposed to collaborate, build their skills, and assist each other to reach their full potential. On paper, it had seemed like a good idea.

With their abilities, they could become exceptional. If they worked hard, each of the four had the potential to pursue successful careers. It wasn't lost on Principal Elmhurst that some healthy competition among the four would push them all to do better and reach new goals faster.

But in practice, things weren't working out very smoothly. The two Seelie and two Unseelie were having a tough time cooperating, and the struggle showed when they met to hone their skills and work on new abilities. Principal Elmhurst didn't care about the tension. She had no patience for the politics and deep-rooted conflict between the Seelie and Unseelie Courts—neither of which were excuses she'd accept. The four had reluctantly resigned themselves to spending at least their foreseeable future at the academy together.

"Actually, if you would stop flailing around long enough, I could show you," Luna, the silver-haired Seelie fae, said.

She had always tried to encourage cooperation in the group and had made an effort to be nice to the others, but today Vivi was pushing Luna to her limits. Even Carson, Vivi's fellow Unseelie, put more effort into cooperating and making the most of their forced alliance. Not so much with Vivi. The somewhat embittered wild card of the bunch made no secret of her frustration at being stuck with a pair of inferior Seelie fae.

Vivi was absolutely confident in her belief that she was the best halfling at the academy. She would complete her education there, go on to graduate college, and have no problem at all in obtaining a job at the embassy. It was what she had to do. Her father expected it of her, and he would tolerate nothing less. She wasn't alone in her aspirations to land one of the highly coveted jobs at the embassy. Securing such a position was the only way a halfling could gain admittance into Faerie, and Carson also had his sights set on the same goal.

Though both had the potential to achieve such an impressive accomplishment, the most skilled fae in the academy was actually Luna. Quieter and more studious, she possessed a better mastery of her magic and tried to help the others—like Vivi—as much as she could. When Vivi would accept it, that is. Far more often, the antagonistic Unseelie pushed away any offer of help. Sometimes this meant choosing to do her own thing and figure it out for herself. And sometimes it meant creating trouble for the group just to make a point and have a laugh.

"We've been at this for hours." Zander, the other Seelie fae, strode toward the girls. "I'm hungry. Let's all take a break and cool off." This was his way of telling the pair to take a step back from each other before they started another fight.

"I'm hungry, too," Luna said. "Let's go to the café. My mom will make us something."

Meeting at Luna's mother's café was one of the few ways the four willingly spent time together when they weren't training. Like everyone but Zander, Luna had a human mother and a fae father. But she didn't know her father, didn't even know his name. She attended the halfling academy on a scholarship, and the only way Nicoletta was able to open the small café near the campus was through the secret support of an unknown investor.

Luna had always suspected that her father had sent the money for her mother to start her business. But Nicoletta had rejected the possibility immediately. She didn't believe he would go to such an extent to help them.

It wasn't that he'd had absolutely nothing to do with Luna. Not wanting to be a full-time father to a halfling child, he had left Nicoletta as soon as he'd found out she was pregnant. But over the years, he had been a part of Luna's life from a distance. Every once in a great while, he would send money for Luna. Usually, these moments of fatherly attention came when she demonstrated a special skill, accomplished a major task, or had done extremely well in a class. She pushed herself to excel for many reasons, but a fundamental part of her drive to do well was for her father. She craved his attention, even though she didn't know him or anything about him.

Nicoletta had refused to divulge even the most basic details to her daughter. She didn't tell Luna her father's name, or where they had met, or anything about their relationship. The only thing she'd revealed was that he was very powerful. Of course, to a human like her mother, Luna was also very powerful, so *that* piece of information didn't mean much.

This was another thing setting her apart from the other three in her group. She was the only one relying on a scholarship to pay for her tuition at the halfling academy. Even Zander had his dues paid by his fae parent. He had been left on his human father's doorstep by his fae mother and had never met her, or had anything to do with her, but she'd seen to it that her son attended the school and received a monthly stipend like the others.

But the café did well for Luna and her mother. Though humans often came by to indulge in Nicoletta's delicious cooking, the spot mostly catered to the fae, which included the halfling students. Few local eateries provided vegetarian menus. Montana was beef country, where restaurants offered heavily meat-based menus, so the fae had limited options when it came to grabbing a bite to eat. Nicoletta's diner ensured that the students at the academy, and any family who visited or lived in the area, had somewhere to rely on for a meal consisting of more than a plate of iceberg lettuce and a handful of meager cucumber slices.

There wouldn't be many halflings or fae in the café. Summer meant most of the students were gone. The summer season was supposed to be spent at home with their families, or on vacation with a fae parent. Usually, the only students who lingered around the campus during breaks were those who needed extra tutoring to hone their skills and abilities, and the orphans surrendered to the academy for training.

Neither case applied to Luna or her group. This summer, Principal Elmhurst had insisted the four halflings stay behind at the academy to give them more opportunity to gel. It was the first time in which students had crossed Courts to work together. These four were a unique unit. Never in the history of the Elmhurst Academiae Superiorum had a group of Halflings succeeded in harnessing the Power of Five. But the academy board and the principal believed it might be possible with the collaboration of these four, even with the unusual combination of two from the Seelie Court and two from the Unseelie. All they needed to do now was find the right fifth person, and they could accomplish this incredibly rare and amazing feat.

It had been centuries since any group of halflings anywhere had created the Power of Five. Most fae didn't even believe it was possible anymore. But Principal Elmhurst was convinced and had insisted on the four students working closely to try to achieve it. Which had meant foregoing their summer away from the school in favor of spending the weeks working on their skills and learning to deal with each other more effectively.

And while they trained, they also waited. Searches were being performed across various academies around the world to find their fifth member. Though conducted among the most powerful and highly skilled of all the halfling academies, the search was yet to discover anyone who came even close to matching the power required to complete the group.

They arrived at the café and sank onto the benches arranged out front. Vivi groaned and dropped her head back against the bench.

"I'm so tired of working with these Seelie scum," she muttered to Carson.

Vivi and Carson were from the Unseelie Court, while Luna and Zander were from the Seelie Court. Neither fae Court played well with the other. The fae could be nuisances, but the Unseelie seemed to have a bit of evil bred into their souls. Of the two Courts, a human would fare better after meeting a Seelie fae. Most human interactions with the Unseelie ended in disaster or broken hearts.

The lucky humans worked for the different Courts in menial labor positions, or they were used for consensual breeding purposes.

Luna and Zander ignored Vivi, which only made her angrier. She wanted a reaction. She intended to make them just as uncomfortable and frustrated as she was. Her gaze lingered for a brief second on Zander, but she looked away, forcing down the thoughts and feelings which always crept up on her when she glanced at him. She focused instead on utilizing her magic in a new way, a way to at least allow her to have some fun if she was going to be forced to work with the Seelie. A practical joke would bring Luna down a couple of pegs, and that was exactly what Vivi needed.

Zander looked at Vivi, not for the first time curious about the expression in her intense eyes when they flickered over him before she turned away. The possibility that she might like him sometimes flashed through his mind, but just as quickly as it did, he pushed it away. It was impossible. Simply being from the different Courts would stop it. No one ever crossed Courts for romantic relationships, not that he had ever heard of.

"I have an idea," Luna said, pulling them all out of their own thoughts and bringing their attention to her. "We've been having trouble working together to make anything happen. We can't just keep focusing on our individual skills and abilities. If we're going to accomplish the Power of Five, we have to be able to work together. I think we should try to create a Faerie circle of purple pansies. We will have to merge our powers together to make it happen. We'll have to be in harmony, or it could end up just becoming a jungle or some other disaster."

Vivi snorted. "Are you kidding me? That's your big idea? How could you be so childish?"

"We have to start somewhere," Zander said. "So far, all our other attempts have failed. We're stuck together, so we might as well put some effort into making something happen."

"Are you suggesting we sprout up some purple pansies right out here? Right out in the open in front of everyone?" Carson asked.

"No. We need to go somewhere out of the way," said Zander.

"How about the field outside the academy?" Vivi suggested. "Where we *always* practice."

"No. It's not isolated enough. We need to be able to focus completely," Zander said.

A tension simmered within the group as to who truly held the leadership position, but in almost all situations, the Seelie male was the one who rose to the top.

"There's another field on the outskirts of town. It's not too far from here, but no one is ever there," Luna said.

"Perfect. Let's get something to eat and then head that way," Zander said.

After lunch, they made their way toward the field. The two pairs walked along separately, each fae speaking only to their Court-mate.

"How am I supposed to survive the school year living with her?" Luna asked, glancing over her shoulder at Vivi and Carson. Their heads were close together, and the brief snippets of the conversation she caught told her they were also discussing the impending moves that would force the two girls and the two boys to live together.

"It's going to be fine," Zander said.

"That's easy for you to say," Luna said. "Anyone can get along with you. You're going to convert Carson into your best friend by the end of the first night."

Zander let out a short laugh. "I doubt that."

It might have been a bit of a stretch to imagine the two fae guys suddenly bonding and creating a tight friendship within the first few hours of forced cohabitation, but Luna could still believe it was possible. If anyone could make something like that happen, it was Zander. He was the undisputed golden boy of the academy, the type of student every teacher longed for. A parent could fill all the walls in the house with pictures of amazing things, running out of space long before *he* ran out of accomplishments. He led in any activity he chose and achieved straight A's in all his classes with seemingly little effort.

But his grades weren't so unique among the group. With the exception of Vivi, they all maintained A averages in their classes. Only Vivi coasted along just behind them, her report cards cluttered with B's. Not because she wasn't smart enough to score the same high grades and achieve the academic awards as the other three. In fact, she was brilliant. Vivi simply didn't apply herself to any of her work.

She used to work just as hard as the others, but her enthusiasm had faded. She'd given up pushing herself all the time after last Christmas. She'd been excited for weeks about the upcoming ski trip she was going on with her fae father. It had been only the two of them after her mother had died, and the time they spent together had meant so much to her. She would never admit that, of course.

Everyone knew how hard Vivi's father was on her, and the pressure he put on her to excel at everything. She wanted nothing more in the world than for him to show her love and approval. But she couldn't let anyone know that. To an outsider, she appeared to not even care. Giving up on trying for more impressive grades meant he didn't give her the approval she wanted, but it also meant she didn't get hurt as often.

Christmas had been her breaking point. She'd been looking forward to it, had worked hard to make sure there would be plenty for the two of them to talk about, and she'd silently longed for the praise he would give her. Then, exactly two days before he was supposed to arrive at the academy to pick her up, he'd bailed on her.

He had no big excuse, no reason for why he couldn't be with her. Only a terse phone message delivered by someone from the office. It wasn't just that he hadn't come or that they weren't able to go on their skiing trip. Her father punking out on her meant Vivi spent the Christmas holiday at the academy by herself. Her only companions were the unsociable halflings who got off on being alone...or had been abandoned by their fae parent.

Since then, she'd been pissed off and had carried an even bigger chip on her shoulder.

"I don't know which I'm looking forward to less," Carson said. "Being in such close quarters with Zander all the time or the swarms of Seelie girls who will darken my doorstep."

"Don't even try. You know you're going to enjoy every single second of it. You might only date Unseelie girls, but you'll mess around with anyone who has breasts. Zander living with you will just be like a funnel bringing in a constant supply of fresh girls. When he rejects them, you'll be right there to scoop them up and make the most of all their desperation," Vivi said with a laugh.

Carson had the reputation around Elmhurst of being a male slut, and he did his best to live up to it.

They arrived at the field and reluctantly gathered in a loose circle at the center.

"I can put up a shield to keep the humans from seeing what we're doing," Carson volunteered.

It took him only a few moments to create the enchantment that would prevent any wayward human from happening by and seeing them conjuring flowers and creating little bursts of magic. It was a caution they had learned to employ early in their education. Their academy didn't exist in some different realm or in a place inaccessible by anyone other than their kind. They were right smack in the middle of a very human town, which meant always having to be careful and avoid being caught.

When the shield was in place, they started their attempts to conjure the Faerie circle. Every time they got close, Vivi derailed them. Her concentration wasn't there, her mind too far away with her plans to punk Luna.

"Seriously, Vivi," Carson finally snapped. "Unless you want to throw up camp out here and rough it until this thing happens, you need to get yourself together and stop screwing around."

His threat was enough to make her focus, and they made one more attempt. All around them, the Faerie circle formed. It was large and impressive, and the group was briefly excited until they realized the blooms around them were black instead of purple.

"Vivi!" the three shouted at her, but she only responded with a smirk.

Zander cleared the field of the black pansies. "Again," he snapped.

"Who are you to decide what we're going to do?" Vivi asked.

"You're the one who's making this so difficult," he replied angrily. "Shut up and focus."

A few hours later, Luna scanned the large circle of purple pansies that finally surrounded them. She smiled and nodded. "It looks good," she said. "Let's try another one."

Carson and Zander murmured in agreement, but Vivi scowled and backed away from them. With a slight sweep of her hand, she turned all the purple blooms black again and crouched to gather some in a bouquet. She presented them to Zander with a mocking smile. Instead of taking them, the Seelie male snapped his fingers and the flowers disintegrated in her hand.

"Don't be too impressed with yourself because of your little parlor trick," he said to Vivi. "Any of us could change the colors of the flowers. In fact, any of us could create the entire circle on our own. The difficult part of this is creating something with the four of us merging our powers together. It's the combination that matters. We have to be in harmony in order to accomplish tasks together."

The reason they were attempting to obtain the Power of Five was the level of power it would bring them. If a full-blooded group of fae obtained the Power of Five, they could do anything. Bring down planes, build a skyscraper in a day, make an entire neighborhood disappear, really anything they set their minds to. Of course, the fae knew not to mess with humans on such a grand scale.

But for a group of Halflings to obtain the Power of Five meant great respect from the Faerie world. They couldn't do quite as much as a full-blooded Power of Five could, but if records were correct, a halfling Power of Five could do more than any individual fae could.

The Seelie and Unseelie Queens could use them to keep the rebels at bay. The Power of Five could be harnessed to defend the Faerie Courts, or any large group the Courts deemed worthy of protection. They could also be used as a weapon against their enemies.

Vivi didn't want to hear it. She still believed Luna's plan to be woefully childish, and that it offered no real benefit as they worked on their abilities. Creating Faerie circles was something the halflings learned before puberty. A very basic skill, it was a common feature of playtime for the young of their kind. The challenge came when trying to do it as a group. Just the temperaments of such different people working together rendered the task almost impossible.

"It's a huge achievement that we were even able to do this to begin with," Luna said. "We need to keep practicing so we can get better at it."

Zander moved to stand between Luna and Vivi. "Look, we all know these tricks are child's play. The difficulty comes in merging our powers together. That's what the Power of Five is all about. If we can learn to work together in harmony, we will be unstoppable and can do anything we want."

"No," Vivi said. "I'm done. We've been out here for hours, and I've had my fill of silly flowers. I want to leave." Sometimes, she even wondered why they were trying. Sure, if she was one of the Five, she'd get her dream job, or rather her father's dream of what her job should be. But she was beginning to understand that her father would never show her any love. He was using her to advance his own status, exactly like most fae parents did with any of their children.

It wouldn't matter if she was one of the most powerful halfling fae in the world. She still wouldn't be worthy of his love.

CHAPTER TWO

Both sets of students dragged their feet as much as they could when it came to moving in together. The idea of being pushed together to work on their skills while giving up the break all the other students were enjoying was frustrating enough. Having to live in the same small space meant not even enjoying the relief of a break from each other when they were sleeping or relaxing at the end of the day. They were forced to be together, forced to deal with each other from the moment they opened their eyes in the morning until they closed them again at night. And technically even the time in between. The thought was intolerable.

But they could only resist the commands of the principal for so long. Living together was part of being a group. The more time they spent with each other, the better the chances they had of getting along. Even if they never learned to actually like each other, they would learn to cooperate. They could mesh their skills and abilities, increasing their powers to strengthen and improve each other's. None of them had believed that was going to happen, but they hadn't been given a choice. What Principal Elmhurst wanted, she got. It had only been a matter of time before they were ejected from their existing rooms and wedged into new ones with each other.

And that time had come.

Luna surveyed the room. She'd arrived first, which meant it was her choice which bed she wanted to claim for her own. It was an important decision. This would be the only space she'd be able to call hers for the rest of her time at the academy. Two more years. Or until Elmhurst had another idea and moved them again.

Luna considered each of the two beds. They were positioned in opposite corners, which at least provided some semblance of separation between them. It wasn't exactly privacy, but it was something.

Finally, she decided on the bed tucked into the corner next to a window with a view of the grounds beyond the heavy curtains, and it was on the other side of the room from the door to the hallway. It would be less noisy and give her more of a feeling of her own area. She set her trunk on the floor beside the bed and lifted the lid. No sooner had she reached in to take out her pajamas than the door to the room slammed open and stomping footsteps announced the arrival of her reluctant new roommate.

"Who says you get that bed?" Vivi immediately demanded.

"Hello to you, too," Luna said.

"That's the bed I want," the Unseelie fae said. "You're going to have to move to the other one."

Luna scoffed. "No. I was the first one to get here, which means I got to choose the bed I want. This one's mine."

"I don't care if you were the first one here. That's the bed I want," Vivi said, her voice creeping up louder.

"Again, no," Luna said.

Vivi tossed her bag onto the other bed and pushed her trunk up against the side of the bed with her foot. She eyed Luna's trunk, and a vicious smile curled her lips up. Focusing her magic on the clothes stacked inside, she shifted them around until she found what she was looking for.

"Here," she said, "let me help you unpack, roomie."

She lifted the pairs of neatly folded underwear from the trunk and made them float over Luna's head. They unfolded and puffed out in the air, looking like the sails of a ship. Luna let out an infuriated cry.

"Stop that!" She reached up to grab them, but Vivi lifted them higher. "What in Buddha's name is wrong with you?"

"I'm just curious. Has anyone even ever seen these things? I doubt it. Why would you want to show off dingy briefs? I guess this is all the proof I need that you aren't getting any play from anyone."

"Tell me, Vivi. Do you have to distribute numbered tickets for access to yours? Like at a deli counter? Now serving..."

The girls dissolved into a fierce argument, tearing into each other until the door opened again.

"Hey! Stop it, the two of you!" Zander shouted over their voices. "You've only lived together for ten minutes, and you're already on the brink of killing each other. This is ridiculous. At least try to get along. Vivi, put Luna's underwear down. Luna, stop making fun of Vivi. This is a seriously uncomfortable conversation for me, so I'd appreciate it if you just went ahead and cooperated. It's going to be better for everyone if you at least put a little bit of effort into co-existing with each other."

"So, does this mean all is fantastic over at the House of Zander and Carson?" Vivi snipped.

"Why does he get to come first in the title? You know, alphabetical order is the most widely accepted method of categorization in lists, and according to that standard, I would come first, making it the House of Carson and Zander," Carson said, appearing at the door.

No one could tell if he was joking or being serious, but it didn't matter. He strode into the room and approached Vivi.

Though he tried not to let it show, his growing feelings for her would be obvious when he looked at her. The last thing the group needed was the additional tension if she rejected his crush on her.

"Vivi, Principal Elmhurst is looking for you. She wants you to go to her office before practice this afternoon," Carson said.

"Why? What's going on?" Vivi asked.

"Do you have a whole lot of time for me to make a list for you?" Luna crossed her arms over her chest.

Zander muffled a laugh and walked across the room to offer his help unpacking. "Be nice," he murmured to her.

"Why?" Luna asked.

"I don't need her to be nice," Vivi said, tossing one last rude comment to them before sweeping out of the room with Carson.

She hated seeing the way Luna associated with Zander. They were so comfortable with each other. He spoke to her easily, and she was able to laugh and smile with him without the uncertainty and uneasiness Vivi felt when she was near him. They didn't seem to have a spark of interest between them, but their close friendship made Vivi seethe with jealousy.

Carson strode beside her as she made her way to the principal's dark, imposing office at the front of the school. He lingered until she knocked on the door and Elmhurst called out for her to come inside. She glanced at Carson for an instant before going in.

"You wanted to see me?" Vivi asked.

"Your father wants you to call him," Principal Elmhurst said, without even a greeting.

"All right. I'll call when I finish practice this afternoon."

"Now. He says it's important that he speak to you as soon as possible," the principal said.

Vivi's heart jumped a little, and she swallowed hard and nodded. Elmhurst directed her to the small alcove at the side of the office containing the only phone available for student use.

She picked it up and dialed her father's number. The ringing buzzed in her chest. He let it ring longer than usual, and Vivi knew it was on purpose. Each ring increased her anxiety and reminded her of the control he had over her.

"Hello?" he answered.

"Hi, Dad," she said.

It only took those two words to start his onslaught. "What is wrong with you?" he demanded.

"What do you mean?" she asked.

"I've heard of your antics. I know what you've been doing during the time you should be spending studying at that expensive school. I didn't send you there so you could torment your fellow students and make a fool of yourself. Don't forget who you are and what you are supposed to achieve. Only excellence matters. Your grades are abominable, and I believe I have been extremely understanding and patient with you. No more, Vivi. Do you understand me? I'm tired of hearing about your mistakes and failures. If you don't get your act together, I won't be seeing you at Christmas," he growled angrily.

Her stomach clenched and heat rushed across her cheeks. Last Christmas had been a crushing blow. The promise of going on the trip this year dangled in front of her, pushing her through when she was ready to throw in the towel. Now he was threatening to pull it out from under her again.

"Yes, Dad," she said quietly.

"We will go only if you behave. If going skiing in Switzerland means anything to you, you will figure out what has been happening and leading you down this path, and you will straighten yourself out. Am I understood?" he asked.

"Yes, Dad." This was her chance to defend herself, and she took it. "But you have to understand what I'm going through. They are making me work with those people."

"I know, Vivi. I hate that you have been paired with the Seelie as well, but I also see the value in the experiment."

"You do?" she asked, startled by the declaration. Her father hadn't talked much about the pairing other than acknowledging that she'd have to stay on campus at the academy through the summer.

"Yes. Life isn't always easy, and you won't get the luxury of only working with people you know, understand, and agree with. You will be forced into difficult situations and be in circumstances requiring you to work with people of all kinds. Training starts now. If you are able to work with the Seelie, it will go a long way toward helping you get that embassy job."

"Yes, Dad."

She was still juggling with the feeling of conflict an hour later when she and Carson walked out onto the field to meet with the others. She desperately wanted her father's approval but loathed what she had to do to earn it. The anger he'd spewed at her was shocking. Not that she wasn't accustomed to him being upset with her—it was a fairly standard state of being for her father. But this was intense and immediate, and he'd thrown accusations at her which had come as a surprise.

He had to have a mole at the school. Someone had to be working with him, following her and monitoring her behavior so they could report back to her father. It was unnerving and put her on edge. Trusting those around her wasn't something she regularly concerned herself with, but now she knew she couldn't relax at all. She had no way of knowing who was watching her and what incident would be brought right back to her father.

Her mood was dark as she stalked into the middle of the tall grass. She noticed Luna approaching from the corner of her eye and turned to her suspiciously.

"Is everything all right?" Luna asked.

"Why do you care? And what business is it of yours, anyway?" she yelled directly into Luna's face. "You hate me as much as I hate you. Why would you come up to me acting like you have some sort of compassion for me? There has to be some sort of ulterior motive."

Luna glared at her, but then drew a breath and tried to force the negativity from her voice. "Yeah, there is. We need to get along, especially now that we're roommates, and will be until we graduate. The best roommates are friends, and friends help each other when they're down."

Vivi considered the words for a few seconds, then finally relented with a nod. She did her best to shake off the mood. This was what she needed to be focusing on now. Not her father's anger. Not whoever was keeping tabs on her and making sure he knew about her every action. Not even her distaste at having to live with Luna and the Seelie adding insult to injury by taking the bed she wanted. What Vivi's father said made sense. If she could prove herself able to cooperate and be successful with two Seelie, she'd be a much more attractive candidate for a position at the embassy. With such a role would come success, respect, and the all-important pass to enter Faerie. The embassy was the only way halflings could enter Faerie, and she wasn't about to resign herself to an existence stuck only in the human world.

"Fine," she said. "I'll work with you."

"We'll start where we left off?" Zander asked. "Let's make another of the Faerie circles. Purple pansies, right?"

"Training for your career as a preschool teacher, Zander?" Carson asked.

"You would make for good practice," Zander snapped back.

"I thought we were going to try to work together," Luna said.

They went to work, trying to recapture the circle they had managed to create the previous day. Vivi messed up their flow and concentration the first few times, but only an hour later, they finally succeeded. This represented a tremendous improvement from the day before, and they all felt a little boost while studying the purple pansies surrounding them.

Rather than wiping the circle away and starting again, they

decided to continue building on the success they'd already found. Soon the tips of vines pushed up from the grass around the flowers, wriggling and swaying, dancing like thick green snakes as they reached up toward the sky. Almost as suddenly as the creeping plants appeared, they crashed. The group's concentration broke, destroying the focus required to maintain the magic they created, making it disappear.

All four let out growls and cries of exasperation. Seeing their ability to create the Faerie circle together in such a comparatively short amount of time had encouraged them. Which only made the disappointment of having it destroyed more poignant. Carson stalked away, digging his fingers through his hair. Luna closed her eyes, drawing in a few deep breaths to try to dissolve the angry feeling boiling in her belly.

"Crickets!" Vivi shouted. The angry word was the best embodiment of the frustration and disgust she was feeling. The sound crickets made was among the most hated in the world for fae, so using their name as a curse always seemed appropriate. "We have to try again," she said. "That was great. We did it once, which means we can do it again."

"She's right," Zander said with a sigh. "This is what we're supposed to be dealing with. Principal Elmhurst told us it wasn't going to be easy. She said we were going to have to learn to control our abilities and work with each other to meld them so we can accomplish bigger things. It's not just going to happen overnight because we want it to."

"We had it, though," Carson said. "It was right there. We had it."

"Yes," said Luna. "We did it once. It's a start, but it's not enough. Just because we managed to create the circle once and add in a few vines and stuff, it doesn't mean we have this down. We have to keep trying. So, let's just do it again."

"But, without our fifth, how are we going to achieve the true Power of Five?" Vivi asked.

They looked at each other and Carson answered, surprising them all. "If the four of us can get our act together, then when they find the fifth, it will be easy to get him in and get the connection we need."

"Him?" Luna chuckled. "I sure hope he's cuter than either of you."

Vivi snorted and agreed. "It would be nice to have some real eye candy around here."

The tension which had been building now began to break, if only just a tiny crack. It was probably the first time Luna and Vivi agreed on anything. The being who had been watching from a distance smiled and turned to head back to the main campus buildings.

The four kept going, struggling and limping their way back to the point where they were able to resurrect the purple flowers. It took several more tries for them to become more than just shaky, almost translucent suggestions of the pansies.

Finally, the flowers were solid, and the four celebrated their accomplishment for a few seconds. Again, they crafted vines that rose from the ground. This time, the creepers remained. As dusk fell around them, the teenage fae created more dancing vines and guided them to weave in and out of the circle. As the vines moved around, some of them burst into bright, fragrant blooms.

The empty brown field seemed to disappear, giving way to the vibrantly colorful, beautiful scene unfolding around them.

"It looks like *A Midsummer Night's Dream*," Luna murmured, spinning around slowly to take in the gorgeous details.

The magic was stronger now, allowing them to release some of the intense concentration they had maintained while creating the circle. They walked around within it and Zander swept up to Luna dramatically.

He gave a deep, playful bow. "If this is *A Midsummer Night's Dream*, we should be dancing, shouldn't we?" he asked.

Luna laughed and allowed Zander to take her hand and pull

her into a dance. As they spun around, an idea came into Vivi's mind.

"You two are adorable," she said. "But I don't think you're close enough. Maybe I can help you with that."

She sent some of the vines out of the flowery growth, and before Luna and Zander could react, they were tangled within them. The vines wrapped tightly around the pair, forcing them up against each other. Vivi sniggered as they both struggled. The vines kept tightening more and more, winding around their bodies until the two fae tumbled to the ground.

"Vivi, stop it," Zander commanded.

"Why?" Vivi asked. "You look like you're enjoying your special moment. Maybe Carson and I should go and let the two of you be alone."

CHAPTER THREE

Vivi was laughing so hard she could barely contain herself. Every time she saw Zander and Luna struggling against the vines or trying to come up with a way to get themselves loose, she just laughed all the harder.

The circle they created was strong enough now and no longer required the constant concentration and precise focus with meager beginnings of a ring of purple pansies. It was still important for all of them to focus their energy and skills on the beautiful surroundings they created, but the prank Vivi played on Zander and Luna meant the group was all but forced to keep concentrating on the vines.

But her sheer amusement at watching the two Seelie fae was enough to keep Vivi concentrating on sustaining the spell. Carson was so stunned at what he was seeing that he kept contributing his own magic without thinking. As for Luna and Zander, neither could help but think about the flowered vines coiling around their bodies and crushing them against each other. Their thoughts simply continued to feed into the Faerie circle, making the magic more powerful. Finally, Vivi decided she'd had enough and released the spell tightening the vines around them.

Luna was most certainly not in the mood for a joke. She clawed her way out of the vines and took three long, furious strides across the field toward the other teenage girl. Vivi smiled smugly, expecting maybe a few tart words, probably nothing more than another simpering speech about how they all needed to get along and trust each other.

But Luna was way past that point. She was furious and wanted to make sure Vivi knew it, but this time, words weren't enough. She stomped up to the other girl and performed one of her favorite Krav Maga moves. The attack was so fast that Vivi barely had the chance to process what was happening before she crashed to the ground, pain exploding within her head.

It took a moment for what happened to sink in. Pain radiated from her face and around her head. She pushed herself up into a sitting position. Warmth trickled down her cheek, and Vivi touched it with her fingertips. She realized it was blood, pouring from her busted lip. The tender swelling around her eye was progressively getting worse. She'd have one hell of a shiner within the next couple of days. Dizziness rolled over her, and Vivi gave up on her initial plan to scramble back to her feet and attack Luna. She simply crouched in the dirt, waiting for the world to stop spinning and for some of the pain to go away.

"Come on. Can somebody use their healing skills to help me?" she demanded. "Carson, you know you're the best. Come help me. Please."

It wasn't merely a platitude spoken in the hopes of receiving help. It was a declaration of the truth. Luna was the smartest and most skilled of the four of them. But when it came to healing, nobody could compete with Carson. He was unquestionably the most talented, and his set of abilities could prove extremely useful one day. It made sense for her to appeal to the other

Unseelie fae and to think of him and his abilities first should they find the need for healing.

"Not yet," Carson said.

"Excuse me?" Vivi snapped. "Did you just say 'Not yet?' Can't you see I need help? She smashed my face in."

"I think that might be taking it a little to the extreme side," Luna said with a scoff. "It was a basic kick. If anything, your face got right in the way of my foot. You should be able to avoid an attack better than that."

"Look, this is a prime opportunity for all of us. We're supposed to be working on our skills and improving them. No better way to improve a skill than to put it into practice," Carson said.

"Are you suggesting I give myself a refresher on healing skills by healing myself?" Vivi asked. "Somehow that's supposed to make this whole situation better?"

"I mean, it can't hurt to try your hand at some healing. It might be useful later in life," he said.

"Yeah, the next time a Seelie scum gets the drop on me and attacks me, completely unprovoked," Vivi mumbled.

"You turned the Faerie circle we made against her, so it wrapped around her and Zander and nearly strangled them," Carson pointed out. "I wouldn't really call that an unprovoked attack. Let's be honest, Vivi. We all kind of feel like you got what you deserved."

"Fine," Vivi seethed. "Then I'll do it myself. Just make sure the shield is still in place. The last thing I need right now is some human wandering along and calling an ambulance."

"It's in place," Carson reassured her.

Vivi primed herself, trying to get into the headspace she needed to call her healing skills into use. Her lip was throbbing and stinging where it had split open. She wanted to heal that first and concentrated all her abilities on it. She envisioned the cut in her lip and that she wanted it to be better. Suddenly, her lips started to swell. It wasn't a gentle softening or the type of major swelling caused by eating something she was allergic to. Instead, it felt like air was steadily filling her lips, plumping them up like balloons.

She tried to yell, but her voice was stuck behind her puffed-up lips and came out as a high-pitched squeal. Soon she would look like her head was almost entirely composed of lips. Finally, she figured out how to get the magic under control and her mouth returned to normal size—except for the swelling from the cut, which was still not healed. Vivi kicked the ground and let out an angry groan. She moved on from trying to heal the damage to her lip caused by Luna's sharp kick and concentrated on her blackened eye instead.

A few moments later, both eyes were completely black, the whites and irises obliterated with only two dark voids staring back at the other three teens. They burst into laughter, watching as Vivi tried to reverse the effect as quickly as possible. She became more frustrated with every attempt. Carson, Zander, and Luna watched, chuckling as Vivi changed the color of her skin to a wide variety of shades and patterns, made one eye drastically bigger than the other, and shrunk her lips down to almost nothing. When she had grown a layer of skin that covered her entire face, Carson decided she'd had enough.

"Your healing skills are terrible," he said. "But if you could master a few of those things you just did to yourself and figure out how to do them to other people, they could be really beneficial in combat."

Vivi mumbled something through the skin—probably a scathing remark, but none of them could decipher the words.

"Maybe we could leave her like this for just a little bit longer," Luna suggested. "It's nice not having to listen to her talking."

Zander chuckled, but then shook his head. "No. She's flailed around enough for one evening. Carson, go ahead and help her."

Carson approached Vivi and held onto her shoulders to stop

her pacing and spinning in circles—which she'd been doing since the new skin obscured her vision. She seemed to be breathing just fine, which was good, but being unable to see or speak clearly was agitating her.

"You deserved to feel some of this pain before I used my healing magic on you, but if you stand still, I can help you," Carson said.

Vivi thrashed around, making screaming sounds, and Carson moved away. The others laughed, sending seething anger through her. But then something occurred to her. She was livid at them for laughing at her, but her father's voice reverberated through her mind. His words interrupted her raging thoughts. Again, she heard how angry he was at her behavior and how deeply disappointed he was in her grades and performance at school. The threat of not going on the skiing trip for Christmas, not seeing her father at all for the holiday, if she didn't straighten up and start behaving properly, took hold. She had messed up yet again.

Forcing herself to stand still, she breathed in a few times as deeply as she could and then exhaled. She nodded slowly.

"Have you calmed down now?" Carson asked, and she nodded again. "All right. Let's see what we can do about all this."

Vivi stayed as still and quiet as she could while Carson went to work undoing the damage she'd done to herself first before turning his attention to the injuries Luna had inflicted. She really wanted to keep control of herself and not mess up again. She had to remind herself that the behavior was beneath her. She shouldn't allow her anger, frustration, and disappointment to get the better of her.

Vivi wanted to prove she was worthy of her fae heritage, that she had what it took to achieve her lofty goals. But she still had some growing up to do, which meant sometimes she exploded. She had to learn to control herself better and do what needed to be done, even when it was the last thing in the world she wanted to do.

It seemed the others also wished to make sure she understood that.

"You really need to start cooperating," Zander said after Carson had healed her. "None of us are thrilled about this arrangement, but it's important for all of us to be willing to work together. The faster we integrate and start doing what we need to do, the better it's going to be for everyone involved. If we can show Elmhurst we can do this and can possibly achieve the Power of Five, she might get off our backs some, and we'll be taken off lock-down."

Vivi nodded. "I'm just so mad about losing my summer to do *this*. I can't stand it."

"You have some serious anger management issues. You might want to look into getting some help for them," Carson said.

Vivi scoffed at the idea, brushing it off as a joke. But maybe it didn't sound all that ridiculous. She thought it through, considering whether going to see someone about what she was feeling and the way she reacted to things, might help her now as well as in the long run.

Finally, she shook her head. Not willing to admit she had a problem—or that someone might be able to help her with it—she turned the conversation on Carson and changed the subject.

"So, have any of the Seelie girls who are still on campus stopped by your room to see Zander?" she teased. "Even more importantly, how many times have you taken advantage of that particular situation?"

Carson made an over-dramatic grimace and waved his hands as though he couldn't stand the thought of even the words getting anywhere near him. "I wouldn't touch a Seelie girl with a ten-foot pole."

Vivi let out a short laugh. "Don't even try to act like that now that Zander and Luna are around. I'm sure they've heard just as much about you as I have. They probably know all about you and your bad boy ways under the bleachers with the silly Seelie Court chicks, too."

Carson gave a playboy grin and shrugged. "All right. Maybe that wasn't entirely accurate. I wouldn't *date* a Seelie Court girl, but I have had my share of fun. It doesn't really matter which Court a girl comes from once you get her in the dark and all worked up. Even the prissiest of Seelie girls can put on quite a show if they're given the right encouragement.

"As a matter of fact, according to my own personal research, the Seelie girls can actually be even more fun. I think being with an Unseelie guy seems so forbidden it makes them feel naughty. They want to let go of all their inhibitions and see just how bad they can be. Now, I haven't gotten through the whole population on campus to get total information, but my sample size is pretty impressive. Of course, I'm happy to continue finding more specimens. Purely for scientific research." He winked at Luna.

Carson pressed his hand to his chest, holding it over his heart to show his sincerity, and grinned at the faces cringing back at him.

"Seriously, Carson. You are such a man whore," Zander said.

It was exactly the reaction Carson wanted. His reputation was carefully cultivated over all the time he had spent at the academy. He didn't want anyone, especially the three others standing in front of him, to know it was all merely a cover. For as much as he was considered the sex god of campus, Carson actually had no experience at all.

In fact, he was a virgin, and he couldn't handle anyone finding out the truth. He was sixteen—the age when he should be having sex with every girl who was willing, no matter what Court she was from. But he simply wasn't ready. He was embarrassed to admit it, so he just didn't. He preferred that everyone believe he went through the girls in school like popcorn rather than knowing he hadn't gotten anywhere with any of them.

The sky had grown dark while Vivi had struggled with healing herself, and the group decided to return to campus. Zander and Luna strode off with Vivi and Carson lingering behind. Carson watched Vivi track Zander's movements as they left the field, then nudged her with his elbow.

"Are you ever going to act on your crush on Zander?" he asked.

Vivi threw him a scowl. "I don't have a crush on Zander."

Carson smiled and nodded, knowing he'd gotten to her. Which, of course, meant he was completely right.

The next day Carson was sitting outside under one of the large trees dotting the grounds of the academy when Zander walked up and threw himself onto the grass beside him. Carson closed the textbook he'd been studying and stared at the Seelie boy.

"It's summer," Zander said. "What are you reading?"

"We're stuck here at the school, so it's hardly summer. It might be according to the calendar, but as long as I'm sleeping in that dorm room and wandering around the campus all day, every day, it's still the school year. I figured I'd get a head start on the reading list for when the semester starts again," said Carson.

"It's not like you need help with your grades. You already have all A's," Zander pointed out.

"It's just going to get more competitive from here on out," Carson said. "Getting a job at the embassy starts here. Only the best will get into the right colleges and establish the connections to land one of the positions. That's all I want, and I'm not settling for anything less. So I'm going to get ahead no matter how many days I have to spend studying or how many people I have to stomp on to climb my way up."

"That's a cheery thought. But along that line, I came to find you to ask if you think we're ready for controlling the wind," Zander said.

Carson's eyes widened and he grinned. "That would be awesome. Yes. We should totally find the girls and do that this afternoon. No more of this purple pansy nonsense. Let's control some wind!"

He put up his hand for a high-five, but Zander left him hanging, eyeing the palm suspiciously. "Um. I'm good," he said.

Carson waited another few seconds, then his shoulders sagged. He held his hand up, still persisting. "Come on," he said. "I thought we were doing the whole team spirit thing and trying to get our lives back."

Zander finally relented. "All right." In an effort to be friendly with his new roommate and encourage harmony among the group, he sighed and reached up to smack his palm against Carson's.

At the last second, Carson pulled his hand away. "Too slow!"

A group of people who were sauntering past laughed at him and Zander shook his head, wondering why he even bothered. An Unseelie was always going to be an Unseelie. No point in trying to make a connection with them.

Carson was still laughing when Luna and Vivi arrived. They were walking a few feet apart, creating a clear delineation between them while still moving casually along together.

"What's everybody laughing about?" Luna asked as she approached. She caught Zander's taut features and her expression dropped. "Oh. Everybody except Zander, I mean."

"Are we going to do this, or what?" Zander asked, standing up and stalking away from them.

The other three exchanged glances and followed as he made his way toward the field.

CHAPTER FOUR

Shanghai, China

"That thing has eyes, Mia," Becky gasped. "It has *eyes.*"

Mia laughed at her best friend's reaction. "It's not like they can see you. Look," she pointed out, happily using the wooden skewer stuck through the fried eel to dangle the creature in Becky's face. "Deep-fried, see?"

Becky grimaced and tried to duck out of the way. "I thought you were supposed to be a good influence on me," she said.

Mia scoffed. "Why would you think that?" Her brow furrowed and she scrunched her nose.

"You're the older one," Becky pointed out.

"We're both sixteen." Chuckling, Mia shook her head in exasperation at her best friend.

"Yeah, but you'll be seventeen in October, so that makes you my elder. You should be the responsible one," Becky whined.

Mia rolled her eyes. There's no way Becky would say something like that if they weren't in Shanghai. They would both start their junior year in the fall, and the slightly younger girl would never put herself a step under anyone.

It was merely a ploy to stop Mia from teasing her with the freaky-looking street food. She tucked the skewer back into the tall wooden display and looped her arm through Becky's. "Let's go see if we can find something you actually want to try," she said.

They made their way farther into the bustling night market. When they had planned their trip here, Mia had envisioned Shanghai being cooler than the summer weather back home. Instead, the temperature earlier in the day had soared over ninety degrees, and the high humidity made the air thick and steamy. Once the sun had set, the humidity had finally eased and the temperature fell, making it far more comfortable to roam around the vibrant market.

Or at least not as sticky.

The atmosphere was invigorating. Music played, and layers of voices added to the sounds and smells, creating the backdrop for hundreds of people weaving around the stalls and tiny shops. Their energy fed off each other in an almost dizzying experience, unlike anything Mia or Becky had ever seen.

Coming to a new country for the first time had been a culture shock, but somehow being in the market made them feel like part of something bigger. They were among the throng of people, each trying to take it all in. As chaotic and intense as it was, it was also unifying somehow.

Children picked out treats from carts peddling elaborate handcrafted sweets. Mysterious smells, some enticing, some strange, lured people to stalls offering an overwhelming array of food, from the creepy speared creatures to adorable buns crafted to look like little animals.

Women ogled gorgeous fabrics and tried on clothes, while others scoured tightly packed displays of trinkets and collectibles. All around them, languages mixed, bouncing back and forth. People who didn't understand a word of what each other were saying still communicated and laughed. Nearby, an old woman grinned as she clutched a young tourist's hand, and Mia's heart warmed. It was a reminder that ultimately, they were all the same.

She had no way of knowing she was about to discover it wasn't true. Moving among the crowds, she was different.

"How about one of those?" Becky asked, pointing to a nearby stall.

Mia studied the bamboo basket filled with steamed buns in the shape of panda bears. She smiled and nodded. Using some of the words their instructor taught them leading up to the trip, they each ordered a bear.

Mia's teeth sank into the soft dough and found the sweet chocolate paste inside. "Good choice," she said, nodding.

They continued on their stroll, nibbling their way through the buns. Becky stared at hers for a second, then grinned at Mia. "Can you imagine if your dad was here?" she asked.

Mia chuckled. "He would have eaten everything by now," she said. "He would have just started at the first stall and made his way through, trying something at each one."

"How far do you think he would have made it before we needed to roll him back to the hotel?" Becky snickered.

"Halfway down the street," Mia said. "Then he'd just come back tomorrow to try the rest."

A hint of sadness lay behind the amusement. She felt home-sick and missed her father. This was the longest time she had ever been away from him. Her mother died when she was only a baby, and Mia had no memories of her. All she had ever known was it being only the two of them.

The sad feeling didn't last for long, though. She caught Becky staring across the street at Brad, who hesitated at a nearby stand trying to build up his courage to eat a fried scorpion. Another of the high schoolers in China for the Wushu tournament, Brad was also Becky's secret crush. Mia knew her best friend had been studying the form of Chinese Kung Fu long before she met Brad. But that didn't mean he wasn't a bonus.

"Go talk to him," Mia urged.

Becky shook her head. Her attention shifted from Brad to the remainder of the bun in her hand, but then drifted back to him. "I can't," she whispered.

"Why not? He's right there. Like,"—she counted out an estimation—"nine steps away."

Becky sighed. "What do I do? Just walk up to him and be like 'Hi, Brad' or what?" She spoke as if it was the most absurd concept she'd ever heard.

Mia blinked. "Yes," she said. "That's exactly what you're supposed to do."

"I can't do that!" Becky gasped.

"Why not?"

"Because it's *Brad.* He doesn't even know I exist." She threw her hands in the air in exasperation.

"You kicked him in the face when he was standing too close behind you at practice two weeks ago. Then you traveled in the same group with him to *China.* Pretty sure he knows you exist." Mia laughed at her friend's silliness.

Becky groaned and covered her eyes with one hand. "Oh, Buddha. I was trying to erase that whole kicking-him thing from my memory," she said. "Thanks for reminding me."

Mia pressed her hand to Becky's back and turned her toward the group of guys all daring each other to eat the scorpions.

"Look at them. They're all having fun and taking in the new experience. Go join them."

"I'm not eating a scorpion," Becky said firmly.

"You don't have to. Just go talk to him. Tell him he did a good job at practice this morning or something. You know if you don't, you'll regret it." The older of the two girls cast a knowing look at the boys in front of them.

Becky took a resolute breath and crossed the street toward the group. Mia lingered in place so she could watch. Becky approached the stall beside the one where the boys gathered, and she pretended to inspect the items on display. She shifted sideways a few inches, paused, then crept over a few more. This continued until she bounced into Brad. He stumbled slightly, then turned around to face Becky. His wide grin elicited one from Becky, and just like that, the other guys were forgotten.

"My work here is done," Mia murmured.

They still had plenty of time before they were due back at the hotel for lights out. Which meant Mia could do some exploring of the market on her own. Becky would catch up with her eventually.

Mia continued along the same road, browsing the numerous items for sale. Soon the tightly packed stalls thinned out, many replaced by permanent shop buildings. The boisterous crowds had lessened. Mia moved more slowly through this area so she could peek through shop windows and get a glimpse of what was inside.

One particular shop intrigued her. The building appeared to be ancient, and something about it caught her attention. She had taken a step toward it when the door opened and the time-worn face of an old woman appeared. She beckoned to Mia with her outstretched hand.

"Come inside," the woman called out. Mia hesitated, and the woman beckoned again. "No afraid. Come," she said in broken English.

Mia allowed her curiosity to guide her. She walked across the street as the old woman disappeared through the door. A heady, spicy scent wafted out at her when Mia opened the door and slipped into the shop. Inside was a concentrated version of the market. Shelves towering nearly to the ceiling held exquisite teapots, cups, ornate boxes, and other objects. Tables laden with even more curios were arranged with narrow passages between them.

She inhaled the competing aromas that confirmed this was a tea shop, but something about the place wasn't quite like the others they had already visited on their tour. A few steps into the shop, she realized the old woman wasn't in the room.

"Hello?" she called.

Rich silks hung from the walls, draped casually to create different segments in the shop. Mia made her way through the first section and passed lush peacock-blue fabric trimmed with gold tassels, into a second area. This part of the shop was somewhat calmer than the first, but with so much going on, it was impossible to decide where to look first.

"Here," the woman called from farther in the shop.

Mia followed the sound of her voice and finally ducked through the purple drapes hanging over the entrance to the last room. The old woman sat on a cushion on the floor beside a low table.

"Your shop is amazing," Mia said.

The old woman gestured to the cushion across from her. "Join me."

Mia lowered herself onto the cushion and studied the traditional tea service laid out in front of them. An intoxicating smell rose up from the pot.

"I'm Mia," she said.

"I know."

"How do you know?"

The woman offered a wise smile as she filled Mia's cup. "I wait for you come. You call me Grandmother." She touched the edge of the cup. "Here. Drink."

"What do you mean you've been waiting for me?" Mia asked.

The encounter felt strange and part of her wanted to leave, but something else was keeping her there. As odd as the interaction was, it was also intriguing. She wanted to know more.

"Drink," Grandmother said again. "Unique in all China."

Mia picked up the cup and brought it to her lips. The strong, spicy scent filled her lungs before she even took a sip. The flavor rushed over her tongue and burned in her throat, but as soon as it was gone from her mouth, she wanted more.

She drained the cup, and Grandmother filled it again. The second went down well, but her head started to swim. Squeezing her eyes closed, Mia waited for the feeling to pass. When she opened her eyes, Grandmother was gone.

"Hello?" she called. "Grandmother?" The shop was silent. Mia carefully set the cup back on the table and stood. She wobbled a bit before righting herself. "Thanks for the tea," she called. "I have to get back and meet up with the rest of my group. Goodnight."

A tingling sensation crept through her body until it felt like her fingertips should be glowing. The shop was different now as she made her way out. Everything was familiar, but she noticed colors and patterns which hadn't been there before. She told herself it had to be the smells of the herbs and teas getting to her. Fresh air would clear her head.

Mia stumbled through the tea shop door and back out onto the street. The air felt cooler as she drew it deep into her lungs. Letting it out slowly, she waited for the effects to wear off. A flicker of movement to one side caught her attention.

She squinted in the direction of the movement and thought she saw the flash of something black scramble over the edge of a nearby building and disappear onto the roof. A growl sounded behind, and she whipped around. Something glowed in the shadowy space between two nearby buildings. The eyes grew bigger as the thing closed in on her, and long, spindly fingers snaked out to creep across the front of the shop.

Fantastic, she thought. *Trust me to get myself drugged in a foreign country. Everybody else will be competing, and I'll become a public service announcement.* The way everything looked, like a Pink Floyd video, with scary shadows which couldn't be real, Mia suspected that the tea had to have been laced with something. But she couldn't figure it out. All she wanted to do was find Becky and get back to the hotel.

Their coach had warned them many times not to separate. She should have listened to him instead of leaving Becky to flirt with Brad.

She tried shutting her eyes again, but this time the creature didn't disappear when she opened them. It was coming closer and soon strode out of the gap. It appeared almost human, but with disproportionately long arms, legs, and fingers. Long hair hung around a face with huge glowing eyes. Fear gripped Mia, and she ran back toward the crowd. Hallucination or not, she simply wanted to get away from it.

The creature followed close behind her, moving along the front of the buildings. No one else seemed to notice it. Ahead of her, dark purple smoke streamed from either side of the street, joining together to create a mass that blocked her way. The cloud turned solid and writhed, suddenly turning to reveal the massive face of a snake, with sharp, gruesome teeth.

Mia stumbled backward away from the snake, then turned to run in the opposite direction. The creature with the glowing eyes took a step toward her, and she made her choice. She rushed full speed toward the snake, only for it to become a puff of smoke when she got close. The busy part of the night market wasn't far ahead. If she could just get there quickly, she could find Becky, return to the hotel, and sleep this off.

The creature was closing in on her, and still no one noticed. A narrow area forced her to slow down, and she felt fingertips trace her spine. An instant later, a woman grabbed her wrist and yanked her behind an empty stall.

The woman pushed her to the ground and stood to look back toward the creature. She was armed with a strange-looking weapon which she pointed at the monster. No one gasped or screamed. Mia had expected a reaction to a woman brandishing a weapon—something resembling a crossbow strung with a long dagger—at the edge of a crowded market. Yet no pandemonium ensued.

"Crickets. He's gone," the woman said. She crouched beside Mia and searched her face. "Are you all right?"

"You could see that thing?" Mia asked.

The woman studied Mia, her expression strange. "Of course. I've been after it for a long time. Troublesome creatures, boggarts."

"*Boggart?*" Mia asked. "What is that? Why couldn't anyone else see it?"

"Did you hit your head? Humans can't see boggarts. Or any of what they think of as mythological creatures, for that matter. Makes it easier to do my job, I suppose." She shrugged.

Mia's head was reeling. She didn't understand what this woman meant when she'd said humans couldn't see the creature which Mia had just clearly seen and been chased by. And what other creatures? That tea must have been seriously strong.

"What job?" she asked.

The woman extended a hand with a friendly grin.

"I'm Cassia, the best bounty hunter of the fae."

CHAPTER FIVE

The girl stared at Cassia for a few seconds, blinking as if that was going to change what she was seeing. Perhaps she believed if she did it enough times, her eyelashes would brush away the words and she could simply replace them with ones she liked better.

"Are you all right?" Cassia asked.

"Tea," the girl responded.

"Tea?"

She nodded.

"I drank some," she rubbed her temples and wished she was in Kansas again.

"That's lovely," Cassia replied, unsure of why the girl felt the need to share that.

"Mia?" someone called from outside the stall where they were still hiding. "Where are you?"

The girl's eyes widened, and she shot to her feet. "Becky!" she called out and scrambled around the side of the stall and back out into the street.

"What happened to you?" Becky asked.

Cassia rose up enough to watch their interaction. The new

girl looked Mia over and grabbed her hands, holding her arms out to her sides to examine her further. Mia gave her a few seconds, then wrenched her hands away.

"Don't worry," Mia reassured the other girl. "All in one piece. Physically, at least."

Becky stared quizzically at her. "What do you mean?"

Mia shook her head, then glanced back toward Cassia for a brief second. Becky followed her gaze but didn't acknowledge Cassia's presence.

"I think that old woman slipped something into my tea," said Mia.

"What old woman?" Becky asked.

Mia turned slightly to look at the stall. She shook her head, then rolled her eyes as she glanced back at her friend. "Not her," she said. "The old woman at the tea shop."

"Not who? Who are you talking about?" Becky's brows furrowed and she nibbled on her lower lip, wondering what in the world had gotten into her best friend.

Cassia leaned against the side of the stall, knowing Becky couldn't see her. No human was supposed to be able to. Yet when Mia glanced back again, this time almost turning all the way around to face her, it was obvious she was looking directly at Cassia. Mia glanced back at Becky, then closed her eyes tightly and squeezed the bridge of her nose.

Looping her arm with Becky's, she steered her back in the direction of the night market. "I think it's time to head back to the hotel," Mia said. "A good night's sleep sounds like exactly what I need right now."

As they headed down the street, Cassia moved out from behind the stall to watch their progress. The thought of the boggart popped back into her mind. She'd been searching for the creature for too long to just let it go so easily. This wasn't a game of hide and seek they were playing to amuse themselves. The boggart was a nasty, vile creature that had already proven itself to be dangerous to the children of the area. Finding him would ensure the young ones were protected.

Cassia retraced her steps to where she had last seen the boggart and resumed her search. Her tracking skills were strong and precise, the very reason behind her reputation as the best bounty hunter of her kind. Those abilities immediately drew her farther along the street, but she had gone only a few steps when she felt something on her shoulder. It was a cool, gentle touch as if the wind itself had formed a hand to stop her. But the grip wasn't that of the wind. Cassia knew it was her father.

For thirty-four years, the ghostly touch had been there to guide her. Cassia would rather have his earthly presence be there with her, but the transcended form brought her great comfort and helped her along her way, nonetheless. Flynn Tarran had been the greatest bounty hunter of his time, perhaps the greatest to have ever lived. It was that skill and devotion which had earned him the coveted role of protecting the fae princess.

And that devotion had cost him his life. He'd laid down his life to defend the princess, but in the end, it wasn't enough. The princess had been murdered, and Cassia was left with only the lingering of her father's spirit and the duty to take up his mission and carry it on. It was a duty she struggled to take seriously.

The stories her father had told her of the princess and the threats to her life had always been fantastical and had kept Cassia up long past when she should have been asleep. But she never actually believed them. Not until his death had she realized the significance of the responsibility that was placed at her feet. It didn't matter what she believed, she had her assignment.

Her secret assignment.

Cassia would much rather stick to what she knew. She liked chasing the tangible threats, the creatures she understood, had seen, and even gone after countless times before. That's what she wanted to do now. The urge to track down the boggart and dig him out of whatever hiding place he'd found was strong. She wanted to leave the brightness of the night market behind her and delve into the shadows where she was more comfortable.

But the touch on her shoulder stopped her. He didn't often interfere with what she was doing. Usually his spirit watched over her from a distance, giving her a sense of being guarded rather than herded. Occasionally, as he would when he'd been alive, he encouraged her to take another path. It could be as soft as a brush of cool air on her cheek or a map unfolding in front of her. It could also be as unmistakable as this nudge, stopping her from going any farther along the empty portion of the street, turning her back toward the market instead.

She had to follow Mia.

There were too many questions left unanswered.

The two girls had already disappeared far down the street and into the market, and Cassia hurried after them. The same skills that had brought her to the boggart had put her on Mia's trail. None of the humans she pushed her way past could see her, but they would be able to feel her. This meant Cassia couldn't simply shove through with abandon. As much as the frustrating moments—when chatty women stopped, blocking the path to scrutinize a piece of fabric, or men paused to try the next snack— inspired her to elbow them out of the way, she held back.

She had seen before what could happen if she let herself run free. The chaos and fighting that might break out among the humans simply weren't worth the time saved. Finally, Cassia caught sight of Mia. The same thing that stood out to her about the girl before was bold and impossible to overlook in the crowd. Wavy red hair hung past her shoulders, swept into swirls and tangles after running from the boggart and pushing through the crowd.

It was that feature, along with her scent, which made her impossible. Her scent was human. Cassia knew it well. Over fifty years of training with her father before his death had instructed her to easily differentiate between species simply by their scent.

But it was her hair that truly stood out. To have so easily seen both Cassia and the boggart, Mia should have been fae. But the dramatic flash of fiery hair eliminated that possibility.

None in either the Seelie or Unseelie Court had naturally red hair. Those of the Seelie Court, like Cassia, had silver hair, while the Unseelie Court was marked by hair so dark and inky it appeared almost blue in the right light.

This knowledge spurred Cassia's curiosity as she continued to follow Mia and Becky as they wove their way through the city. Mia was human by scent and by appearance, and yet she possessed the ability to see what only those of the mythical realm could see.

Could Mia possibly be another creature? She wanted to know who this intriguing girl was and what it was about her that was so important. Something about her was special, or Cassia's father wouldn't have guided her to follow Mia.

After a long trek through the city, Mia and Becky finally stopped outside a hotel. They chatted with several other people who looked to be about their age. A familiarity existed among them and in the way they spoke. This wasn't an accidental encounter or people meeting for the first time. Aware that none of the others could see her, though Mia might, Cassia stayed back. She crept close to the hotel and inched along until she was able to wait in the shadows for the two girls to enter the hotel.

They paused in front of the elevator, and Cassia slipped into the stairwell. She rushed up to the second floor and peeked through the narrow window to check if they'd come out onto this level. Several seconds passed without the elevator opening, so she ran up to the next floor and the next.

On the fourth level, she finally caught sight of them. They strolled along the hallway until they reached a door. After a few words, Becky took out a key and opened the door.

When Mia paused and glanced her way, Cassia retreated from

the doorway. When she checked again, the red-haired girl was no longer in the hallway.

Cassia hesitated in the stairwell. She had nothing left to do here tonight. Mia was staying inside, which would make it easier to keep an eye on her. So Cassia had time to go back for the boggart.

The crowds in the night market had begun to thin as she made her way back through. She could sense the boggart, but the trail was weak. It must be old, a route the creature had taken in recent days or weeks, but not tonight. Cassia focused harder and found another trail, but this one faded within mere moments of following it.

Her aggravation began to build as she found the fifth old trail that led her to nothing. The boggart could be anywhere. These things were fast and crafty. Their glamour could make them blend in with any humans, but the fae could always see past it. Even if she couldn't see a boggart, Cassia would never miss one. Their rank scent was like a sewer.

This would all have been so much easier if not for that one little boy. Only eight years old, he'd believed the mysterious creature that had taken up residence in the attic of his home could be a friend. Naming it would have been meant to connect them, but that was the last thing anyone should do when encountering a boggart. Giving one of these beings a name took them from mischievous to truly nasty and cruel. This one left the house destroyed and the little boy hurt and barely hanging on in its wake.

But the creature hadn't stopped there. As Cassia continued to scour the city for the boggart's trail, she thought of the others who had fallen victim to it. No one knew if the creature went after toddlers and babies because a child had named it, but going after the most vulnerable only made it more reprehensible. Cassia was unfailing in her determination to find the boggart and stop it from making any more of the little children sick. So far, no one who had been stricken by the illness had died, but she wasn't willing to test it. If the boggart was using a potion to make these children ill, it could make the concoction stronger and worsen the effect.

Then, she caught the trail again. This one was fresher, and Cassia felt a surge of optimism. She rushed after it, her hands tingling to reach for any of the daggers hidden among her leather clothes or the crossbow on her back. This thing had to be stopped.

She rushed along the narrow alleys and streets, blocking out everything around her so she could think only of tracking the boggart. Suddenly she skidded to a stop. Her feet were at the base of a sewer and the trail was gone.

CHAPTER SIX

Mia was shaking Becky awake a full hour before they had to leave the hotel. She knew her best friend well enough to know that mornings were not her favorite time of day by a long shot. Becky would fight against waking up with everything in her. Which meant Mia would need at least four rounds of shaking her and telling her they had to get ready before Becky eventually dragged herself out of her bedding cocoon.

"Come on," she insisted on her fifth shake. "We have to get breakfast before the competition."

Becky made a few indistinct grumbling sounds and rolled her head to the other side but didn't open her eyes. It was time for more extreme measures. Mia jumped onto the edge of the bed beside Becky and wrenched the blankets away from her. That did it. Becky's eyes opened and she gave Mia an angry, if blurry, stare.

"What are you doing?" she mumbled.

"Getting you up so we can go get breakfast. Come on. Carb loading time!" Mia announced.

Becky reached down, feeling around for the blanket, but Mia held it out of her reach.

"I thought you were supposed to carb load the night before you did something," Becky muttered.

"Well, we're doing it the morning of. We'll throw some protein in too. Get up."

Becky finally accepted she was beaten. Resigned to the morning which had come far too early for her liking, she slid off the side of the bed and dragged herself over to the bathroom. By the time she was dressed and mostly conscious, they were heading out of the room only three minutes later than Mia had planned. She decided to take that as a victory.

Everyone participating in the Wushu competition seemed to have the same idea and the hotel restaurant was packed nearly full. The hostess grabbed two menus and led them to a tiny table against the wall. It was sticky and sprinkled with crumbs, evidence of the people who had eaten there before them. The hostess tried to shoo them back to the front of the restaurant so the table could be cleaned before they sat, but Mia shook her head.

"No, no. It's fine," she said. "We'll just sit down."

She wasn't about to give up the spot and risk someone else swooping in and taking it out from under them. Her stomach was rumbling after an hour spent dedicated to waking up her friend, and the effort of the competition also loomed ahead of her.

Becky had perked up by the time they ordered. She was back to babbling about the boys at the night market when Mia spotted something strange from the corner of her eye. At first, she thought it was merely someone moving oddly between the tables. When she turned to look at it, she realized it wasn't one of the teenagers swarming the restaurant. The creature was yellow and scaly. It maneuvered between the tables without effort, floating through the air like a ghost. No one else in the restaurant was looking at it. The only reactions seemed to be wrinkled noses and contorted facial expressions when the spectral figure moved past the tables.

As soon as it came within a few feet of their table, Mia understood the reactions. The strong, disgusting smell of decay and putrid, rotting meat filled her nostrils. Becky put down her fork and shook her head, probably trying to get the odor out of her nose. "What's that smell?" she asked, wrinkling her nose.

"I think it's that," Mia said, nodding toward the scaly yellow ghost.

"What?" Becky asked.

Mia gestured with her eyes. "That," she said.

Becky glanced over her shoulder, her gaze focused on the space the creature filled, but she didn't react.

"What am I looking at? Samuel? I mean, he has some post-practice odor problems sometimes, but it's never been at this level." Becky giggled.

"You don't see that?" Mia asked incredulously. She thought she must still be hallucinating from the tea she drank the night before. *Note to self, never drink tea offered by an old lady again.*

Cassia had arrived at the hotel before the sun came up so she could continue following Mia, still trying to figure out who she was. So as not to cause any panic, she put on her human glamour before entering Mia's hotel.

This brought her to the back corner of the restaurant, where she tucked into a massive breakfast and watched the two girls. Almost immediately, she spotted exactly what she was waiting for—the sluagh came into the restaurant, and Mia could clearly see it.

"How does she see that?" Cassia muttered through a bite of syrup-soaked pancakes.

"Excuse me?" the girl at the next table asked her.

Cassia glanced at her and shook her head. "Nothing," she said, swallowing.

The girl turned away, and Cassia looked back at Mia. The sluagh was moving around the restaurant as though it was looking for mischief, but no one could see it.

No one but Mia.

It was confirmation of the strangeness Cassia thought she'd experienced the night before outside the market. She'd told herself she might have imagined it or that it wasn't what she thought. But this was unmistakable.

Somehow, someway, Mia wasn't fully human.

A few minutes later, the girls finished their breakfast, paid, and headed out of the restaurant. Cassia did the same, waiting in the lobby of the hotel until they came back down, now dressed for the competition. She fell into step behind them and followed them through the city. Her glamours helped her blend in with the groups of teenagers, but they wouldn't do any good if Mia turned to look at her. Mia would immediately recognize her. Cassia thanked the Faerie gods the girl didn't see her.

Instead, the two girls hurried off, their heads bent toward each other as they chatted. As they walked along the sidewalk, they passed beneath the plane trees that lined the streets of Shanghai. Cassia caught sight of fluttering movements between the branches. Anyone else looking at the trees might think the shaking leaves and swaying branches could be the wind. Cassia knew better. The branches were bouncing too much to just be the soft sway of the warm breeze. It was wood nymphs.

The mischievous little creatures danced and played between the branches, watching the world go by beneath them. One caught sight of Mia and Becky and scrambled to the end of a low-hanging branch. Followed by one of his friends, the nymph reached down and tugged at their hair with his long fingers. The other joined in, forcing the girls to stop. Becky brushed at her hair, obviously thinking it was nothing more than the branches catching in her flyaway strands, but Mia looked up. She saw the bright, buggy eyes of the little wood nymph looking down at her while the other played in Becky's hair as though it were a sandbox. She let out a cry and Becky turned to face her.

"What? What's wrong?" Becky asked.

"What are you?" Mia demanded, waving at the nymphs who easily avoided her hands.

Cassia laughed. It was funny to see the playful creatures interacting with the humans who couldn't see them as they tried hopelessly to figure out what was happening. Knowing Mia saw them made it even funnier.

"Mia, who are you talking to?" Becky glanced around but didn't see anyone close enough for Mia to be speaking to.

Mia approached the base of the tree and was preparing to climb when the screech of tires stopped her. Cassia saw the near-accident happen before Mia did. It took the laughter right out of her mouth and tightened her heart in her chest.

A taxi driving erratically came far too close to a moped overloaded with four men and a haphazard stack of boxes. The moped was swerving under its uneven load and overcorrected when the taxi nearly hit it, which sent it careening toward Becky. The girl jumped away just in time. Cassia hurried to the trees, knowing Mia was too distracted to notice her.

"You stop that," she whispered up to the nymphs. "Leave them alone and stop causing trouble."

Tearing her hair away from the fingers of the little brown creature tugging on her, Mia ran for Becky. Her friend sagged back against Mia, her hand pressed to her chest. The men on the moped skidded to a stop a few feet away and stared back at the girls as if debating whether to return and apologize. Mia shot them a glare, dismissing them with her hand.

"Are you all right?" she asked Becky.

Becky stared at her for a long second, then nodded. "I think so. They came out of nowhere. I was so busy trying to get my hair untangled from the tree, I almost didn't get a chance to get out of the way."

Mia nodded. "I saw." She reached down and scooped their bags up from where they had dropped them. "Let's go."

With everything Cassia had witnessed so far, she was still stumped as to who the red-headed girl was. *She couldn't be a halfling, could she?* Cassia knew that all halflings bore the coloring of their Court, even if they had very little fae ancestry within their human DNA, they still looked like they belonged with either their inky-black hair or their striking silver tresses.

Cassia considered for a moment that Mia might possibly be another supernatural creature gifted with the ability of sight. Being able to see past fae glamours was something most supernatural creatures could do, even their various halflings could do it.

But that didn't feel right to the bounty hunter. The girl was out in daylight, so she couldn't be a vampire, dhampir perhaps, but her coloring was too flush. Dhampirs always had a look of the dead with their dark eyes and pale skin. Mia had bright eyes and a nice pink hue to her complexion.

Then she considered the possibility of a shifter. And immediately ruled that out as well. Shifters always smelled of their race. Cassia didn't know of any shifter race who could hide their scent and appear as purely human.

Maybe she was a witch, or at least a halfling witch with very little magical ability? There had to be some reason this girl was left out in the wild without a supernatural protector, at the very least. None of the various races would allow a known halfling—half human and half supernatural—to be with full-blooded humans unless the child had zero skills.

It was rare, but sometimes when a supernatural mated with a

human, the resulting child could be born with no powers, but the supernatural elements of DNA were almost always dominant. A child would have some sort of power. Cassia had seen too many offspring of human/supernatural pairings to believe this girl had been passed over as not having anything worthy of her race's notice.

Mia must have been a pure accident that her supernatural parent didn't even know about. It happened, but it was rare. As a bounty hunter, it was Cassia's responsibility to discover *what* Mia was and send her to the appropriate halfling academy.

She decided to continue following the girl, not only because it was her job, but also because her father had nudged her along this path.

As they continued through Shanghai, Mia looked around, her gaze flitting back and forth as though on edge. The girl was probably hoping nothing else unexplainable would appear on the streets. She wasn't so lucky.

Not two blocks later, Mia stopped in her tracks.

Ahead of Cassia, a bogan stood glaring at Mia. These were even nastier than boggarts. Generally, a bogan was a hired henchman. This particular one used a glamour that made him look like a plain Chinese man, but she saw the creature for what it really was, and from Mia's frozen stature, so could she.

Cassia prepared to eliminate him, trying to figure out how to do it without causing a scene. But the bogan made a grab for Mia's arm, trying to pull her into the alleyway the girls were passing.

Mia screamed, "Monster."

Cassia's heart lurched, and before she could make a move, Mia surged forward. In a frenzy of movement, she wrestled the bogan down to the ground then flipped him over onto his stomach, wrenching his arms behind his back so he was immobile. An older man came out of a shop beside her and shouted something.

Cassia caught a few words of it—he saw the creature Mia was

holding on the ground simply as a punk. Switching to English, he offered to handle the man for the girls. Mia nodded and moved aside to let him yank the man up. The shop owner told the girls to go, and they didn't hesitate. It took only a few seconds for them to disappear in the crowd.

As they ran away, Cassia heard Becky say they would be late to the Wushu Competition. Cassia knew exactly where they were headed and decided to take the bogan in, collect the bounty, and join up with the girls once she was done.

With a quick shift of her glamour, Cassia appeared as a human police officer. She rushed forward and took control of the bogan, rattling off what little Chinese she had picked up what she hoped sounded like an official cop spiel about arresting him. As she dragged him down the street, Cassia held the creature close. The little monster would know what she was. He would be able to see past the cop image and know she was fae.

He leaned his head back so he could hiss into her ear. "I'll split the job with you." His breath was hot and disgusting against her neck.

"What job?" she asked.

She knew what he meant, but she needed more information. He had to know Cassia was a bounty hunter. She was the best the fae had, so most fae would know who she was on sight. His statement told her that a bounty was out on Mia's head. But Cassia knew if it was a legitimate bounty, she would know about it already and likely be after it herself.

That implied a criminal element to the bounty, and Mia might be in danger. It worried Cassia, but she didn't have time to interrogate the bogan about it now. She needed to get rid of him and return to Mia as fast as possible.

It felt like it took far too long, but eventually she found a secure place and opened a portal to Forasaon prison to turn the bogan over. Not all fae could portal into the prison, only those who had been magically *keyed* into the system were allowed access. But even still, there were other precautions in place to stop anyone who found a way past the *lock*.

Her bounty struggled against her grip. The giant ogres stationed at the portal where they landed would be intimidating to anyone who wasn't as accustomed to them as Cassia was. She shoved the bogan toward them and they studied it with distaste.

"What is this?" one asked.

She scoffed. "Losing your touch?" she taunted. "It's a bogan."

"I know," the ogre growled. "But there is no bounty on its head."

Fan, the head jailer, came toward them. "Hello, Cassandra. What are you up to today?" he asked.

"I caught this thing in Shanghai, attacking two human girls in broad daylight." She hated being called Cassandra, and it wasn't even her real name. Cassia stood for Cassia. It wasn't a nickname or a shortened version of her name. But that never stopped Fan from teasing her.

"Thank you for handling that," the jailer said, "but since there is no bounty on its head, there is no pay for bringing him in."

Cassia let out a stream of profanities and stomped away, going back toward the portal to Shanghai.

"She's probably already dead by now!" the bogan shouted the moment before Cassia touched the portal.

She turned around sharply and took a step toward him. "What did you say?" she asked through gritted teeth.

"The girl. There's no use rushing back to her. She's probably already dead by now. My partner will have taken care of her." The bogan had dropped his disguise, and his large beady eyes now revealed his mirth. He was happy.

Fan grabbed the bogan by his throat, turned him around, and lifted him so Cassia was glaring directly into his eyes. "What do you mean by that?" she demanded.

The bogan cackled. "You have no idea what you're dealing with."

Fan's eyes sliced over to Cassia. "What's he talking about?"

Cassia shook her head. Now wasn't the time to explain. She headed through the portal back to Shanghai so she could find the girls.

CHAPTER SEVEN

Mia figured their arrival at the Wushu competition would go one of two ways. Master Chen was going to be angry when she and Becky got there, or he was already so angry they would simply vaporize before they made it all the way onto the competition floor. Either way, she was choosing to see it as a chance to boost her adrenaline before the competition began. Optimism, the power of positive thinking, and all those other things she'd seen splashed across motivational banners in her high school.

The truth was, Master Chen was really a kind person. Originally from Hong Kong, the elderly man had a peaceful, calm presence, and very rarely became upset. When his temper did get the best of him, though, it was time to duck and cover. Fortunately, they had only seen that happen twice in the ten years they'd been training with him. Unfortunately, Becky and Mia had just done the one thing guaranteed to push him over the edge. They were late.

Promptness and punctuality were extremely important character traits for Master Chen. He saw them as a demonstration of commitment and discipline. Being late to something, especially a competition like this, was a display of disrespect, which would never be tolerated. Being late meant doing laps. One mile for every minute of lateness. That was going to be a lot of running to do after completing the first stage of the competition. Mia hoped for some understanding and compassion, considering the circumstances.

It didn't start well.

"Mia, Becky, what is this?" Master Chen shouted as he came across the room toward them.

"I'm sorry." Mia started to explain.

"You are no longer permitted to explore the city. Unless you are here at the competition, practicing with the others, or at an activity with the team, you are to be in your hotel room. Do you understand me?" he said.

"We couldn't help it," Becky replied, on the brink of tears.

"You must take responsibility for yourself and what you do." He stared them down.

"She's right," Mia said. "We were—attacked."

"Attacked?" Master Chen asked.

"Yes. On our walk here. Someone came after us, and I defended us. I managed to subdue him until help came."

"She was amazing," Becky added. "Took him right down before anyone got hurt."

He nodded slowly. "I am proud of you for how you handled yourself in that situation, Mia. That was very dangerous and could have gone much worse. Be that as it may, you were still late, and that has impacted everyone in this competition. You will do laps after the competition. You should have scheduled extra time in your walk for unexpected events," he said before he returned to the group.

Mia watched him for a few seconds, then turned to Becky. "Clearly."

Becky still appeared shaken up by the encounter but she managed a laugh. "I guess that went as well as we could hope."

Mia nodded. "Let's go get ready. You'll be going up in the first group."

Mia slung her arm around Becky's shoulders as they headed for the first event. She decided to take the punishment in stride. As her best friend had said, that had gone fairly well. They were going to have to do laps, but since a special group dinner was set for later that night with the team, Master Chen probably wouldn't make them do as many as technically warranted.

Several minutes later, Mia stood on the sidelines watching Becky. The team had broken up into groups to wander around the large competition floor and watch the competitors. This first day of the competition was taolu. The series of movements required tremendous control and connection with the body. It was an art as well as a show of strength and agility. Becky was competing in the category for sixteen and over, and her skill was obvious. Even in the first minutes of the competition, it was clear she was one of the best there.

Mia was proud as she watched Becky go through the movements and sequences of the taolu. Deep concentration etched her face, but her expression also showed how much she loved what she was doing. Wushu had become an important part of her life, as it had for Mia. It gave her a sense of strength and ability, and she was proud to work her way through the levels.

At the end of her demonstration, Becky surprised and delighted onlookers with an exquisitely executed double backflip. She landed effortlessly facing the judges, bowed, and left the mat with an air of confidence, as though it was no big deal.

Mia wasn't buying it. Becky would be bursting at the seams with excitement over her performance. As soon as she reached her, Becky threw her arms around Mia and squealed. Mia hugged her back, indulging in a few seconds of bouncing up and down in celebration.

"That was amazing," Mia exclaimed.

"Really?" Becky asked, glancing back at the judges even though their faces were totally expressionless.

"Yeah. I think you have a really good chance of winning your age division. There haven't been any other competitors even close to you," Mia reassured her.

Becky's face glowed. She squeezed Mia's hands and looked into her eyes. "Are you ready? It's going to be your turn soon."

A swirl of excitement, nervousness, and anticipation filled Mia's belly, but she nodded. She had the skill to handle it. As his best student back in Pasadena, Master Chen had insisted Mia should compete in the adult division for this competition. He believed in her and had told her repeatedly that if she simply kept a level head and focused, if she reminded herself that she had it in her, she could do very well.

Mia was ready to face the challenge. Confronting the strange creature on the street had given her a boost, and she carried that feeling of power with her onto the mat. When she had first arrived, she had been shaken, then watching the competitors perform their taolus, she began to relax and accept that some part of her knew she was stronger than she thought possible.

Even though she was freaked out by what she'd seen since the night before, something in her subconscious told her not to worry, that she controlled her destiny and had more than enough power to overcome anything or anyone.

She figured it was all the Wushu training she'd done over the past ten years. Master Chen had drilled into them the power of mind over matter, so her subconscious must have already been working to calm her and help her to overcome the freakiness of the past sixteen hours.

With a deep breath and the knowledge that she could perform her moves in her sleep, she strode onto the mat.

With Becky and Master Chen watching, she performed her taolu carefully. She lost herself in the movements, ignoring everything else around her, until she finished in a flurry of applause.

There were no winners on the first day of the competition. That day was only for the taolu and would be followed by two days of hand-to-hand bouts before finals on the fourth day determined the winners of the different categories. Mia and Becky still felt confident in the day's success as they were leaving the venue, bolstered by Master Chen reducing their punishment to only running two miles. Mia took his leniency as a victory.

The group dinner was a special event they had all been looking forward to since before they even left for Shanghai. They had the unique privilege of eating in a monastery that had existed for centuries. Though the monastery and the grounds were essentially a tourist stop now, drawing in huge crowds coming to marvel at the beauty of the structure and the sheer awe of experiencing something so old, the dinner was different. It required a special invitation, and a lot had gone into securing the invite. But Master Chen had managed it. They would be welcomed into the amazing space after visiting hours had ended and would be given the opportunity to see it in a way few did.

They were all excited as they hurried back to the hotel to take showers and dress for the night. Everyone had brought along a special outfit for the dinner, and there was plenty of chatting, giggling, and twirling as the girls revealed their chosen looks.

Mia slipped into the dress she had selected and tucked her feet into the moderate heels she'd convinced her father to buy for her. Now she hoped she'd be able to manage walking in them on the uneven streets. The girls styled their hair and helped each other with their makeup, putting far more time into preparing for this than they had anything else since arriving in Shanghai. Both knew this was a once-in-a-lifetime experience they would always remember, and they wanted to look good in their memories.

They rushed down to the meeting spot in front of the hotel,

arriving seconds before Master Chen. Mia was relieved. She didn't want to fathom trying to run laps in her dress and heels after dinner.

Becky held Mia behind as the rest of the group began to walk off. "Do you mind if we sit with the guys?" she whispered.

Mia knew Becky wasn't talking about just any *guys*. She was talking about a *guy*, the one guy in particular who Becky hadn't been able to get off her mind for months.

"That's fine," Mia said. "I'm just looking forward to the experience."

Cassia watched Mia and Becky giggle as they linked arms and tucked their heads close together, whispering to each other and following close behind the other kids. She fell into step behind them. She had to keep a close eye on Mia after what happened that morning, but she didn't want the girl to notice her. Their stroll through the city was pleasantly uneventful. Cassia was hoping they were done with attacks for the day. Seeing Mia alive after the bogan's declaration at the prison was a relief, and she hoped they could skate through the rest of the day without another incident.

All seemed to be working in her favor. They arrived at the ancient monastery, and Cassia hid in the shadows as the group walked reverently inside. When they were safely within the confines of the structure, Cassia decided it was time for some boggart hunting. That nasty creature was still in Shanghai somewhere, and she was determined to eliminate him.

However, the bogan's promise of a partner waiting for Mia was still weighing heavily on her mind. The possibility of those two related creatures working together was strong. If she could find the boggart and remove him, it would eliminate the danger.

As she crossed the courtyard, something caught her eye. A woman walked along the edge of the grounds. Cassia sighed. Maybe this wasn't going to be the smooth night she had hoped for after all.

CHAPTER EIGHT

Something wasn't right about the little Chinese woman wandering through the monastery grounds. Cassia knew it instantly, and it wasn't because the woman's glamour wasn't working well, or because her dark wig was askew.

Being a fae bounty hunter might give her an edge, but she ventured to guess a good percentage of people who caught a glimpse of this woman would immediately recognize something was a bit off.

The woman, standing so serenely looking out over the grounds and occasionally snapping pictures, just didn't fit the scene. For one, it was after visiting hours, and she was the only one seemingly wandering the grounds. A small woman like her walking around alone in the dark was unusual and would likely arouse suspicion. Even odder, though, was that the frail-looking woman was using an analog camera, an older one. Most tourists these days whipped out cell phones with selfie sticks and snapped digital pictures. Even the older generations had digital cameras to capture their memories when they decided to play tourist. But here was this woman, occasionally raising her ancient camera and snapping a picture in the dark.

Completely in the dark. As in, nothing changed when the little old woman pressed the button. She was walking around taking pictures in the dark, but the camera had no flash. Either she was the world's worst tourist photographer, or she wasn't taking pictures at all.

Cassia squinted, and the magical façade of an old Chinese woman disappeared. Instead, the monstrous visage was something that would send the entire monastery running and screaming for their lives—a redcap.

A particularly nasty creature without the flattering touch of her glamour, she was far less unassuming. She was three feet of bearded, razor-toothed trouble. Cassia needed to make sure this thing didn't get anywhere near Mia. Stepping lightly, but quickly, she closed the gap between herself and the redcap.

Cassia skidded to a halt a few feet away from the creature. The redcap spun around to face her and bared her sharp teeth. Her deep-set red eyes seemed to paralyze Cassia by simply making contact with her own. The camera dropped to the ground, bouncing with a clatter, exposing it as merely a shell made of plastic. Long, sharp talons stretched from fingers that reached out to Cassia, threatening to rip her skin from her bones and shred them, making her easier to swallow. Eating their victims, especially if they could do it alive, was one of the less appealing characteristics of redcaps. Which was saying a lot considering that even the females were bearded and horrible enough to be frequently sought-after assassins.

The redcap's long, thin, scraggly beard blew away from her face on the breeze, curling back up around her shoulder and mixing with the thick, unkempt hair, topped with a cheap wig of long black locks. With her façade now gone, the redcap raced toward Cassia, using her shocking speed to gain an immediate advantage. Leaping into the air, her mouth opening wide, saliva dripping from sharpened teeth that looked like millions of yellow nails, she bore down on Cassia.

Instinct kicked in, and Cassia lifted a leg and shifted her weight forward. She kicked the creature in the face as it fell and sent her skidding away in shock. She had expected easy prey, and while a fight was not a deterrent, it required a slightly different approach. Pulling herself into a malleable defensive fighting position, Cassia prepared for the next attack.

She was ready for just about anything from a redcap who was capable of viciousness and randomness of attack at equal levels. What she did not prepare for was the broken, shrill voice of the creature as she slinked back a few steps on what could be best described as hooves somewhat resembling feet. It had toes, it had a heel, but it clomped and stomped on the ground like a particularly aggressive, but very short buffalo.

"Cassia, what a pleasure," the words leaked out of her more than they were spoken, eyes sparkling with recognition.

Vowels were elongated and the voice broke between letters, making it sound like it came from somewhere beyond her body, a dimension of darkness far away. A dimension where monsters lurked and waited, never needing to speak because their anger was always present and filled the space around them like a whirlwind of malice.

"Trust me, the pleasure is all yours," Cassia responded, trying to shake off the nerves accompanying her encounter with one of the most despicable creatures in any universe.

Her knuckles cracked in anticipation, and she scanned the redcap, looking for any potential weak spots. Maybe the knees, maybe the collarbone, but probably not those teeth. Those teeth were capable of so much more than a mere bite. So much more than just death.

"Are you really going to try to take me in?" the redcap asked in a condescending tone. "Many have tried before."

"We have your partner," Cassia said. "Forasaon is waiting to make it a complete set."

A mirthless sound that resembled a laugh escaped the redcap's grimy mouth. "That won't be happening. But I appreciate you coming up to say hello. It saves me the need to seek out another morsel to tide me over until my next meal."

"I've heard I'm a bit salty," Cassia quipped.

Keep talking, that was the key, and it would give Cassia more time to form a plan. The more she kept the nasty thing off guard, the less time she had to worry about those teeth biting into her skin and ripping her apart.

"No bother. You're just the appetizer. That girl is the main course. I want her friend to watch while I devour her bones. I want her to hear her screams while I rip her skin off. I want her to see her eyes while she begs for me to end her life. And then," the redcap smiled, its hundreds of sharp, randomly sized, pointed teeth scraping together as she did so, "I'll have her for dessert."

"That's a lovely menu you've got planned out for yourself," Cassia said. "Too bad you're not going to have much of an appetite when I'm finished with you. You know, once you have your stomach kicked in and all your teeth missing."

The redcap roared and pounced again, this time swiping at Cassia's legs with her long talons. Cassia jumped to avoid them then delivered a kick that missed the creature's head by inches. Continuing her spin to avoid having her back to the creature meant planting her feet, but doing so gave the redcap something to aim for. Blinding pain shot through her as the long, sharp talons pierced her leg, pulling at her with an iron grip and surprising strength.

Falling on her back was the last thing Cassia wanted, but the best she could do was to straighten her body before she landed in a seated position. Bouncing hard on her rear, she used her free foot to kick at the face of the creature. A blow connected and sent her head snapping backward, and her grip loosened. Another connected with the mouth and Cassia heard several teeth crunch under her foot.

The creature leapt in a rage, and Cassia rolled in time for it to miss her. She scrambled to her feet and swung a fist into the redcap that buried deep in her stomach and crumpled her to the ground. A flurry of kicks to the downed monster sent her rolling away, but Cassia wasn't planning on letting her foe escape.

Cassia jumped after her, narrowly avoided a swipe of the talons, only to find her face smashed in by a sweeping hoof-foot. Her vision exploded in stars and lights that danced and obscured the real world. She rolled away as far as possible to give herself space to recover, which was when she saw the blood all over the ground. And on her shirt. Her nose was broken, and a cut above her eye was gushing. These injuries—combined with the tears in her leg—meant she was experiencing a cacophony of pain. And she was seriously pissed off.

As the stars faded from her vision, she focused again on the creature now crawling toward her, but half of what she saw was colored red. The taste of iron filled her mouth and ignited a new sense of purpose in her. She had to try to control herself. Her father had always said, "Anger without discipline is suicide, but anger with discipline is revenge."

She waited until the last second, lying prone on the ground and pretending to be semi-conscious. The redcap got within a few feet of her and a long, gray tongue swept around her mouth, broken teeth falling out and littering the ground around her. Her arms raised as she prepared to bring her talons down and rip into Cassia's body, when Cassia jumped up, ramming her palm into the creature's nose and spinning into a kick to the knee. The creature slumped, a sound of shock mixing with a roar of pain at what had to be a shattered knee. The thought of her knives ran through Cassia's mind, but she shook it off. Alive. She wanted it alive.

The redcap lifted her face toward Cassia and bared her bloody, stained teeth. Taking a moment to aim, Cassia strode forward and thrust a kick from the center of her body, using every bit of strength she had in her to plant her foot in the creature's jaw. The kick was perfectly placed, just low enough, at just the right angle, with just the right power, to knock the brain out for a little nap. The redcap splayed on the ground, her arms loose noodles with sharp pointy ends.

Breathing through her mouth, and wiping globs of drying blood from her nose, Cassia tied up the redcap and sat beside her, taking a moment to wipe the blood from her face and take stock of her handiwork. She had captured a redcap *alive*. Fan was going to hate that. Or love it. It was hard to tell with him sometimes.

"What in the living Hades did you get yourself into this time, Cassia?" Fan boomed.

Well. That eliminated the 'love it' possibility.

"I caught this one outside the monastery. She was pretending to be human and stalking two human girls," said Cassia. "I think she is the partner the bogan was talking about earlier."

Fan studied the redcap, then gave Cassia an almost-approving nod. "I'm surprised you were able to bring her in—especially alive."

Cassia couldn't help but be offended by the comment. "What's that supposed to mean? I'm a bounty hunter. Bringing all forms of nasty creatures to you is kind of my thing. It's what I do," she pointed out.

"That might be true, but this is different. *This one* has a very large bounty on her head. Her list of crimes is extensive. Mostly murder," Fan said.

"And you know every single one of them," the redcap spat. She had come to right after Cassia had brought her through the portal. The ogres held her down while Fan inspected her.

"What does that mean?" Cassia asked.

Fan eyed the creature with disgust. "She likes to leave just enough bones behind to make sure that we can identify her victims," he grumbled. "It's her calling card."

The creature's smile grew more maniacal, and Cassia felt her stomach turn. This was a serial killer who took great pleasure in making sure everyone knew what she had done. Her cockiness didn't just show she had no remorse and very much enjoyed every horrific murder, but that she believed she would do it again. There wasn't a bit of her entitled, self-absorbed mind that believed she had been stopped.

"That's just lovely," Cassia commented. "You can go right ahead and stuff her under a rock somewhere and pay me my bounty."

"Late for something?" Fan asked flippantly.

"It's never too soon to get the Hades out of here." Cassia suppressed the shiver threatening to surge up her spine. Had she known how awful the redcap truly was, she would have killed it when she'd had the chance.

Behind Fan, the ogre guards watched Cassia and Fan's exchange. It was obvious they were amused by the back and forth, their shoulders shaking as they tried to cover up their laughter. Faylynne barely tolerated them referring to him as Fan without exploding. They knew it wouldn't do them any good for him to catch them laughing at him.

"You sure know how to charm, Cassia," Fan said.

"Does my eagerness to get out of the depths of despair and get back to doing something productive offend you?" She arched an eyebrow.

The ogres were quickly losing their resolve to show respect to the lead jailer, and their growing chuckles were audible.

"Maybe it wouldn't be as bad if you hung around and carried on a real conversation for once." Fan's half-smile unnerved her.

A touch of something suggestive echoed in his voice, but Cassia would shut that down fast. She couldn't stand Fan. At least, she didn't think she could. She did not have the mental space to handle an awkward flirtatious conversation right then. Behind Fan, one of the ogres rolled his eyes at the comment.

"You're right, Fan. Why don't you go find me someone I can do that with?" The snark was beginning to return, and Cassia was ready to put the redcap out of her mind.

"There are times when I really want to snap you in two, you know that?" Fan asked.

Cassia glared at him and at the redcap, then back again. "If I keep collecting these death threats, I'm going to develop a punch card system. I have to say that hers was a lot more creative."

That was all it took. The ogre trying his hardest to hold back his laughter let it out, and the deep sound made the building rumble around them.

Once Cassia was back at her hotel and cleaned up, she focused on who Mia really was. To send a bogan after a human wasn't unheard of. It was possible a fae, or some other creature, had taken a liking to Mia and now wanted her as a trophy. But to send a redcap? Especially one so vicious? This was personal.

Some fae lord or someone else really high up had it in for Mia. No, she wasn't a human. The girl had to be the descendant of an important fae. *Why else would there be so much muscle after the teenager?* Cassia went through everything she had learned about Mia and came to the conclusion that, if not for her red hair, the girl appeared to be a halfling fae. She hadn't demonstrated any real power, other than seeing past glamours and an uncanny ability to fight.

So why wasn't Mia back in the States in one of the halfling fae academies? She may not gain entry to the Elmhurst Academiae Superiorum, but she would deserve a spot in one of the lower level academies, at the very least. If nothing more than to learn how to protect herself from the various monsters of their world.

No, she must be a halfling. Maybe she was a distant relative of a witch and somewhere else along the line a powerful fae was mixed in? She couldn't be sure, a red-headed halfling was a first for Cassia.

All halflings attended special schools in their home countries to learn about their abilities and how to master them. Then, the leaders of their different races would choose the most promising candidates to work for them on Earth.

The fae rarely allowed halflings on Faerie, but sometimes it happened. However, most of their organizations on Earth were staffed by halflings. The halflings were more loyal to their fae family than the humans who worked for the fae.

Mia deserved a spot in an academy, and Cassia was going to find a way to take the girl there.

CHAPTER NINE

Phillipsburg, Montana

"We're here so much we might as well just pitch tents and start living off the land," Vivi snipped, as they made their way into the field again.

Carson rolled his eyes at her. "What would you know about living off the land? That doesn't mean you call a waiter over to bring you a drink while you're lying on the beach during a vacation, you know."

Vivi glared at him. She was tired of his jokes and of the way he seemed to want to push her until she cracked. There were times when she thought of him as a close friend and other times when he made her want to pop his head like a pimple. She wondered what it was about him and why he felt the need to tease and make fun of her.

"You're right. Why don't we just go back to the school and ask Elmhurst if we can practice controlling the wind in the banquet hall? I bet it would be a lot of fun to see the peas swirling around the ceiling," Zander said sarcastically. "Maybe the kitchen wants to make lemon meringue pie for dessert, and we can provide the air."

"Maybe we should get a little bit of atmosphere going here." Luna tried to diffuse the tension. "If it didn't just look like the same giant field we keep coming to, it might be more interesting."

"What do you suggest, Little Miss Sunshine? If you're thinking about making another circle of purple pansies, you can just keep it to yourself. I don't want to see another one of those ridiculous flowers for as long as I can possibly avoid it." Vivi rolled her eyes.

"All right, that's enough. I'm not interested in wasting any more time standing around here bickering. The whole reason we're stuck here at the school this summer rather than being able to be off living our lives is that we can't get along. I don't know about any of you, but I'm seriously done with having this be my entire existence. I'd like to see something other than the two miles around the school at some point before graduation," Zander said.

"I don't take saying this about a Seelie lightly, but he's right," Carson said. "If we ever want to get our lives back and not tempt Elmhurst to force us to do everything in tandem, we have to start gelling better. So, let's stop trying to one-up each other and start working together."

"Listen to that." Luna laughed. "I think you're having a good influence on him, Zander."

Carson chuckled. "Maybe I'm the good influence, did you ever think of that?"

Zander gave him an unconvinced look. "How do you figure?"

"I saw the look in your eyes when you were checking out my...textbook," Carson said.

The four laughed, some of the tension lifting away from them.

Luna performed a few quick lunges and rocked her neck back and forth to loosen the muscles. At five feet, eight inches, Luna was particularly tall for a fae girl. But her height had served her well. Growing up in a rough neighborhood hadn't exactly given her the opportunity to be delicate and demure. She'd had to learn to take care of herself and had trained in Taekwondo from a very young age.

Continuing with her martial arts study had resulted in her taking Krav Maga as her PE class. Half the time, she had her face buried in a book, trying to absorb everything she possibly could about magic, and the other half she was learning to kick butt and defend herself. It was a valuable combination that made a meaningful contribution to the group. Of course, it had also given her the skill to bash Vivi's face in after her nasty practical joke.

It was something she was going to have to learn to balance. Like the other three in the group, learning to understand her abilities and utilize them to their highest potential was how she would help elevate their skills.

"What are you doing?" Vivi asked.

"Stretching," Luna said.

"Does doing magic frequently require stretching ahead of time? I must have missed that little tidbit in health class," the smaller girl quipped. But she spoke with a smile, and Luna grinned back.

She was under no illusions that this meant the two of them were friends. At any given time, Vivi could go right back to tormenting her. It was the Unseelie way. They were what they were.

"I don't know what I might have to be preparing myself for," Luna teased.

"I think Vivi is willing to call a truce for today," Carson said. "What do you say, Viv? You'll avoid the temptation to bounce Luna around like she's in the tumble cycle of the dryer?"

"Fine," Vivi said. "No practical jokes today."

"I'm just going to note that you did say today," Luna pointed out.

The other fae girl nodded and shrugged. "I reserve the right to change my mind and resume the hilarity at any given point beyond today."

Carson shook his head and chuckled. Sometimes he just couldn't get enough of Vivi. He was attracted to her, and his feelings were growing progressively stronger, but she was way too much to handle. It was far easier to stay friends and occasionally tease her for the fun of watching her get flustered.

"All right. Let's do this thing," Zander said.

All it takes is focusing tremendously hard on something and wanting it to happen badly enough for it to occur to you just how infrequently something really crosses your mind. That's what all the young fae were thinking as they stood in the field, anticipating the wind. From stiff gusts to gentle breezes, the wind wasn't ever really something any of them had given a tremendous amount of thought to. When it was there, it was; when it wasn't, it wasn't.

Occasionally, on a particularly hot day, each of the teens had hoped for something to break up the stillness in the air and give them a little bit of cooling relief. And in the bitter cold of the Montana winter, there was always the hope of avoiding one of the stinging spirals of air carrying ice crystals and snow. But the wind itself wasn't a strong enough contender for their attention.

Until now. Then it was the only thing any of them could think about. Today was about learning to rein in their abilities and use them to control the movement and intensity of the wind. Doing that as a group was already daunting enough. Now was not the time to try to actually conjure the wind as well. They agreed to wait for some natural breezes and maybe one day build up to creating it. Maybe.

They had already talked about how they were going to harness the power of the wind and what they were going to do with it once they had it under their control. After the purple pansy circle debacle, they knew working together from the beginning was essential to achieving any type of success. They were ready, but the wind refused to cooperate.

The four had been standing there waiting for almost half an hour when a gust finally built up in the trees along the edge of the field. The branches rustled, and the grass around them was flattened. They braced themselves, and when the wind grew stronger, they put their plan in motion.

They focused on every aspect of the wind. How it felt on their skin, what it sounded like in their ears, even what it smelled like as it whipped up the dampness from the trees and the summer-warmed dirt beneath the grass. Finally, they were ready and concentrated their abilities on harnessing the wind in an effort to pass it around among themselves.

Nothing happened. It should have been fairly easy. They should have been able to take hold of the breeze, draw it down, and pass it around like a ball. They had all seen other students doing something similar before. Of course, they were older and weren't being required to work together. The wind quieted and they all expelled the breaths they realized they'd been holding.

"Let's just try again," Zander said. "It's fine that it didn't work the first time. We just need to work on it a little. Are you ready?"

The other three nodded, and they went back to waiting for another breeze.

For the next several hours they went through the cycle of waiting for the wind, attempting to gain control of it, then dealing with the inevitable screw up and having to move on. Unlike during their first practice sessions in the field when trying to create the Faerie Circle, this time they couldn't point directly at Vivi and blame her lack of concentration for them not being able to accomplish what they set out to do. There were a few times when she'd been distracted or frustrated and the effort had failed, but the others had done the same as well.

Zander kept pushing them right into the next attempt. A few times, he tried to scrap all the plans they made and create a completely new approach. They'd only been working together for a short time, but the other three young fae were already accustomed to him. As intense as his icy blue eyes and silvery Seelie hair was, Zander was focused almost to a fault. He would rather drive himself into the ground than let up for even an instant and threaten the future he saw for himself. Even more than any of the others, his sights were focused on obtaining the elusive pass into Faerie. But he was acutely aware that only one percent of halflings ever achieved such a status.

He didn't allow the knowledge to deter or intimidate him. Instead, it pushed and motivated him to constantly work harder and accomplish new levels of success and esteem within the academy. It also put him in the position of being de facto leader of the little gang Principal Elmhurst had constructed. He resented being yoked together with them and having to associate so closely with Unseelie on a daily basis, but he took the assignment as an opportunity to showcase himself and hone his skills even more.

As far as Zander was concerned, they could accomplish the Power of Five on their own, despite only being four. Not technically having enough people to accomplish the power wasn't a deterrent for him. Instead, he figured each of them just needed to work a little harder to make up for the open spot in the group.

Finally, they started to get the hang of controlling and manipulating the wind. But that didn't mean it was going well. The wind seemed to be manipulating them right back.

"Vivi, I thought we agreed," Carson said.

The dark-haired girl shook her head, making the fading light of the afternoon shimmer on the bluish sheen of her glossy strands. She held up her hands innocently.

"That one is not me. I said I wasn't going to do anything today, and I didn't," she protested.

They both turned to watch Luna tumbling around in the air.

"Well, you have to admit it's a little convenient, considering that crack about the dryer and the whole underwear incident," Carson pointed out.

A few minutes earlier, one of their attempts to control the wind went sideways and Luna was sucked up into the air. Now she was trapped in a current, spinning and rolling around as gusts came from both sides of the field and collided.

"Can we just stop with conversation about who did this and get me down?" Luna shrieked.

The three fae went to work, trying to regain control of the wind. They didn't want to just suddenly take away the wind and risk injuring Luna if she crashed to the ground. Instead, they needed to gradually release the power of the wind so she could ease back down. It took several minutes, but finally, they managed to lower Luna onto the ground with only a small thump and a grunt of frustration.

She pushed to her feet, brushing herself off and glaring at the others around her. "Well, that was delightful," she muttered.

She tried to take a step, and the world spun around her. She stumbled a little, twirled, and dropped back to the ground. Zander rushed to her side, kneeling and lifting her head.

"Are you all right?" he asked. "What happened?"

Luna managed a smile and shook her head, which only made the swirling worse. She groaned and pressed the heel of her hand to the center of her forehead and squeezed her eyes closed. "I'm fine. Just dizzy. That was a bit on the intense side," she said.

"Just think, though. Now you are fully prepared in the event you ever decide to go into astronaut training," Carson said. "You've already got that spinning around thing down pat."

"Thanks for that," Luna said. "Way to see the silver lining."

After a few more minutes of sitting and trying to let her head assimilate to being still again, Luna was able to climb to her feet.

"Feeling better?" Zander asked. Luna nodded. "Good. You up for going for another round?"

"Of course, she is," Vivi said. "She's always up for everything, aren't you, Luna? She has to be the best at everything. Wouldn't want her grades to slip or Principal Elmhurst to get disappointed in her and risk her scholarship."

Luna glared at the smaller fae, her arms crossed over her chest. "Oh. There's Vivi. Things around here were just getting too pleasant, and I knew that couldn't be happening with her here. But, never fear, I found her."

"Vivi, you promised," Carson said. "Luna, stop provoking her."

"Who put you in charge?" Vivi asked.

"I didn't provoke her. She was just born like that," Luna argued.

"The wind is picking up," Zander told them. He'd checked out of their petty bickering partway through the attempts to lower Luna to the ground and was done dealing with them for the day. He was going to figure this out and make the group successful if he had to drag the other three behind him the entire way. "This time, let's just try to stop it halfway across the field, change its direction, and send it back the other way. We've done it before. That will be our reset point."

Two days later, that was still their reset point. All four sat in the middle of the field, exhausted from pushing themselves as hard as they could from the time they woke up until they went to bed. As it had been for the last two days, a picnic basket lay tipped over a few yards away. They'd packed it before leaving the academy so they wouldn't have to take a long break in the middle of the day to go back and eat lunch. Both days they ended up having to hunt down various elements of their meal after the wind picked up the basket and sent it flying around the field, making it rain down wax-paper wrapped sandwiches and pieces of fruit.

They all looked a bit worse for wear after their battle against the wind these past days. Vivi sat with her legs sprawled in front of her, her black hair sticking up from her head at drastic angles, as though she had stuck her finger in an electrical socket. In reality, she had just been hit directly in the face with a massive blast of wind, right after trying to toss it to Carson and not moving fast enough.

Zander had long, shallow scratches along his arm and one side of his face from twigs broken off from some of the trees in the woods. They had come along with a particularly intense stream of wind and he didn't move out of the way fast enough. Carson was streaked with dirt and grass stains from being picked up and thrown several feet, then skidding across the ground.

But they'd done it. The wind had chewed them up and spat them out over the long hours they spent in the field, but finally their powers merged, and they'd mastered the skills. Once they'd figured it out, it seemed almost ridiculous that it had taken so much effort. Simple wind control was a skill halflings learned when they were thirteen or fourteen. These four had learned it when they were twelve, demonstrating their exceptional skill and ability. But it wasn't just the ability to control the wind they'd needed in this situation. They were still learning to collaborate and utilize their powers as a unit rather than individuals. Doing that with a skill far more advanced than just conjuring up some flowers took considerably more control and effort. Once they'd realized that and began to truly apply themselves toward combining their powers rather than just exerting their own skills, it became much easier.

Now their bodies were sore, and their minds felt wrung out and exhausted from the exertion. It was still fairly early in the evening, but none of them had any energy left.

"Can I interest anybody in dinner at the cafe to celebrate?" Luna asked.

"Absolutely," Zander said.

"I'm starving," Carson agreed.

"At least you got to eat most of your lunch," Vivi added. "My sandwich got blown into the woods and was stolen by a squirrel."

"I offered you part of mine," Carson argued.

"Your chickpea version of tuna fish isn't something I'm getting anywhere near. I've never even eaten tuna, and I can tell you that yours is so wrong," Vivi countered.

"I think it's delicious, Carson," Luna offered.

"Thank you," Carson said. "The cooks at the academy think so, too. That's why they make it for me."

"They make it for you because you're spoiled," Zander said.

They all dragged themselves to their feet and brushed away remnants of grass and dirt.

"Let's go back to the dorms and clean up, then we'll go get something to eat. Mom made her more than meat meatloaf today, with mashed potatoes and mushroom gravy on the side."

Luna's announcement was enough to fuel all of them to hurry back to the academy. Even though the prospect of long, hot showers was extremely appealing, the dinner waiting for them outweighed it. They met up in front of the dorm and headed to the restaurant, ready to relax.

CHAPTER TEN

Shanghai, China

The next few days saw Cassia keeping a close eye on Mia. When Cassia returned to the monastery after dumping the redcap off with Fan, she was relieved to see the girl was still safe and there weren't any other creatures going after her.

While she had taken care of the immediate threat to the girl, Cassia knew that more would come. Only she still didn't know why or what to do with the girl. A tiny voice in the back of her mind told her to leave the teen to her own devices. Cassia had saved her twice, and the girl needed to figure out how to protect herself.

On the other hand, Cassia reminded herself that her father wanted her to follow the girl for a reason. No regular halfling would have such powerful enemies. Maybe it had to do with her fae parentage?

Cassia kept enough distance to ensure that Mia wouldn't see her, but she had noticed the girl looking at her a few times with a curious stare. No matter what glamour Cassia used, Mia seemed to recognize her but had never approached her. And Cassia had no need to speak to Mia, not until the final day of the Wushu Championships.

Mia had just bowed to the judges after trouncing her opponent and smiled brightly at Becky. When the halfling's entire body stiffened and her eyes bulged, Cassia knew something was wrong. She followed the direction of Mia's stare and recognized the figure glaring at Cassia's new charge. At that very moment, she knew without a doubt that she would be ensuring the girl's safety forever.

The Unseelie fae bounty hunter who had Mia in his sights began to stalk toward his prey. Cassia wasn't sure how Mia knew she was in danger, but from the look of fear on her face, she was all too aware. It was time to make Mia disappear.

In order to do that, Cassia would have to use mind-warping. She hated to use it on innocent humans, but she had to extract Mia without sending up any red flags.

Quickly changing her glamour to that of a middle-aged redheaded woman, she made her way to Mia and her friend. "Mia, darling!" Cassia pulled the girl into a hug and whispered into her ear. "Follow my lead if you want to get out of here alive and leave your friends safe."

"What? Who?" Mia didn't know what was going on, but she did recognize the person hugging her. It was that fae bounty hunter she'd met almost a week ago in the night market. The same one who had been following her all week.

The girl had never made Mia feel worried for her safety. In fact, whenever she had seen the fae, she had felt safer, as though the woman was her personal bodyguard. When she looked over the bounty hunter's shoulder, she spotted the man with the pointy ears glaring daggers at her and knew that she was in danger. But she couldn't leave her friends in the lurch either. If Becky thought Mia was in danger, she'd insist on going with her.

And Master Chen would never allow Mia to leave without him. He *was* responsible for her safety while they were in China, after all. She might be able to escape for a few hours without any trouble, but with everything she'd seen the past week, danger was following her. Her greatest wish was to finish the competition and go home, leaving the monsters behind in China.

At least she'd had part of her wish granted.

Now, she wasn't sure what to do. Her teenage self wanted to scream "Monster!" and run for cover. But that small soft voice in the back of her mind screamed for her to trust the woman hugging her and save her friends.

When Cassia pulled back, she winked. "Mia, I'm so glad I was able to see your final performance. Your father will be so proud."

Mia frowned, wondering if the bounty hunter knew her father. She was about to ask when Cassia grabbed her hand and squeezed it.

"Master Chen?" Cassia looked to the Asian man who stood calmly as he watched the interchange between the two women.

He bowed slightly. "I am."

"My name is Cassandra Jennings. I'm Mia's Aunt." She put her hand out, and Master Chen shook it.

His brow furrowed. "Excuse me, but I thought Mia's only family was her father?"

Still holding the man's hand, Cassia looked into his eyes and initiated her magic. "Mia's father is my brother. I live and work in Asia, so we rarely see each other. But James has given me permission to take Mia for a couple of weeks. I have paperwork for you." She pulled out a blank piece of paper and handed it to Master Chen, who studied it.

He nodded and smiled at Mia. "Well, Mia, it looks like your Chinese holiday gets to continue. I'm very happy for you." His stilted voice worried Mia, and she looked between her Wushu Master and the woman standing next to her.

Becky had been quiet during this exchange, but in her confusion, she spoke up. "But I know you don't have any other family."

Cassia turned to the young girl and took her hand. "You've probably just forgotten all about me. I haven't seen Mia in several years. My work has kept me here in China. But we've met before, Becky. Four years ago, at Christmas."

Becky's eyes glossed over, and she swayed just enough to grab Mia's attention. When Mia put her hand on her friend's arm, she felt power surging through the girl.

"Oh, that's right. Yes, I just forgot." Becky's monotone voice had Mia even more concerned.

"What are you doing?" Mia whispered, glaring at Cassia.

"I'll explain when we get out of here, but you're in imminent danger. You must leave with me now." Cassia smiled and let Becky's hand go.

Mia was confused and scared. Should she go with Cassandra? Or should she stay with her friends and hope whatever that other monster wanted, Master Chen could take care of her and Becky. After all, the entire team was adept at fighting, even though Mia was the only one with real-world experience fighting creatures. She was confident they'd win out.

"No, I'm not leaving with you. I don't even know who you are." Mia looked at the bounty hunter and at Master Chen. "I've never seen her before we arrived in China."

Master Chen only smiled and nodded. "Of course, you want to leave with your aunt now. I understand. Enjoy your holiday, and we will all see you when you return home at the end of the summer."

Becky hugged her best friend as though she really thought all was well and they'd part company only to meet up again later this summer.

"What's going on?" Mia studied her friend and instructor. "They aren't even here with us, are they?" She noted the glossy eyes and vacant stares on them both and shivered.

"It's for their own safety. Trust me, you don't want to deal with what's waiting to grab you here. It's much better for everyone in this stadium if we go outside. Now." Cassia pulled Mia with her, and Mia stumbled for a few steps before looking back at the scary man eyeing her.

Mia bit her lip, righted herself, and joined Cassia in their hasty retreat. "You had better tell me everything, and I mean all of it, the second we get outside." Not sure if she made the right choice, Mia went willingly with the fae.

Cassia wanted nothing more than to find a discreet place to create a portal and take Mia away from China. But she had to get far enough from the other bounty hunters to create a safe portal —one they wouldn't be able to trace. Not all fae could trace a portal, but enough of the bounty hunters were able to, and she had to assume the one following them could too.

With Mia in tow, Cassia wove through the throng milling about outside of the conference center and went several blocks before turning down an alley. While the sun hadn't set yet, it was late enough in the day that the shadows were long and helped to cover their movement.

Once Mia no longer felt the oppression of the person hunting them, she came to a stop and glared at Cassandra. "All right, who are you? I remember you from the other night at the market, and I've noticed you following me around the city this week. What's going on?"

Cassia sighed and scanned the area around them. "This really isn't the best place to have this conversation."

"I don't care. I demand to know what's happening. I'm not going anywhere with you until you explain what happened back there." Mia put her fisted hands on her hips and stood her ground.

This wasn't the way Cassia wanted to do this. But with their safety at risk, she had to. She placed a hand on the wall next to them and thought of where she wanted to go.

Underneath her palm, a shimmering portal of blues and purples swirled out from her hand and created a space that was large enough for a person to walk through.

Mia stared in astonishment at the anomaly in front of her. "What?" She shook her head and rubbed her eyes. "What is that?" She pointed to the wall and took a few steps back.

"Don't worry, it's completely safe. And my name is Cassia, not Cassandra." She shook her head and thought of Fan for a moment before refocusing on the current situation. She shouldn't have used Fan's teasing name for her. Later on, she'd have to evaluate why *that* name came to mind instead of the many other aliases she used.

Mia blinked. "But what *is* it?"

Smirking, Cassia pulled her hand back and the swirling colors coalesced into a doorway of sorts. "It's a portal. The fae use it for traveling between our two worlds as well as to transport ourselves all around Earth. Come, follow me and I'll explain it all once we are in a safer location." She held her hand out for Mia to take.

The teenager shook her head. No way was she going to walk inside a wall. Who knew what was on the other side?

"I promise it's much safer than standing here and waiting for Narco or one of his henchmen to find us." She nodded in the direction they had come from.

"You'll tell me all once we get through that thing?" Mia gulped and steeled herself for the impossible. Of course, she'd read sci-fi novels and even watched movies where portals had been used for travel. But she had never ever believed it was real. If this *was* real, how many other things were real? She now knew monsters existed. What else would she see?

CHAPTER ELEVEN

Shanghai, China

Cassia wanted to believe that she'd gotten them away from danger. After the run-in with the fake old lady tourist on the grounds of the monastery, she wanted to tell herself they were going to be safe now. It made it easier to whisk Mia away when she could convince herself the danger was past. But that wasn't the case.

As they moved through the city, she sensed someone following them. It wasn't another of the creatures or even one of the bounties she'd been trying to track down when she stumbled upon this mysterious girl. It was someone much more dangerous.

She grabbed Mia's arm and pulled her into a narrow alleyway, crouching behind a stack of rough wooden crates and boxes. She held up a finger to her lips to keep Mia quiet.

"What's wrong?" Mia asked.

Cassia shook her head, insisting the girl not speak anymore. She didn't want to take a chance on Mia being heard by the person pursuing them. Footsteps came into the alley and Cassia pushed back against the cold, damp stone wall of the building beside her. She put an arm over Mia to crush her back so both of them were fully concealed behind the boxes. It wouldn't take much to find them.

In retrospect, she should have gone for a more concealed hiding spot than behind a bunch of crates built from slats which anyone could see between if they crouched low enough.

It wouldn't have mattered where she portaled to, the hunter following them had to have had the ability to trace portals since he was already on their trail. Knowing this, Cassia was even more grateful she hadn't portaled to somewhere she *thought* would be safe.

It was much better to try and lose them in a large city such as Shanghai, before portaling around the world to a safer spot. No need to burn any of her secure hideouts yet.

They needed to get off the street and out of sight as fast as possible. With any luck, they had confused their pursuer, and he'd go back to trying to scout them out among the crowd.

Cassia held her breath. It was pointless, but it made her feel better. It was a habit from when she was a little girl. If she was hiding like a child playing hide-and-seek with her father, or when she grew older and began finding herself in sticky situations, she would hold her breath, She had almost believed the act of drawing in air and letting it out again was what made her visible. Or that the little bit of movement would give the person on the verge of finding her the advantage.

The footsteps came closer and stopped. Cassia hazarded a peek through the slats in front of her and scanned the visible portion of the person's legs. They told her enough. Seconds stretched on and felt like hours before they stepped back and walked out of the alley. She rose for a second, just long enough to catch sight of the full person before he disappeared around the corner and onto the street.

"That's what I was afraid of," she muttered.

"What?" Mia asked. "What's going on? Who was that?"

"We need to get you somewhere safe," Cassia replied.

She sat on her heels, her head resting against the wall while she considered their options. They had to find somewhere secure where she could protect Mia and keep her out of the wrong hands until she figured out what to do with her.

A thought flashed into her mind and she stood, reaching down to help Mia to her feet. "I know where. Come on. We need to hurry."

The fae led Mia along the alley in the opposite direction from where they'd come. Squeezing between the buildings and scrambling over low walls and trash cans would make their way more challenging, but it would keep them off the street where they would be easily found.

"Cassia, what's going on? Who was that person following us?" Mia demanded.

"His name is Narco. He's a bounty hunter," said Cassia.

"Like you?"

"Not exactly. He normally works for the Queen of the Unseelie Court. Let's just say he doesn't follow the rules very well."

"What does that mean?" Mia asked.

"He's a bad guy. Like, a seriously bad guy. By all standards, even Unseelie fae. If he has set his sights on you, it's dangerous, and we need to stay far ahead of him." Cassia stopped at an intersection of garbage cans and overthrown boxes of expired produce. She waved a hand in front of her nose and looked for the best way through.

"How do you know about him?" Mia worked to keep up with Cassia as they headed who knew where. Her face scrunched in disgust as she passed the stench of the overturned trash.

Once they were down the next street, Cassia inhaled deeply and let the breath out slowly, trying to calm the trembling of her heart in her chest, while clearing her sinuses of the offending odor. She stood on her toes to look over a low wall then pulled herself up to balance on the top. There were a few loops of old barbed wire, but she used one boot to flatten it so she could help Mia up and over it.

"I've had dealings with him in the past. It's a fun game for him to find out what bounties other hunters are looking for, use the tracing and work they've already done, and swoop in to make the claim himself. But that's just obnoxious more than anything. Narco is dark and won't hesitate to destroy whatever is standing in his path if he thinks it will make it easier for him to accomplish what he wants. I have reason to believe he is the one that killed my father."

Mia drew in a sharp breath and went quiet.

They continued through the city toward the outskirts. Cassia knew of a place to stash Mia for a little while, at least until she could figure out what to do with her.

There had to be something more about her. She must be very special. There were too many people after Mia, too much interest in her. She wasn't displaying special powers, but that didn't mean anything. Depending on who and what she was, Mia might not have total control over her abilities yet. In a way, that could make it even more dangerous.

They were silent for the remainder of the journey, and finally their destination lay in front of them. The abandoned apartment complex was tiny, featuring only eight units.

"What is this place?" Mia asked.

"It used to be an apartment complex. Well, I guess it still is, but no one lives here anymore. It was condemned a few years back and everyone was forced to move out. It's been on my radar for a little while. I meant to come here and check it out when I was searching for the boggart we ran into at the market, but I never got around to it."

She didn't mention that the main reason she hadn't gotten

around to pursuing her instincts about the complex was that she was so focused on following Mia and trying to keep her safe.

"And you think we'll be safe here?" Mia asked, eyeing the sagging building and overgrown patch of grass around it suspiciously.

"It's shelter," Cassia replied. "And that look on your face underscores why I chose it. No one is going to think of somewhere like this when searching for you. We'll lay low for a while and then decide where to go from there."

Mia still looked confused and concerned, a twisted blend of emotions flowing through her vibrant eyes. Cassia couldn't blame her. Everything she'd been through already was a lot for anyone to handle, much less a teenage girl. A slight shudder went through the young halfling as they continued.

They walked over the cracked sidewalk, crushing blades of grass that had forced their way up through the concrete. Cassia made a conscious effort to avoid the tiny flowers sprouting in places. She didn't like the idea of destroying something so delicate and beautiful. It was an odd thought, but she tried not to dwell on it too much.

Two thick pieces of wood were nailed crossways over the front door of the first of the two buildings, preventing them from opening it. Cassia could have broken through one of the windows but didn't want to call more attention to them as they prowled around.

They made their way around to the back of the building. Here, the door that accessed the breezeway at the front of the building was open, possibly smashed in by a kick or two. It hung away from the doorframe, hinges rusted and decayed.

Cassia stuck her head into the room and listened for any signs that someone else had chosen the spot as their own place of refuge. When the building remained silent, she slipped inside. Mia followed behind her. The air was dusty and unpleasant, but they couldn't expect anything else in a place abandoned and closed up years ago. The building was set up with four apartments, one on either side of the hall on two floors. Cassia tested the first door, but it wouldn't budge. The second was crushed, the middle nearly split in two. She eyed the metal steps that led up to the next floor.

"Let's try up there," she suggested. "If there's nothing better, we'll try our luck with building number two."

They climbed the stairs and tried the first apartment. The door resisted, but Mia stopped her.

"Can't you just use your magic to open it?" she asked.

"It's kind of bad form, but I guess whoever locked it in the first place probably doesn't care if we're in there," Cassia replied. "We could go back to the one on the bottom floor, but I'd feel better with us up here. Being off the ground always feels more secure."

She used her magic to release the lock and opened the door to the apartment. Dank air rushed out at them, but the windows allowed enough light inside for them to see the room. It was overflowing with dirty mattresses, discarded clothes, and trash. Cassia slammed the door shut and shook her head. They moved over to the second apartment and found much of the same.

"On second thought, let's not jump straight to the first option. Let's check out what's behind door number two," Cassia said.

They made their way to the second building and up to the second floor. After scouring the first three apartments, they found the door to the fourth standing partially open. Cassia went inside first. It was cluttered like the others, but not as much. But they'd wasted enough time, and this was probably as good as they were going to get. They entered the apartment and closed the door behind them.

"Home sweet home," Mia murmured.

"Not forever," Cassia promised. "Just for now."

"And then?" Mia asked.

"And then, well, it won't be," Cassia replied. She studied a hallway across the room. "Should we explore the rest of it?"

Mia nodded. "Why not?"

They picked their way through the living room and into the hallway, where a familiar, sickening odor wafted to Cassia. The farther inside they walked, the stronger the smell became. She cringed. Eight apartments and she'd had the bad luck to choose this one. Or the good luck, depending on how she decided to look at it.

The stench was almost palpable and forced Cassia and Mia to wrinkle their noses in disgust. Covering her face with one arm, Cassia opened the door to the bedroom, and the handle turned easily in her hand. The door swung open slowly, hinges creaking, halting only when it hit a stopper that made an audible springy sound. Everything beyond a few feet into the room was masked in pitch darkness. There should have been a window in there somewhere, but it must have been covered by a thick curtain which blotted out the light.

"Nope, nothing creepy about this at all," Mia said under her breath.

"I know that smell," Cassia said. She'd smelled it countless times before. She had been right about her suspicions.

"Ick?" Mia asked.

"Not exactly. Come on, the boggart's in here, I smell it," Cassia said, her voice just above a whisper. Reluctantly, Mia followed. Cassia reached for a battle knife on her belt and pulled it from its sheath. Just before they entered the complete darkness, she made eye contact with Mia and waved the knife in the air. "Want one?"

"Why would I need one?" Mia asked, her eyes snapping toward a dark corner of the room. Something had moved. Perhaps it was a mouse or another small rodent, or maybe it was just the rattling of the stuff piled everywhere or falling over.

"This boggart has hurt little children. He's a mean and nasty creature, and the reason I'm in China to begin with," Cassia said, dashing Mia's hope.

"Thanks, but I don't need a knife to protect myself," Mia said, feeling her way into the room with one hand on the wall, the other lightly brushing against Cassia to make sure she was still there.

The smell of mildew was almost overwhelming, burrowing deep into their lungs and bringing them to the verge of coughing every time they inhaled. This complex must have suffered badly from the flooding a few months back, and the summer heat and wet carpet would have combined to create the perfect environment for mold. Furniture and possessions, haphazardly thrown together, stacked against the walls, relayed a sense that at one time, someone had left this room with hopes of coming back for their belongings.

Now a boggart lived there. The nasty little thing had moved in and would not be happy about their intrusion. Cassia held an arm in front of Mia, stopping her progress just at the corner of the wall Mia was holding ended and where the main part of the bedroom likely began.

"Do you hear it?" Cassia asked.

Mia heard a low grumbling sound, like an angry animal mumbling to itself.

Taking a huge risk, Cassia flung herself into the room, crashing through stacks of stuff to where she hoped the window would be. When she felt the drape under her hand, she gave it a hard yank, but only part of it fell. It was enough to let in some sunlight, though, and give the room a sickly cast.

Just a few feet away, she saw it.

Three feet high, the creature stood with its arms hanging at its sides. The light from outside just barely illuminated its outline, but even in the darkness, she could see the ugly human-like form it had taken. Hair sprouted in spirals from the sides of its head, leaving the top bald like a clown. It wore what appeared to be overalls, stained and dirty, and its eyes glowed a deep orange. It stared past Mia to Cassia. Its mouth was a black hole which seemed to wriggle and writhe as if it were made of thousands of ants.

"He is not happy," Cassia muttered. "I've never seen that particular look on one. I'm not sure if I should be encouraged by the gross makeover or not."

Suddenly, the thing sniffed deeply three times, its head following the scent like a blind dog looking for a treat. Then it halted, and its eyes bored a hole into Mia. Even though the mouth shifted and moved, it appeared to curl into a smile. It had smelled her, and its eyes widened, impossibly large, taking up most of its face. Still, it made no sound other than the breathy grumbling.

Mia expected to be scared at this moment, standing in the dark, staring at a malevolent boggart with orange eyes, but instead, she straightened up. Her body filled with adrenaline, and her mind went blank of any thoughts other than action. She had two choices: run or fight. She had chosen.

"I got this," she heard herself say as if her voice came from far away. Cassia raised her hand in protest, but it was too late. Mia was already moving toward the boggart.

It screamed.

Not the scream of a fearful beast, but the scream of one who is unbelievably angry. Mia and Cassia had invaded its space and had dared to make eye contact with it. Now it wanted blood, and Mia knew it was something she should do herself. A part of her that she didn't even know existed screamed at her to take down this beast and prove her worth to the bounty hunter.

The boggart launched itself at her, its mouth widening to become an endless black hole of violence. Without a second thought, Mia sidestepped just as the boggart reached her, and she punched it in the jaw. It crumpled to the ground at her feet and she punted it almost across the room. The creature crashed through a soggy table and into a bookshelf that fell apart, sending cracked moldy books across the floor and temporarily burying it.

Mia dove after it, and Cassia stepped back. She had intended to join in the fight, but frankly, it seemed like Mia had it handled. She winced as the girl performed a roundhouse kick that sent the boggart across the room where it landed. The small man-like creature stood and shook its head—probably to get rid of the dizziness. The grumbling grew louder, and it charged again, its stocky legs—like those of a toddler who did weighted squats—churned and allowed it to move unnaturally fast.

The boggart swiped at Mia, who dodged it before it flung itself at her waist. She ducked and it sailed over her into a glass table, shattering it and sending shards all over the room. The creature got to its feet, unaffected by the little nicks and cuts all over its body. Then it dove again, but this time Mia caught it mid-air with a kick directly to the face. Its head snapped back while its body continued moving forward, then it landed with a heavy thud.

When the boggart didn't move again for a few seconds, Mia turned to Cassia. "So, what now?" she asked, a smile on her face as if she had just done a particularly demanding gardening job and was ready for the next chore.

"Now," Cassia said, unraveling a rope from one of the many pockets of goodies on her belt, "We tie it up. Here," she said, tossing Mia some of the length. "You get the legs. I'll get the arms. Then, we can carry it...him out of here." She studied the creature and noted the Adam's apple in the boggart's throat and said, "Yup, it's a him."

"On it," Mia said, grabbing the rope. She was surprised at herself.

Cassia stared at the boggart. They'd moved him into the living room away from the destruction, but that was as far as her plan went. She'd been chasing after him for so long, and now he was suddenly at her mercy. At least, at Mia's mercy.

Cassia was happy to go along with it. She was impressed by the mysterious young woman's ability to take down the creature, but now that she had him, she wasn't sure what she should do next. This little guy could pad her finances even more, and he was technically her assignment. Bringing him in would open her up for another bounty, or allow her to focus more on Mia and keeping her safe.

"What's wrong?" Mia asked. "Was I too hard on him?"

Mia moved toward the boggart as though she was going to comfort the smelly little being, but Cassia shook her head, rushing to stop her. "No. That was fine. You were amazing, actually. I was just thinking about what to do with him. I can't take you with me to turn him in. But I also don't want to leave you here alone."

Cassia looked down at the boggart again as it grunted and shifted. Leaving Mia alone was a terrible idea. No telling what else could be lurking around here. But she didn't have many options when it came to handing the boggart in. She released a long breath, debating with herself about what she should do.

CHAPTER TWELVE

Montana

The Beyond Meat meatloaf Luna's mother made was just as delicious as they all expected it to be. Meatloaf and mashed potatoes may have been a heavy meal for a summer evening, but they didn't care. All four of the young fae were famished after working so hard, and a filling, comforting meal was exactly what they needed.

As soon as the plates hit the table in front of them, they dove into their very large portions. The diner might not be like other restaurants in the area because of the menu, but one thing it shared with other Montana eating spots was the plates were always piled high, and customers went home satisfied. If the meatloaf and mashed potatoes weren't going to be enough for the teens, the large basket of homemade yeast rolls and butter sprinkled with coarse salt would top them off.

And if in the extreme circumstance that they ate it all and still needed something to push them over the edge, Nicoletta was always good for a slab of home-baked cake or one of her famous pies. Luna was secretly dreaming of a couple of slices of cherry pineapple pie even as she filled herself with mashed potatoes and mushroom gravy.

"If there's one good thing I can say about being stuck in this place all summer, it's that at least I get to regularly gorge myself on your mother's food," Carson said. His fork made it into his mouth before it closed after the last words.

Luna smiled. She was proud of her mother and enjoyed it when the others at the academy acknowledged her. Only a few students were there on scholarship, and the vast majority were extremely prosperous, if not wealthy. Many of them saw a separation between her and the other students. While they received their monthly stipends and were able to look forward to luxurious vacations and other indulgences, she and her mother lived a far simpler life.

Sometimes Nicoletta slipped Luna spending money and also made sure she received the money her father sent, but it wasn't nearly as much as what the others were given. Luna wasn't ashamed. The life they lived now was a major step up from the challenging, often rough neighborhood where they had lived before she'd entered the academy.

Vivi reached her fork across the table and quickly filled it with a scoop of Zander's mashed potatoes, raising her eyebrows and laughing around the bite when he protested. The momentary lapse in tension and anger between the two Courts brought the realization to Luna's mind. She picked up her third yeast roll and coated it heavily with butter. As she sank her teeth into the rich, fluffy bread, she was thankful for the millionth time for her athletic build and fast metabolism.

"You know what I just realized? The summer is already half over, and we have barely done anything together as a team," she said.

"What do you call all those hours we just spent trying to

master being in control of the wind?" Vivi asked. "And the ridiculous purple pansy circles from last week?"

"Work," said Luna. "That's all just us working together because we have to in order to improve our skills. It's not really about us getting to know each other better or making any real connection. Principal Elmhurst wants us to gel and become a team, rather than four individuals. That's not going to happen if all we ever do together is practice our skills and occasionally sit down for a meal."

"Luna's right," Zander said. "If we're ever going to really come together and make a cohesive team, we have to actually spend time together. Doing something away from campus and finding out about one another in an unstructured environment would be good for us."

"Wow. You Seelie fae really do enjoy all the warm and fuzzy moments, don't you?" Vivi said.

Luna rolled her eyes. "Are you ever going to let up? You know, you're not the only one whose life was disrupted by Elmhurst deciding the four of us are her best chance at bringing glory to the academy. Did it ever occur to you that you are just as much of an interference in our lives as we are in yours? The least you could do is put a little bit of effort into not having all these walls up. I'm not asking you to have a slumber party with me or paint each other's nails while we dream about our futures. I'm just asking you to tolerate me for a little while and see if you can actually learn something about me, and about Zander, too. And, while I know this is a revolutionary concept, maybe you could let us find out a little something about you too."

Vivi looked a little taken aback by Luna's intensity, but a smile flickered briefly on her lips. "I mean, we are already kind of stuck in a perpetual slumber party."

Luna offered a hint of a smile in return. "And if I whip out the sparkly nail polish and ask you to create a dream journal with me, you are more than welcome to tell me I've gone way too far."

"Deal," the dark-haired fae said.

"Awesome," Carson said. "Look at all this progress. So, what are we going to do?"

"Let's do something fun. How about mini golf? Or is there anything playing at the movies any of you would like to see?" Luna suggested.

"There's really not that much to do around Phillipsburg," Carson said. "I've done the mini-golf so many times I could probably be blindfolded and still get a hole-in-one at every hole."

"And there's nothing good at the theater. They only show a couple of movies at a time, and I'm not interested in either one of them," Zander said.

"I wish we could go somewhere else. Somewhere interesting where none of us have been before," Luna said. "I'm so tired of being around Philipsburg, Montana. There has to be something more out there we could do."

"Well, we could, if we had a portal," Carson said.

"None of us have the power to open a portal," Zander replied.

"No halflings do," Luna said.

"Why don't we try combining our power to open one?" Vivi asked.

The rest of the group quieted and stared at her. The waitress came by and cleared away their dinner plates. They waited while another server came up with huge slices of cherry pineapple pie, a massive bowl of almond ice cream to put on top, and spoons.

Three sets of eyes stared back at Vivi as though she were crazy, but she didn't back down. She just let them keep on staring as she used her spoon to scoop up some of the ice cream and drop it on top of her pie.

Finally, Carson spoke. "You think we could do that?" he asked.

"I've never heard of a halfling being able to open a portal," Zander said.

"Neither have I," Luna said.

"It takes too much power. It's just not possible," Carson added.

"That's the thing. I'm not suggesting that just one of us go wandering out into the field and create a portal to send us on an adventure. One halfling can't do that. But the four most powerful halflings this academy has ever seen might be able to do it."

Zander thought about the proposition for a few seconds. It sounded ridiculous. But the prospect of combining their skills into a power far exceeding what they possessed individually and using that to create a portal was intriguing. There was no guarantee it would work, but now that the idea was in his head, he didn't want to just let it go.

"We should try it," he said.

The other three turned their attention to him now.

"Really?" Vivi asked.

He nodded and attacked his plate of pie. The crust and filling were still warm, making the vanilla almond milk ice cream melt into a sweet pool around it.

"It's not like we have anything better to do. If we manage to make one, it will be ridiculously amazing, and we'll be able to go wherever we want. And if we don't, at least it's something we did that isn't what Elmhurst would be expecting," he said.

The others laughed and agreed. They finished their dessert and went to thank Luna's mother. She happily offered hugs to them all, and they complied. Luna noticed their casual response and how they pretended to be put-off by the hug, but all three willingly curled into her affectionate arms and even rested their heads on her shoulder for a moment, savoring the attention. Did any of them ever receive the affection and acknowledgment they wanted from their own parents?

When they left the diner, they returned to what they had begun to think of as *their* field. It offered them the ideal combination of an isolated, yet easily accessible location with adequate space and separation from the rest of campus. There were still a few signs of the aftermath of their wind experiments in the form of branches, trees, and leaves scattered across the grass.

"Do you think we should go ahead and put up a protective shield this time?" Carson asked.

They had purposely not put up the shield when working with the wind out of worry it would block too much of the air currents from coming in. It had put them at risk of being caught by any humans who happened by, and they'd seen at least one elderly man wander past at the edge of the field when Luna had been tumbling around in mid-air.

He'd looked right at the group but hadn't said anything, nor did he react in any way. Either he couldn't see far enough to know what was happening, or he'd just figured he had lost his marbles years ago, and it was really just showing up now.

But this was different. Manipulating the wind was one thing. Playing with the possibility of portals was another thing entirely. A portal could be an exceptional tool, providing immediate transportation from one place to another. It could allow them to travel easily and access places they'd never be able to go otherwise. But it could also be extremely dangerous. If not made correctly, a portal could send them somewhere they didn't want to go and not allow for a way back. They might even enter the portal and never emerge.

They were willing to take on the risk, but they weren't going to do it out in the open. The last thing they needed was to have to explain to Principal Elmhurst that a wayward human had been drawn in by the fun of watching them do magic and had ended up tumbling through a portal never to be seen again. That would not bode well for the future of their education or their chances of securing one of the coveted spots at the embassy. Generally speaking, fae who allowed humans to be harmed or lost through magic weren't looked upon kindly. That type of exposure threatened their entire world.

"Go ahead," Zander said. "Make it big. Encompass the whole field if you can. I think we should start small and try to create a portal that brings us just from one end of the field to the other. If we can get that down, we'll move on to a longer trip."

As soon as Carson had the protective shield in place, they gathered at one end of the field. They readied themselves for the challenge, all concentrating hard on the creation of the portal. They focused intensely for as long as they could keep it up, but nothing happened.

"Maybe we're thinking about different places," Luna suggested. "I've heard portals have to be created with a very specific place in mind. If the person creating it isn't focused hard enough on that specific place, the magic can't do what they want it to do."

"Are you saying the magic gets confused?" Vivi said. "Or lost?"

"All right. Everyone look across the field. Do you see that big stick with the two pieces coming off it in the shape of a Y? If you look directly through that Y, you'll see a patch of grass that looks a little different than the rest of the grass. It's thicker or something. Focus on that. Concentrate on that being the spot where we want our portal to go," Zander told them.

They regrouped and tried again. A few minutes later, it still hadn't happened.

"See, I never heard that the person had to concentrate so hard on the exact spot they wanted to go to," Carson said. "It doesn't make sense. What if they're creating a portal that goes somewhere they've never been before? They can't exactly focus completely on that place if they don't really know where they're going."

"Then what do you know about portals?" Luna asked, slightly frustrated to have her theory questioned.

"It's not necessarily about pinpointing the exact place you want to end up when you go through the portal," Carson explained. "It's about your intention and your needs."

"Well, I *intend* for this to work so we can be the first halflings to make a portal," Vivi said.

"And I *need* to have something impressive to add to my resume," Zander said.

Carson nodded, his hands planted on his hips. "Very funny. Both of you. I'm serious, though. I knew someone who knew someone—"

"Who knew someone who knew someone who had a cousin whose neighbor's sister's cat—" Vivi said.

"They created a portal," Carson said, pushing right past her sarcasm. "And it worked. But they said it took having very clear intentions and knowing why they needed the portal for it to happen."

"It wouldn't hurt to try," Luna said. "I guess our intentions are to use our powers together to create a portal we can use to get away from the academy every now and then."

"And we need it because we don't want to be trapped here all the time," Vivi added.

"And because it would help us to mesh better and become a stronger team," Zander offered.

"All right. Let's try it," Carson said.

They positioned themselves at the end of the protective dome again and focused their powers. Combining their energy and concentration, they envisioned the portal forming at their feet and connecting them to the other side of the field. As the intensity of their shared magic grew stronger, they reached out and held each other's hands. The physical connection linked their abilities even more and they felt the power strengthening.

Suddenly a loud popping sounded, and purple smoke billowed up from the ground. It filled the dome of the protective shield and obliterated their vision for several seconds. Luna coughed and swiped at the smoke, trying to clear as much of it as she could.

"Well, that didn't go as planned," she said.

"Yeah. Which one of you *intended* for the field to explode in purple smoke?" Vivi asked. "Because I definitely didn't *need* that to happen."

"It's taking revenge for all the purple flowers we made," Carson said. "It just couldn't take it anymore."

"Let's get this smoke out and try again," Vivi said.

They tried to wave away the smoke, but it didn't work. A spell to clear it helped some, but eventually they had to remove the protective dome for a few seconds to let the smoke dissipate before putting the shield back up. If anyone happened by at that moment, they would see a puff of purple smoke suddenly appear, but no source for it. Fortunately, the smoke seemed to disappear quickly once beyond the protective shield. It could easily be explained away as being from a campfire or stupid kids playing with fireworks, as such things so frequently were.

"Look," Carson said, pointing at the ground at his feet.

Luna came to stand beside him and studied the grass, which dipped down several inches in a perfect circle, as though a large stamp had crushed it. "We dented the ground," she said.

"Maybe it's the beginning of a portal," Carson said. "Like we almost got it, but it didn't quite get all the way through."

Zander stood to the other side of Carson and tilted his head, looking down at the impression. "Nope. I think we just dented the ground."

"Then let's crank up the shield and try it again," Vivi said.

She didn't have the same frustration and aggravation this time as she had when they'd practiced the Faerie circle or the wind control. The possibility of being able to combine with the others to create the first halfling-produced portal fueled her. She was bound and determined to make this happen. This wasn't just about being able to collaborate with the others and please Principal Elmhurst. Vivi also wanted that achievement for herself. If she was going to have to be part of this foursome, she was going to make fae history.

"Let's go," Zander said.

The handsome Seelie boy was just as driven to succeed in this, compelled to create something incredible that would make him stand out. He was convinced that if the four of them were able to create a portal together, it would solidify his chances of securing a pass to Faerie. But it wasn't just the job and prestige he was after.

If Zander was able to receive that pass and enter the fae realm, he could seek out the fae mother who had left him on his father's doorstep so many years ago. He would finally have the chance to confront her about abandoning him at birth and ask her how she'd been able to do it so easily. He'd never understood how a mother could leave her newborn baby and only think of him again when it was time for him to go to school.

The effect of their combined magic happened much more quickly this time. But it didn't create a portal. Vivi let out a scream as a blast of magic sent her flying across the field to what they'd intended to be the endpoint of the portal. She was quickly followed by the other three, then all four were sent back. They tumbled to the ground and lay there, groaning.

"Crickets!" Carson shouted.

"Well, at least this time, we actually went somewhere," Zander said. "It wasn't exactly through a portal, but it was something."

"It was something, all right," Luna said.

"Come on. Let's try again," Zander said, pulling himself up off the ground.

They focused their minds, concentrating as hard as they could on combining their magic to create the portal. Energy buzzed in the air. Something was changing. None of the four acknowledged it. They didn't want to get too excited, didn't want to be too hopeful that something was finally going to work. Instead, they moved closer to each other and held hands more tightly. A rush of magic and energy flowed through their connected palms. It was happening. The world was responding to their magic, changing according to their will.

Above them, the sky rumbled. They looked at each other, confused and curious, and in the next instant, rain began to pour from the dome around them.

That was not their will.

Gasping, they let go of their hands and stared in shock at the protective shield. Beyond it, the sky was still, and not a single drop of rain fell. Inside, the four fae looked like drowned rats and were already standing in mud. Vivi's hair hung in her eyes, and her shoulders sagged under her wet clothes. She glared at the other three and lifted a finger.

"One. More. Time."

CHAPTER THIRTEEN

Shanghai, China

"What do you mean, *take him in*?" Mia asked.

"You know that I'm a bounty hunter," Cassia said. "Well, this creature isn't just some smelly little interloper who's angry at us for storming his abode. Actually, that's exactly what he is, but that's not the point. This boggart is why I came to China in the first place. I've been tracking him for quite a while."

"Why?" Mia asked.

"How much do you know about boggarts?" the fae bounty hunter asked.

"Including that they smell horrible and are really nasty when they fight?"

"Yes," Cassia replied.

"Then I know they smell horrible and are really nasty when they fight," Mia said.

Cassia laughed. "I guess that's a start. These creatures are spirits of a sort. They inhabit homes and can be extremely mischievous. A lot of times they aren't harmful, just more annoying than anything. But sometimes they can become dangerous. When they live in a home and are relatively peaceful, their smell isn't as bad. It has almost an earthy quality to it. Not necessarily something anyone would want to convert into a scented candle and advertise as the next big trend in home fragrance, but not overtly offensive."

"Then what happened to this one to make it smell so horrible? It's like somebody dipped him into the sewer and then rolled him around in the trash like they were breading fried chicken."

"That is a truly awful visual," Cassia said. "But not an entirely inaccurate analysis. Boggarts develop their distinctly horrible smell if they're given a name. Giving one of these creatures a name also causes it to get more intense and more dangerous. Before, they might play practical jokes and be a nuisance to the family who lives in the house. But after being given a name, these spirits become evil. They can hurt people and cause tremendous difficulties for anyone who stands in their way.

"Of course, it's a natural instinct to name things. People do it all the time. They themselves have a name. They name their children, their pets. Some people even name their house plants. That's the challenge with boggarts. When someone realizes there's something in their home, it's the normal inclination to want to familiarize yourself with it. Giving it a name helps to make it more personal and create a relationship. This is especially true for the families who have had the same boggart in their home for years. It's particularly challenging when there are children in the house."

"Children name everything," Mia said.

"Yes," Cassia said. "It's just something they do. Unfortunately, that's what happened with this boggart. There was a young boy living in the home he had decided to inhabit. He was mischievous and almost playful. The boy decided the boggart might be his friend and would be happy to have a name like everyone else. Of course, that made all Hades break loose. He's had a bounty out ever since. And that's what I've been chasing."

"Is this the same one from the market the night we first saw each other?" Mia asked. It was really sinking in at that moment that she had witnessed something extraordinary at the night market. That night she thought it was just the extremely strong tea the elderly woman had given her. Now she realized she had the innate power to see beyond the plane humans could perceive.

Those crowds milling through the streets and stuffing the intersections at the night market had no idea of the dangerous creature that lurked among them. They couldn't see what she saw, or what the bounty hunter saw. The two of them were the only ones to witness the boggart slithering along the sides of the buildings like a giant snake.

"Yes," Cassia said.

"So, what happens now? Or what's supposed to happen?"

"Now that I have him, I'm supposed to bring him into the Faerie prison and turn him over to the head jailer."

"What will happen to him then?" Mia asked.

Cassia shrugged. "I really don't know for sure. All I'm there for is to turn him over to the authorities so I can collect on the bounty. What happens to him after that is his problem and something he earned."

"But you can't bring me with you to drop him off?" Mia asked.

Cassia shook her head adamantly. "No. That wouldn't be possible. You see, Forasaon isn't an ordinary prison. It's in Faerie. Access to Faerie is restricted. Only halflings with very specific positions are ever allowed in. I can't just bring you. But I also can't leave you alone here."

"Why not?"

"Because it could be dangerous. We managed to take down this boggart, but there are seven other apartments. As we just proved, they might seem empty, but may not be empty at all. We have no way of knowing what could be wandering around in them. I can't leave you alone and potentially vulnerable to really dangerous creatures."

"But you deserve to bring this guy in and collect your bounty. You've been working so hard to track him, and now you finally have him," Mia pointed out.

"I think technically you're the one who actually took him down," Cassia said.

Mia let out a short laugh. "Maybe, but I'm sure if I hadn't jumped in, you could have managed him just fine on your own."

Cassia chuckled. "Probably. But I am really impressed by your fighting skills. You can really hold your own out there."

"Well, up until very recently, holding my own out there meant not getting myself destroyed on the mat during my Wushu competitions."

"The skills are in your blood," the bounty hunter replied. "It's part of your fae heritage. Though you are much stronger and more skilled than I ever could have imagined."

"Thank you. I'm also a big girl. I promise you can leave me here alone and bring the boggart in. Nothing is going to happen to me. I highly doubt this dude had any neighbors. The stench alone is enough to drive them out. You go ahead. Do your thing." Mia waved Cassia off. "I'll just hang around here and wait for you to get back."

"Are you sure?" Cassia asked. "I can stay with you. We can just keep him tied up for a little while longer until you feel more comfortable."

"Honestly, I don't think anything's going to make me a whole lot more comfortable. And I'm certainly not going to be more comfortable hanging around in an abandoned apartment with a tied-up creature that tried very hard to wipe me off the face of the planet," Mia said.

Cassia thought about it. As much as she didn't want to leave Mia alone in the apartment, she really hated the idea of the boggart escaping and running off again, leaving her unable to collect her bounty. It was not one of her career aspirations to dedicate the rest of her life to finding this one creature. She could just quickly take him to Forasaon, make sure the credits were applied to her account, and return.

"It won't take long," she told the halfling. "Just stay here. I'll be back as fast as I can."

"I'll be fine," Mia reassured her.

The moment Cassia crossed through the portal, Mia began pacing, wondering what in the heck she had gotten herself into. She was of fae descent? How was that even possible? Her dad was human, no doubt about that. But her mother....

Hauling an unconscious boggart into the prison wasn't exactly Cassia's idea of a fun activity. But at least it wasn't nearly as hard as some of the other bounties she'd dragged through the portal over the years. He was small compared to a lot of the other creatures she brought in, which helped with navigating herself and his hairy little body into the reception area of the prison.

Cassia dropped him at her feet, flattened her hands on the desk, and stared at Fan. He was wrapped up in a conversation with one of his goons and didn't look her way until the ogre cleared his throat and not-so-subtly nodded in her direction. Fan turned and his eyes widened. A smile curled his lips, and if lips could walk, that would be a swagger.

"Cassia. You just can't get enough of me, can you?" he asked.

"I reached that point quite a while ago, Fan. But, alas, it's part of my job," she replied.

The ogres behind Fan chortled and turned their backs to muffle the sound. Cassia was sure their boss wouldn't be too happy knowing they were laughing at him.

But Fan didn't pay any attention to them. He was just staring at her, his mind drifting to the feeling that built up in his stomach every time he laid eyes on the beautiful fae. "Why do you have to be like that?" he asked. "I'm just trying to be friendly."

"Well, here's the thing. I'm in a little bit of a hurry, and I'd like to be on my way," Cassia replied.

He narrowed his eyes as he studied her, trying to figure her out—which he did almost every time they interacted. "Then why are you here?"

Cassia blinked a few times. It was like Fan had forgotten where he was and what his job was. "You're the head jailer of Forasaon, Fan," she pointed out. "And I'm a bounty hunter. I think the reason I've come is pretty self-explanatory."

"Don't call me Fan," he said. "You know I hate that."

She did. But she never gave it much thought when she was at the prison trying to get her job done. Everybody called him Fan. That probably made it one of those 'two wrongs don't make a right' and 'if everybody else jumped off a cliff, would you go along with them?' situations, but it was what it was.

"I'm sorry. You're the head jailer of Forasaon, *Faylynne*. And I'm a bounty hunter. I'm here to turn in my assignment and collect my bounty," she said.

"Your assignment?" he asked.

Cassia pointed at her feet. Fan walked around and looked down at the boggart. He was still mostly unconscious, but occasionally muttered and thrashed around. The ties were too tight for him to escape, and every time he struggled, he eventually gave up and sagged against the floor again.

"You finally snagged the boggart you've been after, I see," Fan said.

"Yeah. This thing dragged me to China and all over Shanghai, causing trouble."

"How did you finally manage to get it?"

"Invaded his apartment," she said. "Accidentally, actually."

"Ah," Fan said with a short laugh. "Only you would manage something like that."

Cassia wasn't sure what that was supposed to mean. It

sounded like the jailer thought he was being funny, but it came across awkwardly, as though he was questioning her skills.

"You mean only the best bounty hunter of our time could manage to bring in a boggart? Is that meant as an insult?"

He muttered for a few seconds, attempting to retract the comment, but never quite finding the right words. "I mean…" he started again, but Cassia shook her head.

She was done talking. She had to get back through the portal to China and the apartment. Mia shouldn't be left alone for this long.

"This has been lots of fun, but I really do need to be on my way," she said. "If you'll go ahead and send my credits for the bounty to my account, I would appreciate it."

"Sure," Fan said hesitantly. "Let me just get this guy into a cell and I'll be right back to handle everything."

"Put him in a cell? He's practically unconscious. What is he possibly going to do in the forty-five seconds it's going to take you to give me my money?" she asked.

"Just hold on. It's protocol. We need to secure the inmate before any other business can proceed," he said.

Cassia was fairly certain he was making that up. There were plenty of times when she'd brought assignments into the prison in a similar condition to the boggart's and she'd seen no rush to get them stashed away.

Fan and his goons were just as likely to leave them on the floor until they had handled their business because it was just easier that way. Now suddenly, Fan wanted to keep everything organized to the point of carrying away a totally incapacitated boggart.

He scooped the boggart up with one arm and carried it toward the cells. The ogres leaned toward each other, whispering and laughing. Cassia rolled her eyes when she caught them digging their elbows into each other's ribs and she glared at them.

"I'm glad you're finding this so hilarious, but I really do need to get going. What is with your boss today?" she asked.

"Same thing as always," one of them said.

"Which is?"

The ogres laughed again. Cassia felt like she was the butt of an inside joke, and she hated it. Before she could ask them again, Fan came back into the room. He smiled at her.

"So, how have things been? I bet you're happy to have that boggart off your back, huh?"

Cassia narrowed her eyes at the jailer. "Things have been busy. I really am in a hurry, though. I have to get back. If you could settle my account, I'll be on my way."

"Speaking of your account, the claim for the redcap you brought in the other day was paid to your account. You are officially a very rich female." He put his hands on his hips and smiled at her. "What are you going to do with all that money? Any big plans?"

"Right now, my big plan is to get my money and get back to what I was doing before I got the boggart," she said.

"You're always in so much of a hurry when you come here," Fan said.

If Cassia didn't know any better—or at least she hoped she knew better—she would have thought the jailer was pouting.

"This isn't a social call, Fan." She held her hands up. "Excuse me, Faylynne. I'm here to do my job. I'm a bounty hunter. This is what I do. People tell me who the bad guys are. I go find them. When I do, I bring them in here to you so you can do whatever it is you do with them. You pay me for it. Then I go back and do it all again. We've been through this a lot of times over the years," she said.

She turned and moved toward the portal, but Fan approached her.

"What else do you do?" he asked. "I mean, other than finding the bad guys and bringing them in here to me. There have to be other things you do in your downtime."

Cassia let out a long sigh. "I don't have downtime, Fan. This is my life. It's all I was ever meant to do. It's all I do. If I'm not tracking a bounty, I'm sleeping. Sometimes eating. There's not a whole lot of kicking-back-to-relax time in my world."

Cassia started to leave again, but Fan took another step toward her. He didn't want her to go. Not yet. These times when she brought in her bounty assignments were the only times he got to see her, and it wasn't nearly enough for him. He wanted to be closer to her, but he didn't know how.

"But there is," he said. "I mean, there could be. With the money you just earned from the redcap, you don't have to worry about finding any more bounties for a long time. You could just take some time to do other things."

Cassia shook her head. "There's not really anything else I want to do."

That wasn't entirely true. Her focus was on Mia now, but she still didn't know what she was supposed to do with the girl. All Cassia knew was that she needed to get back to the apartment as fast as possible. She'd already taken too much time squaring off with the head jailer. She approached the portal for the third time, and for the third time, Fan stopped her.

"What about your claim for the boggart?" he asked. "Don't you want to wait until it's credited? It's a much smaller one than the redcap, so it won't take as long."

Cassia shook her head. "I really don't have time. Just credit it to my account."

She made her way to the portal, but when she attempted to activate it, nothing happened. She tried again, and still, it wouldn't allow her through. Fan stared back at her when she turned to him. He was behind this. The head jailer was the only one who could turn off access to the portal to prevent anyone from leaving. She couldn't go anywhere.

CHAPTER FOURTEEN

Shanghai, China

Mia stood around in the apartment for a few moments after Cassia left, trying to decide what to do. She was still attempting to wrap her head around it all. Her reality had shifted completely, going from what she thought was a normal life to something decidedly not normal.

At least, not normal to *her*. To Cassia and the creatures chasing them, this was just life. And apparently, it was for her now as well. That was a lot to try to take in, and Mia decided she needed to sit for a few minutes.

The combination of the fight against the boggart and the weighty pressure of everything she'd learned over the last few days had exhausted her, and she felt like all the energy inside her had drained out. She had no way of knowing what was coming next, and she needed to take a break before it all came down on her again.

But maybe it wouldn't. Maybe capturing the boggart was all

they'd have to deal with before Cassia took her home. The bounty hunter would come back, having turned the creature in, and they could move on without any more difficulty. Mia knew the chances of that were small, but she let it buoy her spirits as she searched around the apartment for somewhere to relax.

It wasn't the most welcoming environment now that the fight with the boggart had left it in tatters. It hadn't really been the most welcoming environment before. But now the stacks of boxes and discarded items were thrown around, some broken, and the contents of others spilled out across the floor.

She thought she'd noticed some scurrying movements in what had tumbled out of one box, but she didn't want to put too much thought into it. She could handle a spider or even an ambitious mouse who decided to call the apartment home. But now was not the time for her to discover a species of micro-creatures with the same attitude problem as the boggart.

Even if something tiny and strange was lurking around in the apartment with her, Mia could probably handle it. What she'd learned about herself in the last few days was confusing and disorienting, but what really stood out was the empowerment. She had discovered one thing for sure. Monsters were real and she could see them.

That meant she wasn't losing her mind or hallucinating when she'd thought she'd seen the creature at the night market, or in the restaurant at breakfast. She hadn't imagined things when she'd seen the tiny monsters in the tree that caught her hair and annoyed Becky into almost getting hit by a moped. Those monsters were really there, and not only could she see them, but she could fight them. And win.

This gave Mia confidence in herself and in her abilities. She could trust herself to know what was going on around her and to defend herself when she needed to.

Her only real concern now...was her father. Becky and Master Chen should be good for a little while, but her father's mind hadn't been messed with. Mia wasn't sure if that was a good thing or a bad thing. She'd have to remember to ask Cassia what they were going to do about informing him.

Although, if the boggart was at the center of the creatures attacking her, then maybe she could go home as planned and wouldn't have to keep hiding out in disgusting, moldy apartments.

As she picked her way through the apartment, trying to find somewhere at least halfway clean where she could make a little nest to relax, she thought she heard something. Wondering if it might just be things falling over in response to her moving around, she paused. Staying as still as she could, Mia listened to the building around her. She heard it again, this time louder. It wasn't in the apartment with her, but out somewhere in the rest of the building.

Curious, she crept through the debris and out into the hallway between the two apartments. The noise came from the hallway toward the front of the complex. Although she knew the dangers, Mia decided to have a look anyway. After fighting the boggart earlier today, and handing it a beating at that, she felt like she might be ready for harder challenges.

As she crept down the hallway, she hyped herself up, thinking of the training she received and the fight from earlier in the day. Even Cassia seemed impressed by her ability. Maybe this 'fighting bad guys' stuff wasn't so hard after all. She had told Cassia she could handle herself, and she'd proved it once already. If this was something that needed her to use her training, she could prove it again, too.

Light pooled from the edge of the entryway, and Mia slowed down. It was hard to see, but she could tell that someone was there—or possibly more than one person. Hiding in the late afternoon shadows as best she could, gave her the element of surprise as well as the ability to turn back if she thought the fight would be too much for her.

A faint murmuring sound, like two people having a hushed conversation, floated back to her, and she strained to hear it. She could only catch snippets of sound and not a language she knew. Maybe it was just two foreign people, hanging out at an abandoned apartment complex. Where a boggart was. She was close now, close enough to see shapes fairly clearly.

Two men stood there in the entry to the complex. At least it looked like two men. Only she wasn't sure they were human at all. One of them—the shorter one—was nearly translucent in the light and had a wide hunched troll-like frame. He nearly shimmered when he moved around, and the light played off of him. It was transfixing in its own way, but a smell wafted from him that reminded her of the boggart, although admittedly, it wasn't as bad. But just barely.

It was more like the smell of rotting meat, or a dead animal on the side of a back road in the middle of summer. It was terrible for sure, but terrible was relative when talking about the boggart whose stench had made her want to rip her own nose off.

The translucent creature seemed to walk on air. It reminded Mia of how she moved in her dreams sometimes, where she had the sense of being underwater, even when she wasn't. Whatever the creature was, it was sniffing the air, as if it sensed something.

The taller one, a thin man with tufts of platinum blond—practically silver—hair sticking out from under his red baseball cap, was striking in appearance. He had an attractive jaw and deep blue eyes and full lips. She imagined he must be a leader of some kind. People who looked like him weren't often yes-men or assistants. Tall, good looking men with blond hair like that often ended up running whatever business they were in, if only because people naturally gravitated to them.

He was beautiful, until suddenly he wasn't. For a split second, it was as if he had been replaced by a short, fuzzy brown creature. The red baseball cap was still there, but the eyes, so sharp and almond-shaped, had turned large, round, and wild. His nose had grown and was pointed, and his lips had thinned enough to bare his sharp jagged teeth. Then the image of him returned to normal, as if it was a blip in an old movie where someone had replaced a frame. When she was back to seeing the attractive man, she found it hard to remember that the other image had ever been there at all.

But it was. She'd seen it. And she knew what that meant. These two weren't just troublemakers hanging out at an abandoned apartment complex, they were the real deal. The pair might be a little more difficult to fight than a boggart, especially considering there were two of them and one of her. Perhaps she should just go back to the apartment and wait for Cassia to return.

Mia tried to take a step backward, but the men turned with their noses in the air as if sniffing her out. Now their eyes were aimed in her direction, and she turned to run. Her feet took her quickly to the only place she could think of—the apartment where she had fought the boggart.

She flung the door open and slammed it shut. After flipping the lock, she moved back into the shadowed room. Figuring it would be easier to fight in a room she had some knowledge of rather than a hallway, she shifted to the same spot where the boggart had stood. They would come down the hallway, break open the door, rush into the living room and, then...what exactly?

She'd beat the crap out of them, that's what.

Her Wushu training prepared her for various styles of martial arts, but it did nothing to equip her to fight a being who didn't appear the same when you looked at him twice in rapid succession and really missed out on the whole troll ghost thing. Still, she was confident in her abilities at hand-to-hand, and if she could get them one-on-one, she might be able to do some serious damage in short order.

The face-shifting one should be easy. Find a weak spot and hit it hard. Repeatedly. That was something she was good at, and as long as she could keep her cool, she could ramp up the violence fast enough. Being a young girl would work to her advantage. They wouldn't expect someone like her to fight the way she could, so she would at least mop the floor with the one on the right before he even realized what was going on.

Of course, the one on the left looked translucent, like someone had formed air and given it a sheen. How the heck was she supposed to fight a ghost? Would the rules regarding ghosts in the stories of her childhood apply to this thing? Maybe, just maybe if she couldn't touch it, it couldn't touch her. It was worth a shot. Either way, she was going to have to figure it out quickly because just then, the door to the apartment banged open and splinters went flying down the hall and across her vision.

Nothing could have prepared her for the creature coming around the corner. For a flash of a second, it was the tall, good-looking man, but instantly it switched, and the creature it truly was bared its teeth. Saliva dripped from its mouth and puddled on the ground.

Something brown dipped in red liquid hung on its head in place of the red baseball cap. As it scanned Mia, its wide round eyes focused only on her. They were yellow with black slits like a cat's, and they appeared to see more than just an easy target in her. The thing wanted to hurt her, to rip her to shreds.

Instinctively, she knew it would attack her with fury and use her as a trophy. She realized with horror what the creature was... a redcap. She'd read some scary fairy tales a few years back about fae and their various monsters. The thing licking its pointy teeth and staring at her like she was its next meal, looked exactly like what she'd read about.

Suddenly, she wished Cassia hadn't left her there all alone.

Redcaps were notorious for vile, evil behavior in literature, and this one seemed particularly nasty. Or maybe since it was her first experience with one, she just thought it was extra evil.

All elements of the handsome man she'd seen earlier had

faded away, leaving a short hairy monster with a long beard and human skin standing in front of her. It would leap to attack soon, and she would have to respond. As a matter of fact, why wait?

She never was one to wait for an attack on the mat, so why wait here?

Without another thought, Mia slammed her fist into its pointed nose, and it howled as it flew backward.

Rather than chase after it, to try and ground and pound, Mia pivoted to the side and just narrowly avoided a book thrown by the spectral creature. It was nearly invisible, only its glowing eyes were easy to see, and it seemed to be concentrating hard on reaching for a book on the ground nearby. Mia ran to it, kicking out sideways to connect with its body, but she went right through it. Landing awkwardly, she turned around and found herself being punched, albeit somewhat weakly, in the gut.

For a moment, the two of them stared at each other, as if neither knew what to do next, then the redcap came flying into Mia's vision. Gnashing its teeth, it narrowly missed her, and she ducked and rolled away to another side of the room. Grabbing a chair, she tossed it as hard as she could, smashing it over the thing's back. Then she had to duck as the ghost creature threw a lamp at her.

Thinking quickly, she picked the lamp up and tossed it at the redcap, hitting it in the back of the head as it tried to stand. It howled and fell to its knees, shaking off the effects of the blow as best it could. Running to the redcap, Mia kicked it hard in the ribs, and it lashed out, swinging its arm at her in an effort to create some distance while inflicting damage. Its claws left a long scratch on her leg.

Mia jumped back, wincing in pain as blood trickled down her leg, pooling in her sock. It could have been much worse, but thankfully she'd avoided the full brunt of the attack. As the redcap ran at her again, its terrifying face switching between the glamour and the real monster underneath, she grabbed a chair from beside her.

The old metal seat would have been just as at home at a church banquet as a pro wrestling show, and now she swung it like a baseball bat, the seat connecting with the side of the monster's head and sending it crumpling to the ground.

Mia lifted the chair high and slammed it into the redcap a few more times, making sure to hit it as hard as possible on the legs, hoping to slow its progress. Satisfied that she had done some decent damage, she tried to run, but something caught her ankle.

Mia looked into the face of the translucent creature, who was focusing all of its energy on wrapping itself around her leg and holding her in place. She tried to kick it, but it did no good. The thing held her just long enough for the redcap to stand again, tackle her, and force her to the ground.

When the translucent creature lost its grip, Mia rolled as far away as possible. Slowly, the redcap stood up, showing little in the way of damage, and she knew this was going to be much more of a fight than she'd assumed it would be.

The redcap was strong and fast, and it was obviously trained in some fashion. But Mia's experience had taught her that no matter how well-trained a fighter is, they are never prepared for one thing. Chaos. It was time to bring a little confusion to the fight.

"Okay, now that we have met each other," she said, with a confidence in her voice that she hoped didn't sound false, "I think we should lay down some ground rules."

The redcap growled deeply in response, and the ghost creature peeked around its shoulder. The ghost held an iron and was busy winding up for a toss. Better make this quick.

"First ground rule: don't get mad when I kick your butt to kingdom come."

CHAPTER FIFTEEN

The steam iron flew over Mia's head, narrowly missing her and crashing into the window behind her. The glass shattered, sending the appliance outside and an idea into Mia's head. Between the fact that she was still inexperienced at fighting for her life and that one of them was a freakin' ghost thing, she decided her best plan of action was to try to escape.

This would require two things: a way out and some distance between them. She had no idea what lay beyond the apartment complex and the area surrounding it seemed like it had been abandoned for a while, but it had to be better than being locked in a room with two malevolent monsters.

She ducked behind a couch as an ironing board sailed over her head and she checked it off the list of items the ghost thing could grab. The creature didn't seem hindered by the shape of an object, only weight, and the iron had looked particularly difficult for it to wield. While the appliance had crashed through the window, it had flown at an arc that would have required a lot of force behind it. For the most part, if she could avoid being trapped by that thing, she could ignore it. Its primary job was distraction.

That left the redcap. His teeth were sharp and vicious, and his claws were even more terrifying. So far, Mia had avoided any major damage, but she was going to have to go hand to hand with it, and she might not be so lucky for much longer. Her training had taught her how to absorb impact and take damage, but nothing in it had prepared her for a bearded goblin-thing that seemed intent on actually devouring her. After beating her to within an inch of her life, obviously.

Mia popped up from behind the couch, grabbed the bottom of it, and flipped it, then tossed it in the direction of the two creatures. The redcap tried to bat it away, and the ghost simply let it fall through him. Oddly enough, the pair of them were never more than a few feet apart, but right now wasn't the best time to figure out if their proximity meant something. If she could just survive the fight and gain the upper hand, she could get out of there and figure out a theory for their interpersonal relationship later.

Moving closer to the living room was Mia's priority. She dove and rolled in that direction, her plan depending on the giant glass windows in the room. The redcap was on her quickly, and it tackled her to the ground. She thrust her knee into his stomach and flipped him over her head, rolling aside to avoid a vase the ghost tossed at her head. The stubby creature—having shed his glamour as a tall, attractive man—crawled toward her, and she planted a foot in its nose. This didn't seem to deter it, so she repeated the action twice more. With each kick, the redcap seemed to slow down.

Taking the opportunity, Mia bolted for the wall of the living room, then dove behind a table as the redcap tossed a chair at her. It bounced off the wall a foot from the huge window. It was now or never.

She stood, curling her fingers at it as she beckoned the thing to try again. Enraged, the redcap grabbed another chair, a heavier one this time, and flung it at her hard. She ducked and it crashed through the window, landing on the ground outside. Before she could do anything else, the creature was on her again, and they both tumbled to the side as they struggled with each other.

Sharp teeth ripped down Mia's arm, and she elbowed the redcap in the nose to get it off her. The creature scrambled to its feet as she checked her wound. The injury was superficial, but a stream of blood was trickling down her hand and dripping on the carpeted floor. Rather than making her afraid, it angered her.

Instead of taking her chance with the window, Mia charged, barreling into the redcap and knocking it back into the wall, creating a crater in the plasterboard. She punched its head repeatedly, more brawling than using the techniques she'd learned, and she mentally scolded herself for it.

Moving back just a step, she used a roundhouse kick to drive the back of its skull into the wall. The redcap moaned as it slumped to the floor, and Mia spun around and went in search of the ghost creature. It had disappeared. Now was her chance, and she knew it, so she barreled for the window. No time to worry about the landing, she just needed to jump.

As she approached the window, she caught sight of the grassy hill outside. If she built enough momentum, the fall wouldn't be too bad, and she would land about one and a half stories down. She increased her speed and tried to judge how best to dive through the broken glass—she would have to go out like a missile, as if she was diving off a board into a swimming pool.

But the potential landing for a dive like that could be ugly, so she had to make sure to tuck and roll and land as flat on her back as she could, taking the force spread out over her body rather than in one place. All this ran through her mind in the span of a second, and suddenly she was at the window. Without hesitation, she elongated herself into a projectile, cleared the window arms first, and performed a swan dive outside.

She spun in the air and landed with a dull thud on the still damp grass. Having closed her eyes after making the flip, Mia opened them again, looking up into the gray-blue sky. She marveled that she wasn't hurt. A little out of breath, maybe, but otherwise, she felt fine. Chalking it up to luck and good conditioning, she hopped to her feet. She didn't know exactly where she would go, but it had to be somewhere and quick. Shadows were moving in the apartment above, and soon enough, they would be coming after her.

Mia frantically looked for a place to hide. Somewhere not easily visible from the window and which might help to put some distance between her and the two creatures. If she ran across the open field behind the complex, it would take her to a side street, but she would be easily seen and caught.

The complex itself seemed like the best bet in which to lose them, and she could run back inside and get out of sight faster. Then she could duck between the buildings and get to the other side.

The last thing she wanted, outside of being eaten for dinner by the redcap, was to go somewhere Cassia wouldn't be able to find her. She needed to be close enough that when Cassia came back and saw the chaos caused by the fight, she would know Mia was nearby and could reach her.

Just as Mia crossed into the hallway between the apartments in the building, she heard the redcap shouting near the window. Either they'd seen her and were coming, or they had missed her and were now searching.

Either way, she needed to hide. Darting between the apartments, she made her way to a second building. The doors of the two apartments she passed were locked solid, so she kept moving until she reached the other side of the building. There she stopped, her back pressed to the mildewed stonework façade, to catch her breath.

She strained to hear—while calming her breathing so as to not be conspicuous—she thought she could just make out the voice of the redcap back at the first building. It was grumbling, as if it was angry and cursing itself, and she had a problem. It was getting closer.

Mia closed her eyes for a second to steel herself. Up ahead was a dead-end road and a store that appeared as abandoned as the apartments. If she could get inside without them noticing her, she could hide and wait for Cassia. Undoubtedly, when the bounty hunter showed up, there would be a ruckus as she took the redcap to task. Mia could come out then and help, but staying alive and safe were her top priorities now.

The store was about two hundred yards away, and in a sprint, it would still take her close to a minute to get there. If she was lucky, they wouldn't see her at all, and a door would be unlocked or a window open. If not, she would have to break in and hope they didn't notice. If she was really unlucky, the fistfight would resume. The cut on her leg and the bite on her arm were draining her far more than the fall. Something about the creature's scratch and bite seemed to affect her more.

Taking a deep breath, Mia tried to push everything else out of her mind. It wasn't a blind terror but a focused mission. Her training had given her a lot of practice in katas to be performed in high-pressure situations, and while she'd been able to use precious few of them in the fight in the apartment, if she was caught out in the open, it would be easier. Consoling herself that she had a plan for every eventuality, she took off, barreling across the large open area between the apartments and the store. Behind her, in the distance, she heard the howl of the redcap.

No!

Still, it seemed pretty far away, and unless it could outrun her, she was going to make it to the store first. Maybe she could find some weapons inside or lock the creatures out somehow. It was worth the shot. Her legs churned until the muscles in her thighs burned and her lungs felt like they were being squeezed. She reached the store at such a speed she didn't have time to fully stop, and she ended up sliding on her heels into the wall next to the door. She yanked on the handle, but it refused to budge. The lock was old and rusted, just an old padlock, probably thrown on in desperation when the area had flooded. A good kick might knock it open.

Mia hazarded a glance behind her. The redcap and the ghost were halfway there already. They knew where she was going, so her best chance was to get in and get ready for them. The fight wasn't over, but maybe she'd find something in there to hit back with. She kicked at the lock, and it broke easily under her foot. She dashed inside, slammed the door shut and flung a file cabinet to the ground to block it from opening. They were almost to the building now, and she stacked a couple of chairs on the file cabinet then backed away.

She had no clue if somewhere in the building another door had been left unlocked, or if there were windows that could be broken into or were broken already. All she could hope was they would try to come through the main door. She waited for the inevitable crash, squinting in the dim light as she searched for a weapon.

When her eyes adjusted, she inspected the room, which appeared to be a small abandoned hardware store. Most of the shelves were empty, but a few things still sat on shelves or hung from the walls. She dashed to the back of the store, just as the front door shook with the first attempt by the redcap to gain access. She vaulted over a counter where an empty register sat, cash drawer still open, then entered the backroom.

A desk sat in the middle of the room, covered with water-stained paper and various office equipment, including an ancient ruined computer. She scanned the room until she found something near a poster of some swimsuit model.

Jackpot.

A sledgehammer lay on the ground, likely forgotten in an attempt to remodel and fix the building before it was deemed unsalvageable. Lifting it, she felt like the mythical Thor, and she smiled for the first time since the beginning of the battle with the redcap. Hefting it to her shoulder, she strode out of the room.

The door was caving in, falling backward, and the ghost figure had already walked through the wall and was trying to grab the chairs and fling them away. Occasionally he would grasp one leg and move the chair a bit, but not enough. Every time he failed, he would curse and thrash, but it didn't matter. The redcap was almost in.

The door cracked open, and a piece of wood fell off. The redcap peered inside and made eye contact with Mia. It roared and charged again, this time sending the filing cabinet skidding off to the side, and the chairs flying in all directions.

Mia braced herself. She only had one good swing with the sledgehammer, after which it would be faster and more effective to use her hand-to-hand skills. The redcap bore down on her, and rather than swinging for its head, she aimed a little lower, concentrating on hitting center mass.

With a swing resembling a golfer teeing-off more than anything else, she brought the sledgehammer down in an arc the redcap couldn't see in the darkness. The weapon connected with the monster's stomach, lifting it off the ground and into the air. The creature landed with a thud on one of the shelves.

A shrill cry came from the ghost creature, who inexplicably ducked behind the door as Mia made her way to the redcap. It tried to stand but she laid a kick into its ribs, further attacking the area she'd injured with the sledgehammer. It rolled on its back and coughed up a bubble of blood that stained its shirt.

It wobbled as it tried to get to its feet again, and it almost managed to stand, but Mia hit it with a series of blows to the face and stomach. It fell backward, and she put her hands on her knees to catch her breath. The legs of the beast twitched, and she stood to hit it again, but the shrill scream came from behind her. The ghost creature was flying at her, its hands clenched around the blade of a table saw. She ducked just in time for it to miss her and it dropped the blade. Screaming unintelligible curses, the ghost thing swooped to pick it up again, a desperate madness in its eyes.

Rather than trying to avoid it, she turned and ran for the back of the store, near the now-defunct electric exit sign. The door there may be locked, but it was probably a lock like the one she'd broken already.

If she hit it with full steam, she had a chance at getting outside, and possibly to escape. Running as hard as she could with whatever energy remained in her body, she kicked at the door and it flew open, sending her sprawling onto the cold floor of what was once the back storage room of the store.

CHAPTER SIXTEEN

"What in blazes is wrong with this thing?" Cassia asked, kicking at the wall where the portal should be. She had done everything she needed to do and now had to get back to Mia before all Hades broke loose. Not that she knew of any specific evil about to break loose, but knowing her luck, something was happening, and she wasn't there to handle it. She had a nagging feeling that she may have made a mistake by bringing the boggart in.

They paid well, though.

Still, enough was enough, it was time to get back to Mia and figure out what to do next. If Cassia could just get this stupid portal to work... Above the area where the portal normally opened up, a wooden sign in bright letters said, THANK YOU FOR VISITING. It had always bugged her. This was a jail. The only people ever going through that portal had to be there, either because it was their job, or because they were a prisoner. No visitors ever came through.

It was a stupid freaking sign.

Despite this being a stone wall, Cassia was determined if the portal didn't open soon, that sign was getting knocked down, kicked into pieces and turned into firewood. From behind her, Fan was chuckling, which at first made her more frustrated.

Then, as the realization dawned on her, Cassia's spine stiffened and she spun around to give him a deadly glare. His chuckling stopped abruptly, and he appeared to swallow hard. She marched over to him and slammed her hands on his desk.

Fan jumped a little, but the smile hadn't left his face. Either he was too stupid to know how angry she was, or he was too cocky. Cassia was leaning toward stupid because if it was cocky, he was going to end up with a broken nose.

"What is wrong with the portal?" Cassia asked, her voice level and low. She was trying to keep control of herself, but not only was the anger rising to nuclear levels, panic was starting to have a parade in her stomach. Something was going on with Mia, she just knew it, and she needed to get back there right this minute.

"Nothing. It works just fine."

"Then why isn't it opening for me?" Cassia asked, enunciating her consonants heavily. Her t's especially screamed a tremendous amount of a warning to the listener who should have known she meant business.

Unfortunately, the listener was Fan, who seemed unfazed and continued smiling like a goon, tapping his pen on the desk. "Maybe you didn't ask it nicely enough," he said.

There was a moment where Cassia stood in place, trying to make sure she was processing the words correctly. If this empty-headed, dumb-faced jackanape—

"He's so bad at this." One of the ogres from behind the desk was speaking to a second ogre, both holding mugs of steaming coffee and casually discussing the entertainment of the moment in their loudest possible voices.

Ogres were not known for their ability to keep their voices down, which made them such good jailers. When an ogre yells that it was lights out, people on the other side of the town would begin to turn off their lights. Then there was the effect their voices had on the movement of the earth.

Humans usually confuse the deep baritone yell of an ogre with an earthquake. They don't actually cause earthquakes, but some of the 4.0 quakes were really only the earth transmitting the vibrations resulting from groups of ogres yelling or partying.

"Yeah, even *I* would be better at getting a date than Fan. I bet she doesn't even know he has it bad for her. Ha, ha." The second ogre was blatantly making eye contact with Cassia as if she were a cartoon he was watching rather than a living being.

"That's true," said the first ogre. "And you haven't had a date in...how long?"

The words were reverberating as loud as rumbles of thunder, and Fan's face turned a shade of red Cassia had never seen before. Ducking his head, Fan held out one finger to Cassia and spun his chair around.

"Been down here too long," said the second ogre, unaware that Fan was now looking at him. Or not understanding what it meant. "He forgot how to hit on women. No smoothness."

"Hey." Fan spoke with enough bass in his voice to stop their conversation, though he still sounded defeated. "We can hear you."

The ogres stared back at Fan, then looked to Cassia. Their big dumb eyes blinked a few times, and they slowly nodded. "So, did you hear about the...uhh...new keys?" asked one of them, not so subtly changing the subject.

"No. What keys? I thought we were talking about Fan and the pretty lady."

"Oh crickets," mumbled Fan, and he spun back around to Cassia.

"It's fine," Cassia held up her hand. Poor guy. She thought he was just an idiot, or a dingleberry, but he was just an awkward guy who liked a girl who wasn't interested. It was sweet.

"Just open the portal, please."

Without another word—and with his head in his hand—Fan pushed a button on his desk and the portal sprang to life. Cassia looked back one last time before walking through.

He *was* cute, though.

The last thing she heard before going through the portal was one of the ogres saying, "Boy, you sure screwed that one up, Fan."

Cassia shook her head, laughter bubbling up in spite of herself as she entered the apartment from the portal.

The laughter stopped abruptly.

The apartment was in shambles. Mia wasn't going to be in there—Cassia could tell by the silence—but she searched anyway. She called out for the girl but received no response. The living room was empty, and so was the bedroom. Mia was nowhere to be found, and it worried the snot out of Cassia.

She clung briefly to hopeful thoughts: Mia may have just fallen asleep, or maybe she'd climbed out the window, or—the best-case scenario—she was simply exploring the complex. When Cassia spotted the splintered door, she held back a string of expletives. Her instincts had been right—Mia was in trouble.

The outside was strangely quiet, and Cassia was torn on what to do next. She could either go wandering around outside or she could try to gather some clues. She turned and studied the room again. It was a mess, but what was different from last time?

It appeared that Mia had been lounging around at some point. There was a spot cleared off on what had at one time been a pretty nice couch. The seats were still a little indented where the girl must have been sitting, and the pillow resting against the arm meant she'd likely been lying on the couch.

Moving over to the porch door, Cassia confirmed it was locked. That made sense. Even if Mia had gone out there and then came back, she would likely have locked it behind her. Make sure the only way in and out of the room was the main door or the portal. That's what Cassia would have done too.

Still curious, Cassia unlocked the heavy metal latch and

opened the door to the patio. The hinges squealed as it opened, years of rusted and moldy metal fighting to stay closed forever. That gave her a clue. Mia wouldn't have come out on the patio for fear of making too much noise. No one likes the sound of metal grinding together, and opening the patio door would have been far too loud for someone who was alone and afraid.

Shutting the door and locking it, out of habit if nothing else, Cassia went back to the couch. Part of her wanted to sit on the couch the way she thought Mia would have, trying to see from her point of view. It was a compulsion she couldn't fight, no matter how silly it seemed, and eventually she gave in, sitting on the couch and turning sideways.

Ahead of her was the wall, empty except for a dent where the boggart had caused some damage. To her left was the patio door which she had already ruled out. To the right was an empty TV stand, the television gone long enough for a layer of dust to collect on the surface, leaving no trace of it ever having been there. Above the TV stand was a cheap long mirror. It reflected the light from the patio during the daytime, she supposed, helping brighten the room without the need for flipping switches.

Switches. Where were the switches? Some of the lights outside the building were on, probably just solar-powered emergency lights, but if the city had at any point taken over the complex intending on using it, the electricity cabling might still run to the building. Maybe Mia had thought the same thing and had gone to turn on a light? Cassia stood and looked around for the switch, finding it on the wall near the door. Flipping it did nothing.

Something wasn't right. Cassia had been gone a good while, and if Mia got a bug in her and wanted to go exploring, she would have returned by now. It was possible she'd gone wandering and gotten lost or hurt herself. Or worse. Something had hurt *her*.

The splintered door worried Cassia. She didn't want to jump to conclusions that someone—or some*thing*—had broken into the apartment, but what else could the broken door mean?

Convinced there was nothing else she could find in this apartment, Cassia decided to search the others in the building. Grabbing a pen from a jar beside the kitchen sink, she held her breath to avoid inhaling the fetid stench from the refrigerator as she ripped one of the grocery lists off its door. She wrote a note to Mia and set it on the couch. If the girl came back and somehow missed her, at least she would know Cassia was looking for her.

Closing what was left of the door quietly behind her, Cassia approached the apartment across the hall. The door was locked and seemed like it hadn't been opened in a very long time. Which meant she'd have to search the other buildings as well as the surrounding area. Most likely, if Mia was still nearby, she would be in one of the other apartments, probably searching through stuff on a damp and disappointing treasure hunt.

Unless something had gotten to her. Cassia shuddered at the thought. The people pursuing Mia seemed like they meant business. What if they'd found her while Cassia was busy being hit on by a shy prison warden? How would she live with herself knowing she'd left that girl in a dangerous situation, and allowed her to be captured? Cassia had the strong feeling if Mia had been taken, she wouldn't remain alive for long. Something about the people chasing her didn't feel like they were the kidnapping-and-keeping-safe kind.

Guilt was wracking her brain as she reached the bottom floor of the building. She tried to shake it away and focus, searching for footprints or any other sign that Mia had gone off in a specific direction. Or a sign of a struggle.

Two buildings were up ahead, the one on the left backed up to an empty yard, and beyond was a street lined with apartments. The building on the right was attached to the office for the complex, with a long winding driveway leading from the main road.

Cassia approached the buildings, not making a decision either way yet, trying to focus on the surroundings and what clues there may be.

A faint noise, like something falling over, echoed from the area of the office. Cassia stopped, her head snapping in that direction as she listened. The hum of the city was distant but constant, and it was hard to pick up individual sounds nearby unless they were loud.

The sound didn't repeat itself, but now Cassia had to know what had caused it. She headed right toward the office and snuck around to the front of the building.

The door was open—just slightly—and Cassia gently pulled it. It swung open without much sound, a pretty good indication of fairly regular use. That only made her worry more. Whoever was using the office could have spotted Mia and done something to her. There didn't seem to be anyone inside at the moment though, but Cassia poked her head in to check.

The office was empty, save for a desk with a few magazines and newspapers on it. The smiling faces of celebrities on the pages creeped Cassia out, and she turned them over before moving deeper into the office. Something was plugged into the wall here, and as she listened, she heard water running in the next room. It was faint, the sound a leaky toilet makes rather than a sink that's been left to drip.

She opened the door and scanned the room. A nightlight plugged into the wall glowed a bright blue, and sure enough, the water ran in the commode. Someone was here, often enough that electricity was turned on in this building. But who? And did they do something to Mia?

Cassia shut the door quietly and turned around, and almost shrieked loudly. A rat—at least the size of a small dog—ran across the room, knocking over a near-empty trash can, sending crumpled paper to the floor. Exhaling slowly, Cassia realized these must have been the sounds she'd heard—just a rat rummaging round in an empty complex.

Where in Hades was Mia? There were two buildings left to search, then Cassia would double back to the first apartment. Maybe the girl would be there waiting for her. Or she would find Mia picking through abandoned possessions in one of the buildings.

"Come on, Mia," Cassia said under her breath. "Make a noise."

CHAPTER SEVENTEEN

Mia didn't really have time to worry about smashing onto the dirty floor. She scrambled across it until she got her feet under her, then headed deeper into the room. She heard the redcap and ghost creature following close behind her. Only seconds after she dove behind a stack of empty cardboard boxes, the door smashed open.

Her body trembled, her heart pounding in her chest so hard she could hear it in her ears and feel the blood pulsing on the sides of her neck. This wasn't good decision making. As soon as she'd heard that strange sound in the apartment, she should have just blocked the door and found the farthest corner to wait it out until Cassia came back.

But, no. She had to go investigate and see what it could be. Because, of course she did. That's what had recently been getting her into these sorts of situations. It's exactly what had happened the night she and Becky had gone out with the other students to explore the market in Shanghai. The area, congested with other people and alive with the sights, sounds, and smells of all the vendors and shops hadn't been enough for her. She had to go farther, deeper, to drift away from the established path and see what she could find for herself.

That was how she'd ended up in the tea shop with the overpowering smell and the mysterious old woman who'd plied her with powerful tea and searched her eyes deeply, as though she were wondering about something just beyond Mia's awareness.

It was the reason Mia had been there to see the boggart for the first time and watch in awe as it maneuvered around the people, unseen and unnoticed. But it was also how she'd met the bounty hunter who had saved Mia and was now guiding her as she learned more about herself.

For that reason, Mia couldn't completely regret how events had unfolded in China. No, they weren't what she'd expected when she had packed her bag and boarded that plane. She had just meant to come here and compete against other students who were as passionate about the same martial arts as she was. She'd even hoped to demonstrate her skill and ability well enough to come out on top.

She couldn't have imagined that coming here would completely change her life. But she had to keep fighting. Her life might be in turmoil and she might not fully understand what was going on around her, but it was *her* life. Hers to toss aside and give over to the creatures pursuing her so viciously, or hers to save. Mia knew which one she was going to try.

The redcap crossed the room, kicking boxes and crates as he stalked past them. Mia clamped a hand over her mouth to silence her gasps and cries of fear. She needed to stay as quiet as she possibly could and not give away her location. If she could wait for them to go to the other side of the room, she would have a chance to slip past them and get away.

They were moving in her direction and Mia looked around, trying to identify her next hiding spot. A stack of wooden pallets sat nearby, similar to the ones she and Cassia had hidden behind in the alley before coming to the apartment. It seemed like the perfect spot. It had worked for them then, so she may as well see if it would work for her now.

As soon as the redcap turned to look at the ghost, she sprinted toward the pallets. Her feet skidded in the dirt and dust that had built up on the smooth cement, and she almost crashed to the ground. She went with the momentum, rolling as she would to avoid a blow, then braced herself for impact with the wood. Her mind raced, hoping she wouldn't hit them, hoping by some twist of fate she'd slip around them and nothing would fall on her.

Suddenly, she realized the movement across the floor had stopped. Her body had squeezed perfectly into a small space between the pallets and a stack of discarded plastic milk crates, leaving everything still standing.

A breath shuddered from her lungs and she squeezed her eyes closed tightly, giving herself a moment to calm down. It couldn't last for long. She had to keep moving. The creatures were getting angrier the more they moved around the room, and soon enough, they would abandon their delicate search technique and simply trash the room.

Pressing her back against the wall, Mia shuffled sideways to ease behind the stacks to a unit of metal shelves. She rolled onto her belly and slithered across the empty bottom shelf. Abandoned products created a wall that blocked nearly the entire shelf from view. Spider webs stuck to her skin, and a thick layer of dust and dirt tickled at her nose. She could taste the filth in her throat as she breathed, but it didn't matter. There were far worse things ahead of her if she let these guys get their hands on her.

Mia slipped off the shelf onto the floor and hopped to the balls of her feet to scramble further. Ahead of her, a faint light glowed at the bottom corner of one of the cardboard boxes. It wasn't the light filtering from the main room of the floor. She followed it as it snaked across the floor and disappeared beneath the far wall.

It took a few seconds for it to sink in—she'd progressed all the way around the room and had found the door leading out the back of the building. Her heart jumped. All she had to do was get through that door, and then she could make a run for it. She would return to the apartment building and hide.

The space in front of the door had little to conceal her. She had to make a choice. Either she could try to slip out and possibly take much more time to escape, or she could burst out of hiding and go full speed until she was back at the apartment.

That tactic had the chance of disorienting her pursuers, so they didn't immediately come after her, giving her a little bit of a head start to find the most concealed path toward the apartment building. She thought about everything her Wushu master taught her. It wasn't just about the actual movements or the katas. It wasn't about physical strength, agility, and stamina.

What she needed now was everything else he had instilled in her over the years of training under him. His strictness and expectation of excellence had been challenging when going through the same movements for the thousandth time or running laps for being late. But they had taught her determination. They'd given her drive and strength. They'd imbued her with a sense of trust and faith in herself, and accountability for her actions. He'd taught her to believe in what she knew within herself and to not question it. Hesitation could be disastrous.

Mia knew what she had to do. Priming her muscles and steadying her mind, she burst from her crouching position. Her body shot toward the light gleaming from under the door. She put her hands out in front of her and shoved with all her strength.

Her palms hit the door before she'd even considered the possibility of it being locked. The weight and speed of her impact broke through the boards crossed over what turned out to be double doors leading out onto a cement porch. She grabbed the metal banister tightly and pushed back just in time to stop herself from tumbling over.

She had already thrown herself out a window that day. Such a maneuver would be unnecessary, especially when a set of cement steps that led to the ground provided a much more controlled and less dangerous route. Mia was so focused on not falling as she made her way down that she didn't pay sufficient attention to her surroundings. It wasn't until she'd left the stairs and was running that she spotted the fence in front of her.

She had expected the back area to be open, probably with a loading dock, but a huge fence loomed only a few yards from her. Mia ran around the side of the store and sprinted down the narrow alley between another fence and the building. Halfway to the front, she hit another fence. She grabbed it, shaking it frantically. She hadn't seen the massive chain-link barrier when she'd run toward the store earlier. Now she was trapped, a cage at the back of the store keeping her from going any farther.

Mia stuck her foot into the fence and tried to scramble up, but sharp points on the metal cut into her hands. Above her were coils of razor wire. There was no way she could get over and to the other side. Her only chance was to run back inside. She jumped to the ground and raced up the alley. But before she reached the other end, the two creatures came around the corner.

Their eyes burned into her as they approached. The redcap rubbed his hands together, a sickening smile on his lips as he moved toward her. "Have you finished your little escape now? I built up quite an appetite coming after you. But that's fine. It only means I'm going to enjoy my dinner all the more," he said.

"No." The ghost stopped the redcap's advance. "You can't do that. We have to capture her alive."

"You saw what I've been through trying to catch her. She wasn't supposed to be this difficult. Look at her. Who is she to make it so hard on us? I will savor every bite of her," the redcap said.

"You can't," the ghost insisted. "She has to be kept alive. You know that. We were sent to capture her, not destroy her. Our employer wants her captured alive."

The redcap narrowed his eyes at the ghost and took an angry step toward him. Mia continued to scan the alley for any way she might be able to get out. She pushed on the fence, yanking at the corners in the hope of finding a piece that was broken and could fold out of the way. But it was secure.

As the redcap faced off against the ghost, Mia formed a plan to get around them. If she could slip past while they were distracted by each other, she might be able to get back into the store. She pressed her spine against the brick wall of the building and started easing her way back down the alley.

"I know what our employer wants of us," the redcap growled. "But the agreement was to bring her in alive if it was within our power. She is to be stopped first. That is the most important thing."

"Yes, she's to be stopped, but bringing her in alive is what he wants. There would be little good in announcing we've found her and had the chance to bring her in, only that we couldn't because there was nothing left of her. She's right here in front of us. Trapped like a little mouse in a cage. We must capture her and bring her in alive," the ghost demanded.

The bricks behind her scraped Mia's hands as she kept them flattened against the wall and moved slowly but consistently along the building. Just a few more yards to the corner, and she could break free and run for the door. Once inside, she could push as many boxes and crates into their path as possible to slow their progress and make a run for the apartment.

Cassia was coming. She had to be. The bounty hunter had already been gone for so long. It couldn't be too much longer before she returned. When she did, they could battle these things together.

"You know, you're right," the redcap said to his companion. "I've been so selfish thinking only of my own needs. I can't just destroy her now and have nothing to bring back. We'll earn our pay, and the favor of our employer, by bringing this thing back to him to do whatever he wants with her."

The sinister note deepened in his voice and Mia squeezed her eyes closed, swallowing hard as she tried to will her legs to keep moving. Cassia had told Mia how impressed she was by her, that she was brave and a good fighter. Mia wasn't feeling it at that moment, but she had to try to channel it. While the two arrogant creatures in front of her were arguing, she had to do everything she could to escape. Just a few more steps now.

"What do you mean?" the ghost asked.

"You said she would be no good if we found her only to have nothing left because she was killed and eaten before we could bring her back. That is absolutely true. But I'm still hungry, and she seems so delicious. Our employer asked us to bring her back alive but didn't say anything about her being intact." He turned sharply to Mia, making her scream and push herself hard against the bricks. "She could easily stay alive, even if she were missing an arm or a leg."

Mia lashed out, burying her foot in the redcap's stomach. He grunted and stumbled back, and the ghost was pulled along with him as if something had blown him out of the way. Mia didn't stay in place long enough to think about it too much.

She sprinted toward the end of the alley, but the redcap surged in front of her. She screamed again and ran the other way, not knowing what to do next, but desperate to stay out of his grasp. Mia whipped around and pressed her back against the wall again.

He was coming toward her, and she pushed back harder against the bricks, wishing more than anything she had a safe place to go. It didn't matter where. She just needed a place, any place where she'd be safe, where these monsters wouldn't be able to follow her. Somewhere they couldn't find her.

The wall behind her began to give way, and Mia's first

thought was that the bricks were crumbling. She couldn't find her feet as they dissolved behind her and the redcap let out a chilling scream. His hand dipped into his coat and reappeared, gripping a gun. The blast exploding from it tore another scream from Mia's throat just as the wall vanished and she fell back.

She didn't hit the ground. She just kept falling. When she opened her eyes, the space around her looked like some strange vortex. Colors and shapes swirled and merged around her, making her dizzy as they spun faster and faster.

Mia had gone down the rabbit hole. It was all she could think. She'd somehow ended up in a confusing, nonsensical dream and didn't know when she would wake up. That's what it had to be. A dream.

CHAPTER EIGHTEEN

Phillipsburg, Montana

"There's a reason it's called the Power of Five." Carson climbed to his feet yet again. "It's because it needs five people."

He groaned and tried to stretch the pain and tension out of his muscles. It was somehow even harder being tossed around by the failed portal over and over than it had been with the wind. It was almost as though the magic they were using kept getting more offended that the four young fae were trying to do something so beyond what their abilities should be able to manage. In retribution, it was building up their hopes and making them think they had accomplished their goal.

At the very last second, their dreams would be dashed when yet again they'd be picked up and either thrown across the field or unceremoniously lifted and dumped onto the ground. At least the sudden thunderstorms had only happened two more times.

Any more frequently and their dome might have turned into a swimming pool.

Then they would have to attempt a water portal, which was infinitely more difficult. Vivi might be up for it, though. Much to the surprise—and pleasure—of the other three, the dark-haired Unseelie girl had maintained her commitment to good behavior even through all their spectacular failures. She'd continued to push them to the next effort and offer suggestions for how to make it the successful one. They had gone past the flowers and the wind to find a challenge that had captured her attention and had brought her focus to its sharpest point. She wasn't willing to let go.

"That's just a suggestion," Zander said.

"No, I think that's actually how it works. If it wasn't, they would call it the Power-of-however-many-people-you-happen-to-have-around-you-at-the-moment-and-can't-figure-out-how-to-make-the-spell-work," Luna said.

"Come on. We can figure out how to do this. How many times has Principal Elmhurst said we are the most powerful halflings she's ever worked with? She's been drilling it into our heads all summer long that we are the ones who can make this incredible thing happen. If she has that much faith in us, why can't we do it on our own?" Zander asked.

"Because she has also spent the entire summer looking for another person to add to our group so that we can have five," Carson pointed out. "We actually do need that other person."

"I'm with Zander," Vivi said. "We can't just give up. Not yet."

Luna and Carson exchanged glances then looked at Zander.

"Let's go, then," their de facto leader said.

"This was all your idea, I want to remind you," Carson said to Luna.

"My idea was for the four of us to do something fun together to help us get to know each other better and take some time away from all the work. It's not my fault we ended up right back in this field doing more work," she replied.

Zander laughed and opened his soaking wet arms. "What are you talking about? This is fun. I'm having fun. Vivi, aren't you having fun?"

"No."

"See? Vivi is having fun. This isn't work. It's a means to an end. We figure out how to open the portal, and we can go anywhere we want and do all kinds of fun things together."

"That was inspiring," Carson said flatly.

They all walked to the end of the dome again and prepared for yet another attempt. It went on that way for another three hours until finally Carson glared at Zander through another pouring rainstorm and shook his head.

"I'm done," he said. "It's late and I'm hungry. Time for a break."

"We've been at this long enough, Zander," Luna said.

Her voice didn't have the same edge as Carson's. Instead, she appealed to him through the softness in her tone, the friendship between them coming through the words. She knew his intensity, his drive to be the best he could possibly be, then push through that and be even better.

But she also knew he didn't know when it was too much. He didn't know when he needed to stop and give himself time to rest. When he was committed to something, it was all he could think about. He would push himself into the ground if it was what it took to accomplish the next goal he set for himself.

That's where the three of them came in. Zander hated for them to try to control him, especially Carson and Vivi. But they were his protection from himself. They stood between him and his own destruction. At least, he hoped they did.

"All right," he finally said. "It's late. We'll try again another time."

"Here, Luna, let me help you dry off."

The voice was so unexpected that at first, Luna wasn't sure

she'd actually heard it. When she turned, Vivi was standing a few feet away, looking at her expectantly. She had actually been the one to offer to help her.

Luna and Zander glanced at each other in shock but didn't say anything. It was unlike Vivi to volunteer to do anything for anyone else. Offering to do something for a Seelie—and Luna especially—was totally out of the realm of their understanding of the girl. They didn't want to make a big deal out of it and possibly spook her.

Instead, Luna nodded. "Sure," she said. "Thank you."

Vivi nodded in return and gestured behind Luna. "Back up a little. Spread your arms out."

Luna did what she asked but did her best to ready herself for anything. There was still a considerable part of her that was convinced she was being set up. Any second now, Vivi could turn on her and make this into another of her humiliating practical jokes. It would just be worse because Luna had actually set herself up for it.

But that's not what happened. Luna spread her arms out and closed her eyes, and Vivi used her magic to sweep warm air over the Seelie girl until her clothes were dry. She told Luna to turn around and did the same until her silvery hair hung smooth. Luna faced her with a soft smile on her lips.

Before either of the girls could say anything, Carson approached Vivi and threw an arm around her shoulders. "That's my girl," he said.

Vivi's face darkened and she shoved him away, turning to sneer at him.

Luna immediately snickered. "There's the Vivi I know and love to hate," she said.

Everyone laughed, including Vivi. "Come on," she said. "Let's go back to campus. I'm sure the kitchen will have something for us."

All four had agreed to get an early start. They met up at the entrance to their dormitory just as the sun was rising in the East in order to catch the first bus of the day. The little field on the outskirts of town was a nice change of pace for them, plus none of the remaining students would be able to watch their failed attempts at obtaining the power of five, so it was the perfect place to practice.

The stop was a few blocks away from the academy. Now, as they made their way to the academy entrance, they walked closer together than they ever had before, possibly a result of trying so hard to make the portal together.

As they strode past the large ivy-covered brick wall surrounding the grounds of the school, Carson paused. He'd spotted something strange about the wall but wasn't entirely sure what it could be. He reached out and flattened his hand on Zander's chest to stop him.

"What are you doing?" Zander asked. But the agitation in his voice dampened when he saw the other boy's eyes focused on the wall ahead of them.

"Look at that," said Carson. "What's going on with that wall?"

Luna and Vivi paused and followed the guys' gaze to the wall. Right beside the towering black gate leading onto the grounds of the school, a portion of the wall looked strange. The thick covering of ivy looked like it was bending in toward the bricks and liquefying at the edges. Beyond the leaves, the bricks had faded into one mass and had begun to swirl.

"Is that a portal?" Luna asked. She moved in front of Vivi and Carson, curiosity drawing her closer to the wall. It looked like a portal was opening on the wall, but that didn't make any sense.

"Could we have—" Carson started, but Zander shook his head sharply to stop him.

"No way. We didn't accidentally make a portal all the way over here from the field," he said. "And the next morning at that."

"It would be awesome if we did, though," Carson said.

Sparks sprang out of the wall, and the four gasped and backed away. In the next second, they were running toward it. This was bizarre. They reached the wall just as the portal opened in front of them.

Something was coming at them fast, and they jumped out of the way just in time to avoid colliding with a terrified-looking girl falling through the portal. She stumbled a few steps and smashed unceremoniously onto the ground.

In the next instant, a shot rang out, and a blazing bullet hit the ground next to Zander's foot. He bent to reach for it, but Luna grabbed his shirt to stop him.

"Don't touch it. It's hot," she said.

They turned their attention back to the wall, where the portal was now closing. When it had fully sealed, the girl lifted her head from the ground and stared around frantically. Her emerald eyes were wild with fear and she scrambled to her feet, jumping away from the four teens as she stared at each one of them in turn.

"Who are you?" she demanded. "Who are you?"

She struck a fighting pose that looked like she seriously knew what she was doing and the four exchanged glances, trying to understand what was happening. The girl whipped around to look at the wall, searching the ivy and staring at the bricks as though she was afraid something was there.

The wall was solid again, but she stared at it like she didn't believe it. She was waiting for something to come after her, even though the portal had closed almost as soon as she'd fallen through it. There wasn't time for anything to follow her except the bullet. She spun around again and resumed her aggressive pose.

The four young fae had no idea what to think. They were shocked. None of them had ever seen a human go through a portal and had certainly never seen one open on the wall like that.

It wasn't even within the grounds, just out on the sidewalk where any of the humans could have seen. Fortunately, it was so early in the morning that no one was walking past, but it could have been disastrous if someone had seen her ungraceful and unexpected arrival.

The only experiences the students had with portals were the ones specifically created in certain areas inside the campus buildings that were put there purposefully and for express reasons. Only specific people from the academy were allowed to use them, and they went to places on exacting records.

To ensure they were kept secure and no one misused them, these portals were always guarded by a group of full fae. Usually the headmistress was among those closely monitoring the portals and every instance of their use.

Something told the four fae that Principal Elmhurst didn't know about this particular portal and wasn't anticipating the arrival of the frightened human. They couldn't just keep standing there staring at the girl and wondering how she had shown up.

Vivi took a step closer. "Who are you?" she asked.

Zander moved ahead of Luna, using his arm to push her back. He stood in front of the group, squaring off against the strange human girl. He was prepared to fight if he had to, prepared to put himself between the intruder and his team so they would be safe.

It should have been a reassuring gesture to them. He meant it as a show of unity. Instead, it got under Vivi's skin after she'd spent all day and night trying to cooperate and to make their group more cohesive.

She pushed to the head of the group, stalking out in front of Zander. It offended her that he would think not only that she would need to be protected, but that *he* was the one who should be providing that protection. That's not how this was going to go.

Zander didn't need to protect her, or the others. He wasn't their leader. That was a role Vivi wanted for herself.

Mia's eyes met those of the girl in front of her. Her hair was so dark it stood out in stark contrast to the sunshine around her and seemed to glisten almost blue in the sunlight. Her eyes pierced Mia's, and the intensity in that stare was alarming.

But it didn't intimidate Mia into trying to get away or softening the strength of her stance. She didn't know who these people were or where she was. If it came down to it, she was going to defend herself.

Fury rushed through her veins, and her hands twitched. "Who are *you*?" she demanded.

They needed to come up with an explanation and fast. They were standing in front of Mia, acting like *she* was the threat and that they were entitled to information about her. But *she* was the one who had spent her day being hounded by monsters and had just fallen down the rabbit hole with bullets chasing her.

It had been a seriously rough day, and she'd had enough. It was time for something to go right for Mia, even if that only meant these people explaining to her where she was and who they were. They could figure out where to go from there then.

Luna studied the girl, taking note of the torn clothes and bloody injuries all over her body. Her red hair was a mess and her eyes were wide with fear or possibly shock and had luggage so big Vivi's entire wardrobe would fit in them. For a brief moment, she pitied the frightened human who looked to have been in a war.

Mia stared at each of the four standing in front of her in turn. They looked like they were about her age, but there was something strange about them. She couldn't quite place it, couldn't quite figure out what it was that was making her feel so odd facing off against them. The group didn't look fully cohesive. Instead, it looked like two sets of two. A boy and a girl each, two were all silver and ice blue, and the others were dark. The contrast was intense, but so was the clear connection among them. There were tension and conflict, but there was also a sense of togetherness, a clear delineation of *them*, and *her*.

Silence fell over them and they stood there unmoving. Their postures were tight, their gazes flickering between each other. The five were stiff, on guard, none knowing what to do next.

CHAPTER NINETEEN

China

Cassia closed the door to the apartment behind her, keeping her concentration on any sounds she might pick up. For a second, she thought she heard something slamming, but it was pretty far off. Most likely on the streets nearby, and not within the complex.

She went over to the first apartment building, just like she and Mia had when they'd first arrived at the complex. They hadn't entered the first apartment then. It had been locked and Cassia hadn't bothered with it, and instead had just moved on to the next building.

It had appeared to bother Mia when she had realized the fae could simply force the door open if she wanted to. Maybe the halfling had given into that curiosity and come over here to figure out her own way into the locked apartment.

Cassia approached the first door and reached for the handle. It was still locked, with no signs of anyone entering recently. She used her magic to release the lock anyway. Finding Mia was critical. Cassia couldn't just skip over a place because it didn't make sense. She had to look everywhere. When the lock was disengaged, she reached for the knob again.

The door opened under her hand and she was surprised to find a light on in the hallway, illuminating the kitchen and living room. It was strange to see electricity working in a place like this, and it sent an eerie shiver along her spine.

The living room was empty, but there was a fresh smell to it, and the carpet had been replaced recently. It looked cared for, and if she hadn't already seen the rooms of the other buildings, she would have assumed this was a new apartment, ready to rent.

"Well, crickets," she muttered. "If I'd just unlocked the door, I could have found this place. Of course, this might actually be creepier than the abandoned places, so maybe I was right."

As hopeful as she was upon finding a clean, empty room and seeing a light on, hopeful that Mia was hiding in there, the place turned up empty too. Cassia stood in the kitchen and tried to think. This inexplicably perfect apartment aside, the rest of the building still looked dilapidated. Where could Mia have gone?

If she was looking for adventure, she would have found it in the other rooms and would likely still be there by now. If she was looking for a cleaner place to stay, she would have ended up in this apartment—if she had found a way in. So, where was she?

Cassia walked to the screen door leading to the porch of the upper floor apartment and stared out over the grounds surrounding the building. The complex looked dark and foreboding. There was something sinister to it that she couldn't put her finger on.

She was just about to turn away when something caught her eye. Cassia spun back around to look out again and spotted a glinting in the dim light. It looked like glass—quite a lot of it— spread out behind the apartment. She could just see it from the porch because it was higher up and sat on a bit of a hill above the other building.

There was a field beside the building, then a street with a small shop. The shop appeared abandoned too, only there was something wrong, something different about the store, and when Cassia understood what it was, she took off running, cursing herself for not seeing it before. The shop door was cracked open.

She bolted out of the apartment without bothering to lock it and ran down the stairs. She leapt off the third step from the bottom, landed in mid-stride, then raced for the shop.

Cassia ran faster than she had in quite some time, spurred on by the need to protect the young girl. From inside the store, she heard crashing sounds and something screeching. Whatever was going on in there was not good, and she had a sinking feeling it involved Mia.

Mia had proved she could handle herself in a tough fight, and she'd impressed Cassia with the way she'd dealt with the boggart. But Cassia didn't know what was inside the store with the girl, and the bounty hunters who were after her certainly hadn't seemed like they were going to be an easy fight.

Cassia was deeply worried that Mia was in the kind of trouble that could prove fatal. She kept running as hard as she could, past the other apartment building and through the field toward the store.

She slammed into the side of the building rather than slow down for the door. Figuring anyone inside might be confused and take their concentration off Mia for a moment, Cassia rammed into the wall, then flung the door open for a second before ducking her head in.

It was dark inside, so she allowed her eyes to adjust for a moment, and eventually shapes within the shop began to form. The room was unoccupied, but the shelves were destroyed. In the middle of the store, a sledgehammer lay on the ground, and everything had that chaotic appearance she recognized quite well. It was the scene of a fight, for sure.

Cassia ran into the room and listened to see if she could hear anything. There didn't seem to be anything close, and she was about to go to the door and look outside when a sound chilled her heart and made her stop cold in her tracks.

A gunshot echoed all around her. It was close, somewhere outside of the building. Across from Cassia was a door to a back-room, and she sprinted for it. She flung it open and ran inside, pushing away a desk as she raced for another door which led outside.

The air was thick with smoke as she entered a passage that led to another alley along the other side of the building. The sound of shouting echoed from around the corner, and of a voice, a female voice. The girl screamed.

Cassia sprinted to the corner and rounded it just in time to see Mia with a portal behind her, sucking her inside. The girl was bent at the waist and was falling. In front of her stood a redcap, its glamour gone, and beside him was a short, nearly transparent troll. A sluagh.

The redcap held a gun, which was smoking, and as Mia disappeared through the portal, he fired several more rounds at her. The bullets all seemed to miss, bouncing off the wall behind the portal and leaving black marks on the concrete.

The sluagh screamed in frustration, and the pair began an argument Cassia couldn't quite hear. It wasn't clear if *they* had opened the portal or if someone else had, but they seemed upset that Mia had gone through it. It didn't matter. They'd fired a gun at Mia, which was all Cassia needed to know.

"I told you," the redcap said to the sluagh. "I needed her to… hey, who are you?"

Instead of bothering with words, Cassia flung herself at the redcap fast enough to land an elbow on its chin and send it barreling backward, the gun skittering off into a dark corner of the alley. The sluagh raced off, undoubtedly to find something to throw at her.

She'd dealt with them before, and they'd been more annoying than harmful. Often, sluaghs tied themselves to someone to feed off their energy and could only use what their host could spare. Considering the redcap was now most certainly missing some teeth and looked like Mia had already put the hurt on him as well, Cassia figured the sluagh wasn't going to be much trouble.

The redcap began to stand, getting to its stubby feet so it could run at her. Dropping low, Cassia swept her legs out, swiping the redcap at the knees and bringing it down to the ground on its back. She jumped on top of it and drove her fist into its stomach. The gun the redcap had dropped was too far away, and every time he reached for it, Cassia slammed her fist into the monster's armpit.

"Where did she go?" Cassia screamed, pounding the redcap in the face with rapid-fire rights and lefts.

"I don't know," it yelled. "I didn't open the portal!"

Cassia didn't believe him and continued punching him in the head. He started to weaken and looked as if he was about to fall unconscious when Cassia noticed something ahead of her. It was the sluagh, and it was picking up the gun.

"Leave or die," it trilled at her.

"You first," she said, grabbing the redcap by the chin and back of the head. As the sluagh raised the gun toward her, she twisted violently, snapping the neck of the redcap, killing it instantly.

There was a slight pop, and the gun dropped to the ground, the sluagh that had held it no longer there. Cassia had been right, it had tied itself to the life force of the redcap, and since that was the case, it couldn't be called back. No one would know what happened here.

She stood slowly, eyeing the wall. It didn't seem possible. Mia couldn't have done that. Not a halfling, not one who didn't know she had fae blood at all.

Cassia approached the wall and lifted her hands to it. Resting her palms against the brick, she felt for the power of the portal. Even though it was closed, the energy would still linger there. Not many fae had the ability to detect the remaining magic of a closed portal, and it was one of the things about Cassia that made her such an incredible bounty hunter.

The special ability didn't stop with just being able to feel for the portal. Once she found it, she could re-open it and follow the trails. She'd done it many times before when in pursuit of criminals. Being able to chase them even when they opened their own portals and closed them the instant they went through meant it was harder to completely avoid her. It was the reason that the majority of fae who had the ability ended up becoming bounty hunters.

Cassia found the center of the portal's power and focused her magic on it, opening it back up. This could be extremely dangerous. She knew that. It was always a risk to go through an unknown portal, but she didn't have the option of hesitating or thinking too much about it.

Whatever danger *she* might be facing, Mia faced even more. Wherever the portal brought Cassia, she was better equipped to manage it than the young halfling. Cassia had to find her and make sure she was safe.

Taking a breath, she jumped through the portal. She was accustomed to traveling this way and barely noticed the swirls of color and twisting feeling that came as she moved through it. An instant later, she landed on a sidewalk in front of four startled teenage halfling fae. It took a second for her to recognize that Mia was standing beside her.

Mia gasped. "You're here."

"I am," she said. "Where's here?"

She looked around and saw the gate to the side of them. It bore a name that she knew very well. Elmhurst Academy. A smile came to her lips. She didn't know how this had happened, but she was glad it had. She turned her attention back to the four sets of eyes staring at her and Mia.

They didn't seem nearly as pleased as she was that she and Mia were there. All four of the halflings were clearly on edge, ready to challenge her new ward in an instant. She positioned herself slightly in front of Mia just in case they decided to get jumpy before she could figure this out. She had to be prepared to keep them away from Mia.

Zander, Carson, Luna, and Vivi couldn't believe what they were seeing. It was shocking enough to see the portal form on the wall and spit out a human girl and a bullet. They weren't at all prepared to see the portal open again and a full fae woman saunter through.

This fae moved with absolute confidence, striding out onto the sidewalk like she owned the portal. She was beautiful, if dressed fiercely and armed to the teeth. This wasn't the parent of one of the students at the academy.

They studied her, evaluating every detail to try and understand who this fae woman might be. The leather jacket over black pants and heavy black boots set her apart from most of the other fae women they encountered on a regular basis. They could see the outline of weapons under her clothes and instinctively knew there were others. When someone who looked like that had one weapon, most of the time, they had a lot of them.

Strength and power radiated off her. She was either a bounty hunter or someone of great power. They didn't know what to take from that. If she was a bounty hunter, was it possible she was chasing down this human girl? That didn't make sense. Fae bounty hunters rarely pursued humans. She would have had to commit truly horrific crimes in order for that to happen, and they doubted that.

"Who are you?" the fae woman asked. "What are you doing here?"

"What do you mean what are we doing here?" Vivi asked

defensively. "This is our school. We're the ones wondering what you two are doing here."

"She came through a portal in the wall," said Zander. "Actually, she fell through the portal. A gunshot followed her."

"It almost hit Zander," Luna said. "It followed right after her, and if she hadn't just fallen on her face when she made it through, it could have hit her."

"What's going on? Making a portal here is really stupid. There are humans around here. If it wasn't so early in the morning, she could have gotten caught falling out on the sidewalk," Carson said.

"She probably didn't even fall. She probably got thrown," Vivi said. "How would someone like her know how to use a portal otherwise?"

"We were on our way back to town and saw the portal forming. She hit the ground right in front of us and got up threatening us," Zander added.

Mia struggled to control herself through the fury coursing through her. She turned to Cassia, who was looking her up and down like she expected to find a grave injury she had missed in their first exchange.

"Are you all right?" the bounty hunter asked. Mia had more injuries than when Cassia had left the girl alone in the apartment complex. But nothing looked too bad. No obvious broken bones, since she was standing in a fighting stance. She also seemed to be fairly coherent, but all the blood did bother Cassia.

Mia shook her head adamantly. "No, I'm not all right. Are you hearing what just happened? What the heck is going on? How did I end up here? And where is here, anyway?"

Cassia smiled at her and took a few steps closer to the large gate. She gestured to a plaque on the stone beside the iron. "You're right where you need to be."

CHAPTER TWENTY

Luna, Vivi, Carson, and Zander were stunned by the declaration. They stared at Cassia in shock and surprise. Did she seriously just say this strange girl was where she was meant to be? What was that supposed to mean?

Vivi looked at the other three, waiting for one of them to say something. Especially Zander. He fancied himself the leader of their group, no matter how the others might feel about that particular issue. This would be the ideal situation for him to use some of those leadership aspirations to figure out what the heck was going on.

When he didn't, she moved forward. "You've got to be kidding me," she said, her arms flying up in the air before falling down by her sides. "Not only is this girl showing up out of some bizarre portal that showed up in the wall of *our* school, but now you're just waltzing in here, too? It's not enough for her to get chased by a bullet that could have hit any of us. Now you're saying this is where she belongs? You are severely mistaken. She doesn't belong here. We don't want her here. And while we're on the topic, who do you think you are, deciding something like that?"

The other three stared at her. The rude, mean outburst was a little more the speed they typically expected from Vivi. But coming in the face of strangers showing up and confronting them seemed both appropriate and out of character somehow. She wanted to exert her dominance and didn't like new people coming around, especially humans. But she wasn't just speaking for herself. That fit had been about all four of them. In her own way, she was defending them.

Zander understood her hesitation, but he was willing to be more open. There had to be a reason this girl had shown up here, and the woman was ready to not only protect her but had declared she was meant to be here. He looked at the girl again.

The suddenness of her arrival combined with her immediately going into fighting mode meant they hadn't had much of an opportunity to really look at her. The first thing he noticed about her was her eyes. Bright, vibrant green, and incredibly wide, they caught his attention even with the fear in them. From there, he saw the tangles of coppery red hair billowing down around her shoulders. It looked like she'd experienced something pretty difficult in the time before she'd come through the portal, but that's not what mattered.

It was the color. Naturally red hair wasn't the mark of a fae. It didn't exist among their kind. It was what had set her apart and made them immediately assume she was human. Of course, it was possible she did that intentionally. It could be her version of glamour. He knew plenty of fae and halflings who assumed a variety of different features when they used their glamour. None of the four of them had taken enough time or paid enough attention into looking beyond any glamour she might be using.

He leaned in a little and squinted at her. "Is she a halfling?" he asked. "This academy is only for halflings."

The girl turned slightly, and he realized she wasn't using glamour. Red was the natural color of her hair.

"Look at her," Carson snapped. "Of course she's not."

"When was the last time you heard of a student showing up through a portal in the wall around the grounds?" Vivi asked.

"But she did use the portal," Luna pointed out. "Have you ever known a human girl who could do something like that?"

"Again," Vivi snapped. "I think someone threw her. She pissed off the wrong fae, and they picked her up and tossed her through. Followed it up with shooting at her, hoping it would finish her off before she got where she was going."

"Vivi," Carson said, almost in warning.

"What? You heard the shot and you saw the bullet. Do you have a better explanation? I don't know about you, but I don't know of a lot of people who shoot at people when they want to give them a friendly goodbye," she said.

"That doesn't mean she did anything wrong," Luna said. "You saw how frightened she was. Maybe she didn't even know the people who shot at her."

"But how did she know how to use the portal?" Zander asked. "It's not like they have them just sitting around out in the human world with a sign explaining how to use them."

The woman stood with her arms crossed tightly over her chest, watching in disgust as the four young halflings argued over the girl. Zander finally pulled his attention away from the bickering to look at her. "Who are you?" he asked.

She tightened her arms over her chest and cocked her hip at him. "The daughter of the greatest bounty hunter ever known and protector of what could be."

Mia peered at Cassia out of the corner of her eye, but the four teens clearly understood the cryptic message. Immediately silent, they moved in a little tighter together. They exchanged glances and looked back and forth between themselves and the two who came through the portal. They communicated their questions and concerns to each other without having to say a word. Their eyes established Zander as their speaker, and he looked at the fae woman again.

"Who is this girl? Did she open that portal?" Zander asked.

The leather-clad woman straightened her spine and faced off with him. "Her name is Mia. She is being pursued by some very dangerous people for reasons we don't know, including bounty hunters, redcaps, and others. Today was a particularly difficult and treacherous day for her. I am acting as her guide and her protector, and I took her to a place where I thought she would be safe. It turned out not to be so. There was already a boggart there, but Mia held her own against it. She fought him and enabled me to capture him without further incident. Unfortunately, that creature wasn't the only danger we faced. A redcap and a sluagh also appeared. As you can imagine, we weren't interested in spending much quality time with them," she said.

"Are you going to tell us she defeated those, too?" Vivi asked sarcastically.

Cassia's eyes moved over to the dark-haired girl. "Is there a reason you refuse to believe that?"

"Because it doesn't make sense. Human girls don't go around getting chased by fae bounty hunters and creatures like redcaps. It just doesn't happen. If it did, there would be chaos all over the place. Even if she did manage to cause enough trouble for herself that some of those creatures might be after her, she wouldn't be able to fight them." Vivi cocked a hip and looked disdainfully at Mia.

Cassia nodded slowly and looked at the others again. "The truth is, those creatures did come after her. We were able to avoid them but got split up when we reached the portal. She came through first and the redcap pursuing her shot at her. I followed after and ensured the portal was closed. It's really that simple."

"That still doesn't explain everything," Zander said. "Why would you say this is where she needs to be?"

"Because she does. She belongs here just as much as any of you. Mia is a halfling," Cassia said.

"She can't be." Vivi snapped. "Look at her hair. There are no fae with red hair."

The others continued to question her, not knowing that in the huge academy building beyond the wall, someone else knew something was happening just beyond the grounds and was going to make it known.

Principal Elmhurst strode down one of the large corridors of the school, heading for the library. She walked the same route several times a day and had done so for the vast majority of her life. It was so familiar to her, she barely thought about it. She didn't count the steps or try to figure out where she was in the walk. She didn't pay attention to what she saw on either side of her.

This academy was in her blood just as it had been for the generations before her. The entirety was imprinted on her mind, and at any given moment, she could describe the sprawling building, every room and nook, every piece of art, and every accolade. That was why she rarely ever acknowledged the gargoyles positioned in the corridor on either side of the entrance to the library.

The gargoyles weren't exactly the most pleasant features of the academy. They weren't all bad. Much of their negative attitudes came from being victims of their circumstances. Neither could leave their post, forced to remain exactly where they were so they could guard the library and as much of the academy as they could see.

One thing they actually enjoyed doing was reporting on the students as much as possible. Whenever Elmhurst came by, they had some little tidbit to tell her about misbehavior among the students, classes being skipped, cheating, or anything they could possibly come up with to cause difficulty for them.

Not that the principal blamed the creatures. Life wasn't easy for them, and the students were rarely compassionate about it. These gargoyles were often the recipient of incessant teasing and had been used for several practical jokes. More than half of which were orchestrated by Vivi.

"Headmistress," one said as she passed him. "You are awake and walking the school very early this morning."

"Hello, Steve. Yes, I had trouble sleeping and thought I could come for a book," Elmhurst said.

The gargoyle cringed at the sound of his name. It was one of the most challenging parts of his life and a tremendous contributor to his bad attitude. It was the same for the statue on the other side of the door. Steve and his partner, Dan, had the names bestowed on them by the first Elmhurst to run the academy.

The gargoyles had taken their place at the library when that Elmhurst established the academy, and he'd given them names he'd thought were unique and interesting. Unheard of at the time, Dan and Steve were compelling monikers the creatures could be proud of. Of course, as time changed, so did the perception of their names.

Those titles became average and mundane, and being a gargoyle burdened with one of them they became even more miserable. They had no way to change their names or even what people called them. They were as stuck with the names as they were with their posts outside the library. It left them hating the students and wanting to cause as much difficulty for them as they possibly could.

Which was exactly what they wanted to do that day.

"I'm glad you did," Steve said. "I have something to tell you."

"Don't you always?" Elmhurst asked dismissively.

Most of the professors and other staff went to great lengths to ignore the gargoyles and not engage them in conversation. They tired of hearing the snippets of gossip and having to think of even more issues with the students. At least Principal Elmhurst acknowledged them. She thought that was enough for the morning.

"It's important," Steve insisted.

"It is," Dan said. "We thought you needed to know immediately."

"It can't wait until later?" Elmhurst asked. "I really do want to get this book. The day starts very soon, you know."

"Sure, it can wait. I'm sure it is not truly a concern that there are strange portals appearing on the grounds," Steve said.

That made the headmistress stop. "What do you mean strange portals on the academy grounds?"

"Not exactly on the grounds themselves, but very close. In the wall. Two opened just moments ago near the front gate. There are people gathered there, Headmistress."

"Thank you, Steve," she said and hurried out of the corridor and to the front door of the academy.

She rushed down the long path to the front gate, wondering what was going on and worrying about who might be involved. The gargoyles had the ability to perceive things happening around the academy. It allowed them to keep the buildings and the grounds safer. But they didn't know everything.

They couldn't tell her who created the portal or who was there. The principal was concerned that humans might have seen the portals form, not to mention whoever came through them. That could have devastating consequences for the academy.

There was also fear that whoever created the portal was trying to come onto the grounds and cause harm to the students. Enchantments prevented unapproved portals being formed within the grounds but having two form in the wall near the school was far too close for her comfort.

As she approached the heavy gate, movement flickered beyond the bars. It was brief, not enough to see the person's face, and Elmhurst moved faster. Finally, she reached the gate and opened it. Six people turned to look at her as she rushed down the sidewalk toward them. She withheld a gasp when she saw that four of them were who she referred to as the Scooby gang, the four halflings who had so much promise.

"Zander, Luna, Carson, Vivi, what are you doing?" she demanded as she approached. "What's going on?"

"We didn't have anything to do with this," Zander said. "We were heading to the practice field when we saw a portal open in the wall. Then this girl fell through. We've been trying to figure it out ever since."

There was something strange about the answer. She didn't want to think it was insincere, but it didn't seem to have the weight of all the information and details it should have. She turned to the other two to question them about them coming through the portal so close to her grounds and was shocked to see Cassia's face staring back at her.

"Did you do this?" she asked.

"The portal was a necessity," Cassia told her. "There was a very dangerous situation, and utilizing a portal was the only way to escape it."

"Where were you when you created it?" Elmhurst asked.

"China. Outside Shanghai," said Cassia.

"And what was the purpose of coming here? Surely there was another place to take this girl where she would be safe." Elmhurst gave Mia a cursory glance.

"Coming here wasn't the intention," Cassia said. "It was an unintended consequence, but it is where we needed to be."

"She already told us that," Vivi quipped bitterly.

"Mia, this is Principal Elmhurst. She is the headmistress of this academy. Her family established it many generations ago as a place for halfling fae to come and be trained in their skills. That's why I brought you here. Principal, this is Mia. I take full responsibility for her coming here today and for the way she arrived. But this is where she needs to be. She needs to be in your academy. Mia's a halfling who was just discovered."

CHAPTER TWENTY-ONE

Principal Elmhurst stared at the young girl who had made such an unexpected arrival at the academy. She looked so afraid, and yet there was also a strength about her, a confidence that radiated from her even through her confusion. This wasn't cockiness from the way she was raised or arrogance that came from ongoing praise for her skills. This was real and deeply ingrained within her. It was the type of strength that ran through her veins as a part of her blood. She was fascinating, and the principal still didn't know what to think of her.

The same couldn't be said about the Scooby gang. Zander, Carson, Vivi, and Luna had strong opinions about her arrival and the assertion from Cassia that this girl needed to stay.

"Again, trying to insist on this girl staying here," Vivi said. "That's ridiculous. I don't know who you think you are, but you can't just walk up to an institution like this and demand that any wayward halfling you came upon is good enough to be among us."

Vivi had heard the cryptic, almost threatening message from the woman when questioned about her identity, but it didn't impress her as much as it had the others. In Vivi's life, she had become accustomed to people thinking they were far more important than they really were. Any number of fae could claim to be whatever they wanted, and it was up to the people they spoke to to choose to believe them or not.

Vivi learned early on to believe no one. Too many times, she had watched this play out as people tried to persuade and impress her father, seeking to create a more powerful image for themselves through association with her family. It never worked.

"Honestly, Headmistress Elmhurst, you can't possibly be considering allowing this girl to join the academy when you know nothing about her," Carson said.

"You know nothing about her either," the fae woman who had come through the portal commented.

"It doesn't take much to know she can't possibly be good enough for Elmhurst Halfling Academy. This isn't a place just anyone can attend. It's extremely exclusive and difficult to get into." The Unseelie boy crossed his arms over his chest and huffed.

"I'm well aware of that," the woman said.

"Then you are also aware of the extensive prerequisites and aggressive learning environment," Luna said. "There are many other schools this girl could attend. She could go to one of the basic schools and accomplish the levels for halflings who aren't particularly skilled."

She delivered the comment as if she thought she was being kind. Luna believed she was being helpful, guiding this new halfling into a more appropriate situation than Elmhurst. The basic schools were the ones attended by halflings who didn't show much promise in academics or in their magical skills, or those who couldn't afford the heavy price that came with an education at Elmhurst. This was an academy only for those halflings who showed tremendous potential in their magic and control of their skills, or those from exorbitantly wealthy families who showed promise in other ways.

Students who went through the basic schools rarely amounted to much. They would get proper training in what little skills they did have and develop them as much as they could. After school, few would move on to college. Instead, they would go into service for wealthy fae families, or take menial jobs, like accounting, at one of the corporations.

"Luna's right," Zander offered. "The basic schools could be the perfect pace for her. If she's only just now discovering she's a halfling, she can't possibly have the understanding of her skills and abilities necessary to keep up here. At this point, she's probably too old to catch up. Going to one of those schools will help to make the most of what she does have and give her a path after graduation. She could get a steady job at one of the corporations and be just fine."

"Don't build her up too much," Vivi snarled. "She wouldn't even be good enough to work as a janitor for my uncle's company."

"I don't know," Luna said, trying to be as gentle as she could and not completely smash the hopes, dreams, and self-esteem of the new halfling. "That's not necessarily true. Maybe she could be a janitor."

Vivi tossed another scathing look in Mia's direction and rolled her eyes. "I doubt it. Maybe a bit lower. An accountant, perhaps. I mean, it's a stretch, but if she really applied herself, she might be able to squeeze out enough intellect and skill to manage that type of position."

In her mind, a janitor was a better position than an accountant, and Vivi had trouble imagining how someone who got all the way into her late teens without knowing she was a halfling would ever have the skills and abilities to take on any role. She would only end up embarrassing herself and causing difficulty for the company who employed her.

Mia narrowed her eyes at the dark-haired girl.

Vivi's hands clenched and her chest tightened uncomfortably. This new girl was beautiful, and it made Vivi's skin crawl. She disliked being around anyone she thought was prettier than her, and the envy this caused often turned those girls into targets for Vivi's unpleasant jokes.

"That's enough," Principal Elmhurst finally said. "I don't believe any of you were asked for your opinion. For people who are acting so proud of the academy they attend, you aren't putting much effort into being kind and welcoming ambassadors. I will say I understand your concerns and have heard what you had to say about Mia. But you must understand that when it comes to who is admitted into the Elmhurst Academy, the decision lies squarely and solely with me. I don't take into account the opinions of young students when determining who will be given the opportunity for an education here. This is only more Court politics, and I won't stand for it. You know that."

"Yes, Principal Elmhurst," all four of the Scooby gang replied solemnly.

The principal gave a nod and smiled at them. "Good. Now, the four of you should be getting to practice. From what I've seen, you still have a long way to go. I will speak with Mia and Cassia in my office."

The name struck Zander hard. He looked at Carson, Luna, and Vivi, who were having the same reaction. They had known the beautiful woman who'd come through the portal after Mia was powerful in some way. She even introduced herself as the daughter of the greatest of their time, and her clothing suggested she was a bounty hunter. But none of them had known just how accurate her comment was.

They hadn't heard her name yet, and now that they had, they were all struck that they were able to meet the legendary bounty hunter. She truly was the daughter of the greatest of their time, and her presence exuded the same type of confidence, telling them she was as exceptional at her job as her father had been.

Cassia gave them all a long and knowing stare before turning to follow Principal Elmhurst through the gate and up the path toward the school. The building loomed in front of them, stately and impressive. It had the strength that came from being established and secure but still felt exciting and full of possibilities. Every student who came through the halls and every new skill discovered created more potential and renewed the commitment to excellence that led to the Elmhurst family establishing the school so long ago.

Principal Elmhurst led them through the huge arched doors into the building. They followed her along the quiet corridors in silence. Mia thought about the four teenagers she'd just met. Actually, she hadn't met them at all. Nobody had offered their names; they'd only demanded to know who she was and why she was there. They had made it abundantly clear she wasn't welcome, and that they didn't believe she belonged among them.

Mia didn't know why that bothered her so much. She didn't know what this place was or what made the four other young halflings they'd just encountered so special. Yet, the insinuation that she wasn't as good as they were and therefore shouldn't be allowed to be a part of their school was deeply insulting. It wasn't just the feeling of being left out or made fun of. It cut deeper in a way she didn't really understand.

Finally, they arrived at an impressive dark wooden door. Principal Elmhurst swept her hand in front of her and the door unlatched, swinging open to allow them inside. Mia and Cassia followed, both looking around to take in as much of the rich, beautiful surroundings as they could while the headmistress led them to another door. Everything around them was in deep shades of blue and purple, with occasional accents of white. Large display cases lined either side of the lobby or reception area of the office. Deeply inset lights glowed on trophies, insignia, and other awards on the shelves.

They went through the second door into the main office. Principal Elmhurst took the tall wingback chair behind an elaborately carved wooden desk and gestured to the two chairs across from her.

"Please, sit," she invited.

Cassia and Mia settled into the seats and looked across the desk at the headmistress expectantly. Her eyes swept across them, evaluating them and trying to decide how to proceed. She was calm, any anxiety that had built within her after finding out about the portals opening had long dissipated. Now she was just curious.

It was unusual for anyone to show up at the academy unannounced. The last term had ended several weeks before and the new one would not begin for several more. Existing students wouldn't return to the campus until a few days before classes began again, and the newest students would only arrive a few days before that. Mia was unusual, and Principal Elmhurst needed to know more about her.

"Tell me again how you came to arrive through the portal," she said.

Cassia and Mia exchanged glances. Mia noticed the changes Cassia made to the story about her arrival and didn't know if she wanted to keep up that story or tell how it actually happened. She chose to stay quiet and allow the bounty hunter to make the explanations. Cassia seemed more secure in what was happening, and Mia was prepared to follow along.

Cassia gave the same explanation to Principal Elmhurst as she had to the two boys and two girls earlier. She'd changed the details slightly, but significantly. It wasn't lost on the young halfling that Cassia had avoided telling any of them how the portal had come to be in the first place.

She skirted around the issue, seamlessly going from the creatures pursuing Mia to them entering the portal in order to stay safe. Mia was curious about this, wondering at the meaning behind the changes made to the story. But she stayed quiet. Cassia knew what she was doing. At least, Mia hoped she did.

"Do you understand just how dangerous it was for that portal to open out onto the sidewalk in front of our school?" Principal Elmhurst asked.

"Yes," the bounty hunter said. "I apologize for that. It wasn't our intention at all to put the academy or any of the students at risk. As I said, we traveled through the portal to avoid extreme danger. It brought us here, which I believe is exactly the place we needed to be."

"So, it was a portal of need rather than one of direction," the headmistress said. It wasn't really a question, but a statement, an acknowledgment of her understanding.

Cassia replied. "Yes. I believe it was."

The principal nodded slowly and turned her attention to Mia. "Would you please step outside for a moment? I'd like to speak to your guardian."

Mia looked at Cassia, who nodded. "Go ahead and just wait right outside. We'll come for you soon," she said.

Mia exited the office and closed the door behind her. When her footsteps faded away, Cassia turned back to Principal Elmhurst.

"This is unprecedented, Cassia," the headmistress said.

"I know," she said. "It is highly unusual, and I apologize for any inconvenience or discomfort we've caused. But I'm telling you, she needs to be here. The portal wouldn't have brought us to this place if it wasn't where she was supposed to be. You know that. She needs to be among her own kind and learn the skills and abilities she's missed out on. This is where she's going to be safest and be able to make the most of herself."

"You understand this is not an ordinary school. While they could have chosen their words more diplomatically, Zander,

Carson, Luna, and Vivi were right when they talked about the other halfling schools. This is an extremely prestigious academy. We turn away students every year."

"I understand that. That's why I'm asking you to recognize that she needs to be here," Cassia implored.

"The deadline is past for any scholarships that would be able to defray the cost of tuition and accommodations while she's here. I won't mince words when I tell you the quality of the education and facilities of this academy come at a premium price," Elmhurst said matter-of-factly.

"I'm well aware of the expense of attending this academy," Cassia said. "I'm prepared to cover it. I will pay Mia's fees and send her a monthly stipend."

The cost of attending the academy was high, but Cassia knew she could manage it. With all of the extra bounties she had brought in recently, she had more money than ever before. Especially after the amount she'd earned from capturing the brutal serial killer redcap. Just as Fan had told her at the prison when she'd brought in the boggart, she was a very rich female. She had little need for so much money. Her living expenses rarely amounted to much, and though she'd enjoy having a little padding in her account to ensure she could cover anything that came up, other than her penchant for anime, she could think of no better use for the money than to support and protect Mia. She could always buy the red sailor moon costume next year. The bounty from the redcap alone was enough to pay tuition, room, and board for the remainder of Mia's high school career, and that was what Cassia intended to do with it.

"Even if you are capable of paying the cost, I'm concerned about her ability to fit in with the rest of the students," Elmhurst admitted. "These are exceptionally talented and powerful halflings. They've been learning skills and sharpening their ability to use them their entire lives. I'm worried having just found out about her fae heritage will mean that Mia will be too far behind in her skills. I have no doubt she would probably be just fine in the academics portion of her education, but what about her magic? She is fully untrained, and according to you, didn't even know she was fae until a few days ago. I'm concerned she will quickly fall behind in such an advanced and aggressive program. She can't expect the other students to slow down to accommodate her, or the professors to take extra time to teach down to her. The goal of this academy is to produce the strongest halflings possible."

"I understand that," Cassia said. She couldn't help the smirk which came to her lips. "But I assure you Mia will be fine."

"How can you be sure of that?" the headmistress asked.

Cassia considered how to respond. She had to be careful with her words and not reveal too much too soon. Just as she had with the Scooby gang and the first time she told the story to Principal Elmhurst, she didn't go into full detail about the portal.

She didn't want to tell anyone yet that Mia had been the one to open her own portal to come here. It was an incredible feat, one that made Cassia believe her young ward was going to be very powerful. But in order to assume that power and make the absolute most of her skills and abilities, she needed the right tutelage. Having the highest quality education available to her would ensure she could rise to what was innately within her.

"I've witnessed it myself," she told the principal. "I have experienced moments of her power and seen her use skills she didn't know she had. I've watched her fight various creatures, even a redcap, and survive. Well before she knew the truth about herself, she could perceive magical creatures and didn't panic. She handled them with confidence and grace. She's courageous and unafraid to defend herself and those around her. She is the one who defeated and captured a boggart I just brought in to Forasaon. If you need assurance of her abilities, you are more than welcome to speak with Faylynne, the head jailer there. He will confirm I brought a boggart in and tell you of the condition it was in upon arrival. Mia definitely has exceptional talents. She is just untrained and doesn't know what all she can do yet."

Cassia knew if the principal heard from Fan how thoroughly defeated the boggart was when she'd brought him into the prison, Elmhurst would have to believe in Mia's skill.

"I don't think that is necessary. I will take your word for it," Elmhurst said.

"Thank you," Cassia said, smiling.

"But," the principal continued, "I will only accept her for one semester. She'll be expected to assimilate with the other students and to the school environment as any other student. She will have the same standards and expectations as everyone else. I will ensure there are others available to help bring her up to speed, but she will need to apply herself and demonstrate that she does, in fact, belong among our students. One semester, Cassia. If she does not prove herself, she will need to be transferred to one of the basic academies at the end of the semester."

Cassia nodded. "I understand. She won't disappoint you."

Before Cassia left, she took Mia aside and spoke to her. "Mia, I need you to stay here and learn as much as you can about your newfound abilities."

"But why? Why can't I go home and find a tutor there?" Mia knew her voice sounded whiney, but she missed her dad already and wanted to go back to a place that felt familiar. With all of the new revelations since that night in the Chinese night market, she craved normalcy. Staying at an academy where she wasn't wanted, wasn't going to help her feel any better about who she'd become.

"There isn't anyone who can tutor you. This place is safe and is the only academy that can help you to uncover all your potential. You need to work hard and stay under the radar as much as possible. If no one knows you're here, then you'll be safe." The bounty hunter still wasn't sure what was so special about this halfling, but there had to be something considering all of the attention she had received lately.

"What about my father? He'll worry about me and call the police. He knows he doesn't have a sister in China." While Master Chen and Becky's memories had been messed with, no one had said anything to her father—that she was aware of. He would worry a great deal about her if she didn't show up when she was supposed to.

"Don't worry about your father. I'll come up with a cover story to keep you safe."

Mia waved her hands. "No, I don't want you messing with my dad's memories. That can't be good for him, can it?" While she didn't know anything about magic, she couldn't believe that messing with the memories of humans was safe. Her dad had to be human, he would have told her who she was if *he* was the fae parent.

While she hadn't had much time to think about it, her mother had to be the fae parent. Was her mom even dead? Or did she disappear on her husband and daughter right after Mia was born?

Cassia took Mia by the shoulders. "Listen to me. You are in real danger. That danger will follow you around. Do you want anything bad to happen to your dad or Becky? Or anyone else you care about?"

She hadn't thought that far ahead. Mia shook her head. "No, I don't want them to have to deal with what I've seen this past week."

"Then stay here and let me talk to your dad. What's your address? I promise I won't hurt him. He'll just think you're in China still, training." Cassia would have to come up with a better story, but it was enough of a start that by the time she reached Mia's dad, she'd have a better one to convince him of.

Mia nodded. "All right, but if you hurt my dad, I swear you'll regret it."

The intense emotion behind Mia's words and the stony stare impressed Cassia.

"As I said, you're right where you need to be." Cassia turned and left the school.

CHAPTER TWENTY-TWO

With so few students around, and a desire to keep them all together, Mia was given a room near Luna and Vivi. As in, right beside them. To say Vivi didn't take it well would be an understatement.

Every night was an adventure in whatever torment and torture Vivi was going to plot for Mia, who, for the most part, didn't react. She kept her cool and tried to accept the practical jokes as the kind of ribbing that should be expected any time teenagers were left to their own devices. Especially when someone new entered their social circles. It still bothered her though, and while she wouldn't let Vivi know, a few weeks into the relentless mocking and tricks, Mia was about done with it.

Vivi, for her part, decided she was going to have fun with Mia. If she could get the new girl to quit and leave the academy, then great, but if not, she was going to enjoy knocking the pretty smile off her face at every possible opportunity. The hot water trick was especially diabolical, she thought.

One morning when Mia went into the shower, Vivi snuck behind her and placed a hex on the water heater. Using an incantation, she raised and lowered the temperature of the water at random intervals, going from ice cold to scalding hot in a matter of seconds, causing Mia to leave the shower, her skin beet red, and shampoo still in her hair.

Vivi laughed for days at the look on her face, the towel wrapped around her haphazardly, as Mia stomped out of the shower and into her room. She had glared at Vivi, but she'd lacked proof she had anything to do with it.

Then, there were the missing pens. That took more planning but was worth the aggravation. Every chance she got, Vivi would cast a vanishing spell on the pen Mia was using. At first, she would stop what she was doing and look around her desk or start digging through her bag for her lost pen, but eventually, she just started bringing whole canisters of pens with her to the library where she was receiving tutoring in advance of the semester. If Vivi made one disappear, she would just grab another. One time, Vivi made the entire canister disappear, but Mia just reached into her bag and pulled out another can and a new bag of pens. She opened the bag, dumped the pens inside the can then bore a hole through Vivi with an icy stare.

But nothing could compare to the knockout punch Vivi planned for this day. It had been a solid week without doing anything to her, and it was absolute torture, but it was imperative for Mia to think Vivi had given up. She needed to get comfortable and trust that things were normal again in order for this trick to work in all of its multiple parts.

When Vivi arrived early for lunch, she scouted out the best possible seat, directly in the middle of the cafeteria, and sat so she could watch people come out of the line and head to their seats. Mia had been sitting at the same table—the farthest away from the line—every day, so she would most certainly come by where Vivi sat. Vivi had brought an apple and a bottled water with her for lunch rather than going through the line to make sure she had plenty of time to wait for Mia.

But Mia was taking her time, and Vivi was getting anxious. The cafeteria was filling up, and some people were sitting near Mia's regular seat, meaning she might choose somewhere else and blow the whole plan apart. Vivi was about to move a little farther down when Mia came out and approached her usual spot with her tray in her hand.

Normally, she walked with her eyes somewhat downcast, but today she seemed more confident, like she was in a really good mood. That was only going to make this trick all the more delicious.

As Mia got closer, Vivi put her plan into action, using a conjuring spell she'd learned just for the occasion. Suddenly, in Mia's path, just under the foot that was coming down, a banana peel appeared. The trick was cheesy, but that was the point. Who actually slipped on banana peels?

Mia did.

Her leg slid out from under her and shot up in the air, and the rest of her body went airborne. The tray flew out of her hands, and a second spell hit it just in time. As Mia crashed to the ground, the empty platter bounced off her head, the food still floating above her.

Struggling to sit up, Mia glared at Vivi, who smiled and waved. Then she pointed up, and Mia followed the direction of her finger to see the food still hovering. Just when Mia's expression shifted as she figured out what was about to happen, Vivi released the spell and the warm, wet pasta and marinara sauce dropped on the new girl's face. The sauce stained her clothes and colored her hair.

For a moment, the only sound in the room was the laughter of the kids who had witnessed what had happened. Mia sat in the mess, allowing the humiliation and shame to wash over her before she slowly got to her feet and stared Vivi dead in the eyes.

The other girl stood, shrugging as Mia picked up her tray. She aimed it at Vivi and swung her hand, ready to hurl it. Seeing it coming, Vivi began a spell to stop her, but Mia thrust out her free hand, fingers curled into a fist as if she had punched the air in front of her.

Vivi flew across the room, crashing into the wall and sliding down. Mia had done something, but even *she* didn't know what. It was powerful though, and Vivi moaned at the pain in her back from hitting the wall. Mia took off for her room, leaving the mess of food on the floor as Vivi tried to stand.

"What are you looking at?" she yelled at the tables full of other students who were now looking at her wide-eyed. No one had ever stopped Vivi mid-trick before. Not with magic like that. No one had ever publicly humiliated her by slamming her against a wall either. Fury built up inside her as she too stormed off to her room, leaving the full cafeteria free to gossip and laugh.

Vivi was still stinging from the embarrassment of the prank gone wrong the next day when Principal Elmhurst appeared in their dorm to get Mia.

"You have a visitor," the principal said.

Mia suspected her visitor would be Cassia. The bounty hunter was the only person who knew where she was. But it still made her smile when the headmistress led her to the courtyard at the back of the school and she spotted the fae woman looking out over a low stone wall at the grounds surrounding the building. Mia came to stand beside her and followed her gaze to see what had captured her attention.

The courtyard was mostly contained between two sections of the academy building, but a gap in the architecture allowed them to see out beyond the campus onto the rolling grounds behind the school. From this perspective, it appeared as though the grounds went on forever. Ahead of them, the early morning fog blanketed a hedge maze making it look eerie against the rest of the picturesque landscape.

"We went into the maze earlier this week," Mia said.

"Is it as confusing as it looks from up here?" the bounty hunter asked.

"No," Mia said, shaking her head. "It's worse. It changes while you're in it to test your memory and thought. And probably something about magic. I don't know."

Cassia laughed. "I'm glad it's been so valuable to be here."

"I was just distracted by Carson. He got frustrated in the first ten seconds we were in there and ended up just blasting a hole in the hedge to get out."

"How did that go for him?" Cassia asked.

"Not well. The hedge swallowed him and held him for about an hour. Then he had to deal with Principal Elmhurst. It wasn't a good day for him. But I liked the maze," Mia said.

"That's good. So, you probably know why I came here today."

Mia didn't look at her. She didn't want to see the expression in Cassia's eyes and know what she was going to say before it came out. If it was going to be bad, Mia preferred to hang on to her ignorance for as long as possible.

She nodded. "You went to talk to my father again?" Mia's whispered words sounded pained.

Mia had spoken to Cassia after she went to see her dad, and Cassia had assured her he was okay. Whenever they'd emailed each other, he had seemed fine, but Mia still worried about her dad and his safety. And about how the memory invasion would affect him long term.

Their cover story had been that Mia had received an offer to stay in China to study under a Wushu Master of some renown. Because she had done so well, no one questioned the story. Mia's dad was so proud of his daughter and knew it was an honor, so even though he missed her, he'd let her stay.

Cassia had promised she would handle it, but Mia worried that hurting the people she loved would become just another part of her challenges as she struggled to wrap her head around the truth about herself.

Now the bounty hunter was finally back to tell her exactly what happened.

"Yes," Cassia said.

"How is he?" Mia asked. "Was he worried about me?"

"He has no reason to be worried," she admitted. "He truly believes the cover story. He looks forward to your weekly emails, so keep them up. What's important is that he's doing just fine and isn't concerned about you right now."

"I'm glad to hear he's doing well." And she was, but she really did miss him. It had been just the two of them her entire life. Or at least for as long as she could remember. Her mom had been around for her first few months, but she'd died before Mia was a year old. Her dad was all she had as far as family went.

Becky was her best friend. They told each other everything. Mia really wished she could tell Becky the truth. She'd know exactly how to handle Vivi and the other students who were treating her so horribly.

"I didn't give him any sort of timeline or anything, so he isn't expecting you back anytime soon. I modified his memories, so he believes you called him yourself to tell him the good news. That way, he can spread the word to friends and family, so they aren't wondering where you are."

Mia drew in a breath. "There is no other family. It's just the two of us. Always has been."

Cassia nodded. "I know how that feels." She gave Mia a quick hug around the shoulders, then rubbed her back encouragingly. "But he's very happy for you. He says you are amazingly talented, and he knows you're going to get really far. I think part of him was hoping something like that would happen for you while you were in China."

"Really?"

Cassia nodded. "He's extremely proud of you, Mia. He thinks you're incredible."

"I think he's pretty great, too." Mia hung her head. "I don't want to upset him. I know it's going to be hard for us to be apart."

"It will. I know you'll miss him and he's going to miss you. Which reminds me, you're going to need to call him at weird hours and send emails home, as if you're still training in China. You should do the same for your friends from the competition and your old instructor. I manipulated their memories the same way I did your father's, so they think you're back in China getting trained as well. It's important to maintain a consistent story for all of them."

"Yeah, I figured as much. I've been sending them emails late at night mostly because that's the only time I can do it," Mia said.

Her voice trembled slightly. She was still getting accustomed to the new life she had been thrown into without any warning. Before she'd left for China for the Wushu competition, her thoughts of the world had been pretty much limited to Pasadena.

She thought of little other than school and training and had never imagined anything beyond that. Going to Shanghai for the competition was the biggest thrill of her life, something she had looked forward to and planned for months. It was so much bigger than anything she'd experienced, and she believed she would go back to Pasadena carrying those memories and never have anything to compare them to.

Then suddenly, everything changed. It was that fast. She went from knowing her life and who she was to all she ever believed suddenly shifting and coming under question. Her life was completely different now, and it would never be the same again. It was exciting but frightening and disorienting at the same time. She missed her father, Becky, and her other friends, and had moments when she felt isolated and alone.

"I know this is hard for you," Cassia said. "But you need to remind yourself that this is where you're supposed to be. You are fae, Mia. That is who you are. The abilities and skills within you are yours. They've been there since the moment you were born, just waiting for you to discover them. Now that you have, you owe it to yourself to learn more about them and make yourself the most you can possibly be."

"I know," Mia said softly. "I'm trying."

"And you're doing well." When Mia only nodded, Cassia took hold of her chin and turned the younger girl's face toward her so she could meet her bright green eyes. "You also need to remember why we came here in the first place. There are people after you, Mia. I still haven't figured out why, but you're being pursued by very dangerous creatures. You need to learn to defend yourself. I know you have tremendous skill in your martial arts, and you are a powerful fighter. I've seen that for myself. But that will only carry you so far. There will come a time when you'll need to face off against those who don't want to just use their hands or weapons to battle. When that time comes, you need to be able to fight on their terms."

"I will," Mia assured her.

Cassia nodded. "Good. Now, I'm going to be away for a while. I have another assignment in San Diego. Principal Elmhurst knows how to get in touch with me if there is an emergency. Everything is taken care of for you, and I've created a fae account for you. There's money in there, and I'll send you more each month."

"You don't have to do that," Mia said.

Cassia nodded again, staring directly into the younger woman's eyes. "I want to. I want what's best for you. Now, come on. Walk me out."

They were headed through the building again when the headmistress appeared. "Cassia, you're leaving already?" she asked.

"Yes. I have to be in San Diego for another assignment tonight, so I have to find a place where I can create a portal," Cassia replied.

"You can use one of the school portals," Elmhurst offered. "We don't have one to San Diego, but there's one that will bring you to a transportation depot where you can move on. Do you have everything you need?"

Cassia patted the bag hanging over one hip and nodded. "Yes. And thank you. That will be very helpful." She knew the school was guarded against unapproved portals, which was just one more reason Mia's portal was so strange. Even though it was on the outside of the school's fence, it still shouldn't have worked. The fae magic behind the blocking spell was just as powerful as the one going in and out of Forasaon. It shouldn't have worked.

At the very least, Mia should have been sent right back to where she'd started, or at the worst, lost in the void.

"Oh, headmistress. One more thing. You might want to check the spell protecting the academy from unauthorized portals. Especially where we opened one." Cassia shrugged. It wasn't like Mia did it on purpose or even knew where she was headed. But still, the portal shouldn't have worked, and she worried they might have left a rift in the wall. Possibly allowing someone else to take advantage of what Mia had done.

Principal Elmhurst smirked. "Did it the second I had Mia settled." She shook her head. "I don't know how you opened it there, but everything is fine. There wasn't even a dent in the spell protecting the school. In fact, if it weren't for the gargoyles, I never would have known a portal opened."

Cassia raised her eyebrows. "You have gargoyles?"

"Of course. The library has two stationed outside, and they are in tune with the entire campus, and even parts of town." Elmhurst stood tall, as though she was proud of the security protections she had. Not many schools had gargoyles. Certainly, none had any as in tune as Steve and Dan.

Cassia whispered in Mia's ear, "Make sure you befriend the gargoyles. They will help to keep you safe."

Mia nodded. She wasn't sure what she was supposed to do with gargoyles, but if they were important, she'd find a way.

They proceeded through the corridors until they reached a

large octagonal room. Fae stood guard at the door but moved out of the way when Elmhurst approached. Inside, more fae were positioned at the junctures of the walls to provide full protection of the room. The principal brought Cassia up to one of the walls and gestured toward it.

"Whenever you're ready. Have a good journey. I'll see you when you return."

"Thank you," Cassia said again.

When the principal left, Cassia turned to the wall and conjured the portal. Mia watched in fascination as the swirling vortex appeared. Cassia said goodbye and waved as she entered the portal and disappeared. The wall closed behind her, leaving Mia staring at nothing but a blank expanse.

Finally, she turned and left the room. She was a few strides down the hallway when Luna and Zander turned the corner.

"Hi, Mia," Luna said. "Are you all right? You look upset."

"No," Mia said, shaking her head. "Not upset. Just..." she glanced briefly over her shoulder, "will we learn how to make portals?"

Luna and Zander glanced at each other, then turned to Mia. "No. We can't do that."

"Why not?" Mia asked.

"We're halflings. No halfling can create a portal," Zander replied.

Mia started to say something, then stopped. She wanted to keep her secret skill to herself, and Cassia must have had a very good reason to take the credit for opening the portal. Mia still didn't fully understand how she'd made the portal appear, or why it had brought her here to the academy. Instinct told her not to share that information until she learned more.

That was the day she started frequenting the library on her own. Foregoing spending time with the others in the mornings, she immediately went to the library by herself and pored over the huge volumes. Scanning their thick pages and complex language, she looked up everything she could find on both portals and what halflings were capable of doing.

As she searched, she tried to find any information that might be available on her mother. Mia needed to know who she was and what had happened to her.

If only she could call her dad and ask him. She couldn't risk it, but he had to know who her mother was, didn't he?

CHAPTER TWENTY-THREE

The rest of the summer, just a few weeks, seemed to be an exercise in frustration for Mia. The headmaster assigned two girls to help her try to catch up on some of the more basic skills and tasks. It hadn't really worked all that well. No matter what the girls tried to teach Mia, it just never seemed to take. Even small, easy spells eluded her.

A lesson in conjuring, in which the girls had showed her how to produce a flower, had gone nowhere. Flower conjuring was something little halfling girls learned before they could write. They'd frolic in the fields creating flowers to play in as tiny children, graduating to Faerie circles when they were only slightly older. But Mia struggled to produce anything.

Frustration built every day that Mia couldn't figure it out. The girls would show her how, she seemed to understand it, then she would try it and…nothing. Nothing would happen at all. It was in those moments she would doubt her abilities and wonder if she were in the right place. Then she would go back to her room, and Vivi would have laid out some trick, and Mia, without thinking, would defend herself.

One day, Vivi tried to trap her inside a room by removing the doorknob and locking the door. Mia realized too late that Vivi had tricked her into entering the room by telling her the headmistress wanted to see her there. When Mia turned around to leave, the doorknob was missing.

"Very funny, Vivi," she said, her face pressed against the door. "Let me out."

"Let yourself out, Mia. It's just a simple conjuring spell. Just conjure a doorknob and come on out."

"Vivi, you know I am having trouble with conjuring. Just let me out, will you?"

"Sorry, Mia, I have a lunch date with Luna. I have to go. Bye," she said, lowering the volume of her voice to make it sound like she was running away. She stomped her feet lighter and lighter to make it more realistic.

Mia wasn't convinced.

"I know you're still there, Vivi." Silence greeted her, but Mia could swear she heard the faintest of snickering. "I swear if I can get out of here and you are still standing there—"

What, exactly? She didn't know how to do any spells to attack yet, and she certainly couldn't promise to return the favor of a practical joke. All she could do, so far, was defend herself, and she could only do that in very specific circumstances, and only when she wasn't thinking about it. If she concentrated on trying to defend herself, her mouth would go dry and she wouldn't be able to think clearly, and then nothing would happen.

Mia let out a groan of frustration and tried to think of something else. It wasn't long before she leaned back against a bookshelf and closed her eyes. As she drifted off to sleep, her mind wandered to all the different ways she would exact revenge if she could control her own abilities. After some time passed, though Mia wasn't sure how long, a loud banging sound startled her awake.

The door flew open, and Mia, struggling to figure out where she was and what was going on, threw her hands up in the air to defend herself. Tables soared into the air and slammed against the walls. Books zoomed off the shelves and clattered into the center of the room, and Mia herself seemed to lift off the ground, defying gravity for just a moment, before she settled back onto her feet. She dropped into a stance from her Wushu training, prepared to fight.

Standing across from her were Luna, Vivi and Principal Elmhurst.

"I do apologize for startling you," Principal Elmhurst said primly. The barest trace of a smile crossed her lips. "I trust this sort of incident will not be happening again," she said, glancing at Vivi before facing Mia, who was still breathing heavily, her heart racing. "But if it does, I will be sure to knock."

Principal Elmhurst turned and left the room. Vivi followed, her face contorted in anger and frustration. Luna, on the other hand, stood there, her mouth agape, blinking every so often, until a giant grin broke out across her face.

"Crickets, that was awesome," she finally said.

"I was surprised. I had to defend myself," Mia muttered, dropping the fighting stance and sitting back down on the floor.

"Remind me never to fight you then," Luna said, sitting down cross-legged in front of her.

Mia stared at her quizzically for a moment. "I guess you need the room," Mia said, "I'll clean up in a minute and leave you to it, I just need a second to calm down."

"Oh, I don't need the room," Luna said.

"Then what?" Mia asked, trying to extract an answer out of Luna.

It took a moment for Luna to realize the words bouncing around in her head weren't coming out of her mouth, and she laughed. "Oh, sorry. I just…I don't see people around here who can defend themselves quite like that. What you just did was really cool."

"It was?" Mia's brows furrowed in confusion.

"Yes, very cool," Luna said, and Mia risked a smile. Luna didn't seem like the type to play practical jokes, and Mia was willing to open up a little around her. "Stuff like that, kids our age can't do. I know Principal Elmhurst was shocked, I could see it on her face. The levitating thing, that was sick."

Mia was grinning now. Getting compliments from Cassia was cool, but receiving them from her peers at the academy was something else entirely. Especially after so much failure at the simple stuff.

"So, do you want to practice sometime? I know a bunch of Krav Maga and Tai Kwon Do stuff I'd love to work on, and the stance you took, was it Wushu?" Excitement filled Luna's voice as she rattled on.

Mia nodded excitedly. "Yes, it was. I've trained for a long time."

"Then come on, we have a great gym that's outfitted with everything we could possibly need." Luna stood abruptly. She held out a hand for Mia, who took it, and they walked out together.

When they arrived at the gym, they wasted no time in getting right into the heart of self-defense practice. Considering this was all martial art and no magical abilities, Mia felt far more comfortable, and Luna was easy to have fun with. Playful katas turned into full-on attack scenarios, and they began to bond over their shared love of martial arts.

Several days later, Principal Elmhurst sat in her office, looking at the pictures of Zander, Vivi, Carson, and Luna spread out across her desk. She'd been sitting like that all morning, contemplating the group she'd created and all they had accomplished together.

But there was still a gap, still a place open in the collaboration.

Filling that place would bring their number from four to the elusive five, giving them the opportunity to accomplish even higher feats of skill and power.

They had the potential. She knew they did. These four young halflings were the most incredible she'd ever encountered. All the years she'd spent teaching and guiding halflings, she had never seen power and skills as exceptional as her Scooby gang possessed. They were phenomenal in their talent and could be even better. The Power of Five wasn't fantasy or an abstract concept. It was very real, and *this* could be the time it finally happened within her academy.

But choosing the fifth member of the group was a major decision. She couldn't take it lightly. Selecting the wrong fifth could hold back the other four and prevent them from ever accomplishing what they were truly capable of. The biggest problem was she would never really know. There would be no way to tell if they failed because they'd never had the ability to begin with, or if they were simply being dragged down by a member who didn't fit the position.

The search for the fifth member was exhausting. The team she sent out had scoured every academy, every training ground. They explored the chance it was a younger halfling, though the potential of that being true was next to nothing. They investigated older halflings with more training. But they hadn't found anyone who could begin to match what these four could do. None seemed right to her and she rejected them as soon as the team gave their suggestions.

But things might be different now. She reached in front of her to pick up the photograph set at the top of the desk. It was a shot taken on the grounds of the academy, with the student standing just beyond the hedge maze. Her long red hair glittered in the sunlight as Mia had glanced over her shoulder at someone or something not in the frame.

When she first appeared through the inexplicable portal just beyond the grounds, Principal Elmhurst never would have imagined Mia could be everything Cassia promised. The possibility of Mia taking the fifth spot hadn't crossed her mind. She was concerned the young woman wouldn't be able to keep up, but her opinion was different now.

After watching her train with the others and seeing how she handled Vivi, it was obvious that the legendary bounty hunter who had accompanied the halfling here hadn't been exaggerating her abilities. Mia was still new and required training, but the talent and ability built into her were astounding.

Principal Elmhurst set down the picture and called in her assistant, asking for the four as well as Mia to come to the office. Gathering the pictures, she stashed them away in a drawer so they wouldn't be seen, and then she waited. It only took a few minutes for them to trickle in, and as soon as she saw the five of them standing there together in front of her, she knew she was making the right decision. There was no way to really explain it —nothing that would make sense—but she felt it deep inside her.

There was no reason to skate around the issue or try to present it gently. She folded her hands on her desk and looked into the faces of each of the young fae in front of her.

"I have decided that Mia is the fifth member of your group," she announced.

Disappointment, frustration, hesitation, and anger flickered across the faces of the original four. Some emotions showed up in greater intensity on some faces more than others. While Luna stared back at her with more concern and hesitation, Vivi was visibly infuriated.

That was nothing Principal Elmhurst didn't expect. Vivi hadn't wanted to be a part of the group as it was. There wasn't anyone they could present as the fifth member who she would accept willingly and happily. This was something she simply had to deal with, regardless of her feelings. Which didn't mean Vivi was going down without a fight.

"First, we had to deal with her coming here and getting shoved into our academy. Then, we had to have her live next door to us and be a part of our training. We had to play with her and try to teach her baby skills. We might as well be helping with her teething, and now you want to force her into the fifth position of our group?" Vivi demanded.

"Yes, I do," Elmhurst said. "She is the right one for the position."

"I don't know," Mia started.

"See? She doesn't think she can do it, either," Carson said.

"I didn't say that," Mia argued.

"But it's true," Vivi said. "There's no way she can hold her own in this group. She's not going to be any sort of real contribution. We're supposed to be getting stronger and magnifying each other's skills. How are we supposed to do that with somebody who doesn't even know what they're doing?"

"I am worried her lack of training and relative disconnect from her abilities could drag us down," Zander said, trying to remain as dignified and diplomatic as possible.

"Well then, in that case, I suppose it is most fortunate that I am the one who makes the decisions around here and not you," Principal Elmhurst said. "The matter is settled. As of now, Mia is your fifth and will be a part of all your training and efforts. As for you, Luna and Vivi, tonight the two of you will move into the larger room down the hall from your current dorm room. With Mia."

Vivi couldn't believe this was happening. It was too much. Being forced to interact with the strange halfling was one thing, but now Elmhurst had dropped Mia in their laps and was making them babysit. Vivi had to work with her, live with her, and rely on her to help them achieve their aspirations.

Vivi wasn't going to take it easily.

As they moved rooms, Vivi figured she had one really good prank left up her sleeve. One that would make Mia so embarrassed that at the very least, she would always know her position in the pecking order of their group was at the bottom. She seethed at the idea that Mia seemed incapable of using her abilities except when it came to defending herself—and specifically against Vivi. It was so unfair that Mia was so terrible except when she was the subject of a prank, so Vivi had to get creative and think of a way to attack her where her defensive abilities wouldn't kick in.

It finally dawned on Vivi after the three girls finished their short move down the hall. The pranks so far had worked for the most part, Mia was simply more capable of fighting back when she became really angry or distressed. What if the prank itself didn't make her upset, but rather it was the humiliation brought on by things she couldn't change?

The idea began formulating in her mind later that night when she went to bed. The next day, while Luna and Mia were busy practicing, she prepared the room for her master plan.

The prank was pretty simple, really, but diabolical. First, she filled a large blanket with enchanted fake bugs. They were tiny little things, smaller than ants, and they were made mostly of liquid so they would squish when hit and would evaporate within a few hours. But they were great for playing jokes on people squeamish about bugs, and if you had a creative mind, like Vivi, they provided many other opportunities. Like covering them in itching powder.

She emptied several cans of itching powder into the blanket with the fake bugs, then enchanted them to wake up and begin crawling all over the first person they came into contact with when they were released. Then she enchanted the blanket to hang just under the ceiling of the room. Now all she had to do was wait for Mia to return, let the blanket drop, and wait for the bugs to fall on her. Then Vivi would trip the fire alarm so everyone would go outside, including a very itchy Mia. The effect would be gloriously funny, and Vivi had a camera ready to capture pictures of the experience.

When she heard the sounds of voices coming down the hall, Vivi stood on the far end of the room—away from the door and far away from the blanket—and waited. Soon, Mia stood outside the door talking to Luna, and Vivi waited anxiously for her to enter.

"I'm going to grab a quick bite to eat and I'll meet you in the library, okay?" Luna asked. Vivi hated that they had become so close. Rarely was there a day when the two of them didn't practice katas together and bore the group to tears with talk of Grandmaster Old Fart or Sensei Older Fart.

"Yeah, I'll meet you there in about ten," Mia said cheerfully and opened the door. Her eyes immediately went to Vivi in the corner of the room. It was like she knew something was up but didn't know what. "Hi—" she started to say.

Vivi began whispering the words to make the blanket drop from the ceiling onto Mia, but Luna burst in unexpectedly. This was even better than Vivi hoped. Luna had it coming, too.

"Hey, I just thought...wait, what the heck?" Luna exclaimed.

The blanket was falling, but Mia grabbed Luna and thrust her hand in the air. A wave of energy burst out of her hand and circled them in an umbrella-like shape. It was a shield, and it was blocking all of the fake bugs from landing on them. Even worse, they were bouncing off the shield and going everywhere.

Including onto Vivi.

Vivi screamed as the bugs swarmed around her, and she began shouting the spell that would de-animate them again, but in her panic and itchiness, she missed words. She kept trying to say it, but more would jump on her, and she would cry out and have to start over. Under the shield, Luna opened her eyes, and both she and Mia were cackling with laughter. The plan had backfired, and Vivi was receiving a taste of her own very itchy medicine.

Mia and Luna backed out of the room, collapsing against a wall in laughter, waiting until the chaos and mild cursing from inside their room stopped. Eventually, all was silent, and they snuck a peek inside. Vivi sat in the middle of the floor, wearing a tank top and gym shorts, covered from head to toe in some kind of cream. It was also in her hair, and while it seemed like it must have covered every inch of her, she was still scratching random places and unable to sit still.

"How did you do it?" she spat, her hands finding other spots where the itching was driving her insane.

"Do what?" Mia asked. She knew what she was being asked, but since she had absolutely no idea how she did it, and Vivi deserved every bit of this frustration, playing dumb only made it funnier.

"How can you be so terrible and do that?" she exclaimed, jumping to her feet and scratching at the thousands of bite marks on her legs. Vivi had used a cream she'd bought for the occasion, one that was supposed to counteract the itching immediately, but either it was a lie, or she had over powdered the little bugs, because she felt like she needed to tear her skin off to finally not itch anymore.

"How can you be so terrible to try to do this?" Mia asked. "You brought this on yourself, Vivi."

Hatred boiled in Vivi's heart. Sheer loathing colored her vision and made her shake with rage. She had to get out of the room, but leaving would expose her to the rest of the school in all her cream-covered glory. Exactly the humiliation she had planned for Mia.

"Who are you?" she finally spat, moving to within inches of Mia's face.

Mia smiled. "I'm your roommate. And you had better get used to it. No more pranks."

Vivi growled and brushed past her, grabbing a handful of clothes out of her drawer and heading as fast as she could to the shower.

CHAPTER TWENTY-FOUR

After the incident with the bug-filled enchanted blanket gone wrong, none of the newly minted group of five was particularly excited when Zander called for their first practice together. It wasn't something he was looking forward to either. But it had to be done.

Principal Elmhurst had made herself extremely clear when she'd established Mia as their fifth member. Nothing was going to change her mind or sway her into not forcing them to work with Mia. They'd already given up their entire summer, and now the weekends, fall break, and holidays all loomed large ahead of them. There was absolutely no question in any of their minds that their headmistress would take away the privilege of them leaving campus during any of those breaks if they hadn't accomplished the goals she had in mind for them.

That wasn't something Zander wanted to deal with. He was more than ready to take his leave of the academy for a while. As much as he enjoyed the challenge of trying to accomplish the Power of Five and honing his skills even further, the stress and tension were just too much for him. He needed to get away, which meant they had to make Principal Elmhurst happy, so she'd be satisfied with allowing them to be apart. If they could prove they'd managed to mesh well enough, she might relent on her never-ending quest to find ways to force them together.

Today was the beginning. It was their first opportunity to really work together in the context of being a unit. Though they had to help Mia at some point, or at least stand by while she attempted to learn skills, this was the first time they'd be actively participating in working with her.

Instead of merely trying to help her pick up on the most basic abilities—which even the youngest of the halflings knew—they'd be expected to combine their skills with hers and elevate them to a new plane of effectiveness.

It was daunting, to say the least. Today he'd decided against going to the field. Instead, he'd reserved one of the practice fields behind the academy. It reminded him of the earliest days with the four of them working together, when they'd barely been able to exist within the same space. In those days, they hadn't ventured far away from the academy and had preferred to do all of their practicing right there on the field. It was time to return there now, time to go back to the beginning and build again. There may be a point in the future when they would introduce Mia to the private haven they'd found at the other field, but not now. She hadn't earned her way up to that yet.

There was little joy and excitement among them as the five trickled out onto the field and gathered in a loose circle in the center. Carson and Vivi looked at the others accusingly, as if blaming Luna, Zander, and Mia for Elmhurst making the momentous decision. Luna and Zander studied Mia out of the corners of their eyes, questioning her presence there, and wondering just how much she was going to delay their success. Mia had no one to glare at. She was alone in her own seething about the situation—solitary in her discomfort and uncertainty.

The others were paired off. The two guys lived with each other and had a camaraderie, even if they did everything to try to both deny and push back against it. There were glimmers of a friendship forming between them, and it was obvious either one of them would choose the other over Mia. The girls were more challenging in their relationship, but even *they* had a history of knowing each other and having lived together before being thrust together with Mia.

But it was more than that. They had their Court loyalties as well. The two Seelie were bonded together by being Seelie, and the two Unseelie were bonded together for the same reason. Their Courts defined and identified them, and they were largely untrusting of the other.

Mia didn't even have that. She couldn't show any loyalty to her Court or connect with the others, because she didn't know to which Court she belonged. Despite all her investigation and exploring at the library, she hadn't found anything leading to who her mother might be.

If she could find just that one detail, she would be able to align herself with either the Seelie or the Unseelie. It didn't really matter to her which one it was. From everything she'd heard, there should be a part of her that hoped she'd find herself as a part of the Seelie fae. In truth, she would have accepted either, just to know where she belonged. It would give her an anchor here, a stronger link to prove this was what she was supposed to be doing.

Hopefully, that day would come soon.

"Let's go ahead and get started," Zander said.

"Hold on. Let me put up a protective barrier," said Carson.

"But we're right on campus. You've never put up a protective barrier when we are practicing in the fields on the school grounds," Luna said.

"Let's just call it extenuating circumstances," Carson said.

"Yeah, like he's worried Mia is going to screw something up, so he's trying to contain the damage," Vivi snapped.

Mia rolled her eyes. "When are you going to get over this?"

"What do you mean?" the Unseelie girl said angrily. "Get over what?"

"That I'm here. That I'm part of your group, and you have to work with me," said Mia.

"Why should we have to get over it?" Vivi asked. "We've been here. This has been our school for years. You just showed up, and all of a sudden, you're Principal Elmhurst's darling. You have her practically eating out of your hand, giving you all sorts of special accommodations and putting you in a group you have no business being a part of."

"What special accommodations is she giving me? If anything, I have to work ten times harder than anyone else and am expected to excel beyond everyone else just to prove I deserve to breathe the same air you do while I'm inside these gates. As for her putting me in this group, I had nothing to do with that. Trust me when I say that I don't want to be here one bit more than you want me here. I don't understand what this group even is or what we're supposed to be doing, or what the point of me being chosen for it is. All I know is my life got thrown up in the air and scattered around just a few days before I came here. I'm still trying to work my way through it, and the four of you acting like this isn't going to help me get there."

"You act like you're the only one who thinks you have had any challenges in your life," Carson said. "It doesn't make you special that you've been through hard times. It makes you just like any of us."

"I never said it made me special. And I'm sure the four of you have faced challenges in your lives. Everyone does. But try to think for a second what it's been like for me. Every one of you grew up knowing you were half-fae, didn't you? From the very beginning of your life, it was a part of you, something you used to identify yourself. You knew what life was going to hold for you and how that identity would impact your future. I don't have that. I grew up not knowing the fae world existed, much less that

I was a part of it. My life went from absolutely normal to something I didn't recognize in a matter of minutes. I'm having to figure out who I am and how my life turned out the way it did while playing catch up to people I'm constantly reminded are the most talented and skilled of their time. So, excuse me if I'm not thrilled about the truly underwhelming welcome wagon you rolled out for me. I'm not going to fall all over myself for you. I'll do my best, and I'll apply myself as much as I possibly can. But that's all I can do, and I'm not dealing with any more nonsense from any of you. I'm not a pushover, and I'm not going to take your crap."

"Crickets," Luna said.

Mia's eyes snapped to her and narrowed. "Is that supposed to be some sort of commentary on what I had to say and your reaction to it?"

Luna shook her head. "Actually, no. I was talking about the word. You should have said, 'I'm not going to take your crickets.' It's the word we use in place of any of those other words you could use. Fae hate the sound of crickets, so it makes sense. If you're going to be here and be one of us, you should at least know that."

The words could have come across as condescending, or even aggressive. Instead, Mia sensed a softness to them, as if Luna was breaking through her resistance for a moment to reach out to her.

The red-headed halfling offered a hint of a smile back. "I never understood why people always loved the sound of crickets and I detested it. I just thought I was strange," she said.

"Not strange. Just fae," Zander said. "Can we get started now?"

"Can I first ask what it is we are supposed to be doing? What is this elusive Power of Five?" Mia had heard the term a few times, but no one had ever explained it to her. She hadn't thought to look it up in her research because she was more focused on learning who her mother was, and what her own abilities were.

Zander nodded. "I guess that makes sense. It might help you if you understood it." He went into the explanation about how if they could merge their powers together, they could be unstoppable. They would achieve something even full-blooded fae rarely did.

With wide eyes and a headache from the absurdity of it all, Mia listened and absorbed the information. It did sound like something she should do. If she could manage this power with them, then no one would be able to tell her she didn't belong there. She was going to prove to herself and everyone else that she *did* belong at the academy.

Mia didn't know how much good the conversation had done, but it felt like they'd reached an understanding, or at least taken a few steps closer to each other. But it didn't mean it would last. She and Luna had started to cooperate while helping her hone her fighting skills, but Elmhurst establishing her as the fifth member of their group and forcing them to live together had driven a wedge in their relationship.

It was entirely possible that the moment they'd just experienced was fully isolated and wouldn't come back. She would just take it for what it was and keep focusing on herself and building her own skills. At least then, she'd be living up to what she'd promised Cassia.

Mia didn't know it, but Cassia was there at the school at that very moment. The bounty hunter had quickly resolved the assignment in San Diego but hadn't told Mia she was returning to the Academy. She didn't want to put too much pressure on the halfling or give her any expectations. Instead, she wanted to check in on her almost anonymously. By coming unannounced, she could see how the girl was fitting in with the others and if her skills and abilities were improving.

Cassia was standing out on one of the massive balconies surrounding the top of the academy and was staring out over the practice field to watch the group work together. It wasn't the first time she had been back. As far as Mia knew, Cassia had left her in the care of the academy, but the bounty hunter had actually returned a few times over the last weeks of the summer to check in.

Not wanting anyone to notice she was there, Cassia retreated back inside the academy. She headed down one of the corridors and entered the front of the library. The gargoyles glared down at her and she almost walked past.

But she hesitated, then turned to the statues. "You know Mia?" she asked Steve. "The new halfling with red hair and green eyes?"

"Of course, the one Principal Elmhurst has taken such a liking to," the gargoyle said.

"I wouldn't say she's taken a liking to her," Dan said from the other side of the library door. "She's only made her a part of the group because she sees something in her."

"Something she's trying to find out for herself," Steve said. "She sure comes to the library a lot."

"I need you to keep an eye on her," Cassia said. "Make sure she's doing what she needs to do and is safe."

"Why would we do that? We have so many other students to worry about, and we report to Principal Elmhurst and the staff, not a bounty hunter," Steve said in a growl.

"I've noticed her many times, and I'm curious about her. I can watch out for her for you," Dan said.

"Thank you. I appreciate it," said Cassia.

Cassia wasn't the only person secretly watching the interactions of the five young halflings. Principal Elmhurst stood at a vantage point only *she* could access and which provided a view of the field. Even if one of them turned and looked directly at her, they wouldn't be able to see her. Her magic was too strong for them, and at this distance, it would be too challenging to counteract a cloaking spell anyway.

Watching them from this distance meant they didn't realize they were under scrutiny. They were more authentic that way. Without them realizing she was observing them, she could truly watch how they interacted with one another and see if she'd made the right choice. There was really no going back on it now. She'd made the decision, and they were starting to work together. Either this succeeded or it didn't, and all she could do was wait and find out.

As of right now, it didn't seem to be working out quite as well as any of them hoped, but Principal Elmhurst wasn't going to lose faith so quickly. It took time for fae to learn to work together with others and combine their powers with one goal in mind. It would be harder for a halfling without much training and who didn't truly know how much she could do. That was proving true for Mia.

Principal Elmhurst watched as each of the four demonstrated how to conjure a cluster of flowers, then they stood together and created a Faerie Circle. She smiled, remembering how much difficulty they'd had with that very thing just a few weeks ago. Now it went smoothly, the circle appearing around them within moments of beginning to focus.

Not so much for Mia. When she joined the squad, nothing seemed to happen. They tried several times, only to drop hands and start shouting at each other for a few seconds before trying again. Elmhurst finally laughed and turned away, returning to her office to continue other work while the five figured each other and themselves out.

On the practice field, Zander was trying for at least the tenth time to explain to Mia how to conjure the flowers properly. Carson was busy watching girls who had shown up early for the semester jogging around the field. Luna looked exhausted. Any second, Vivi was going to explode.

"I think I have it this time," said Mia.

She concentrated hard and did exactly as he instructed. Finally, a few purple blooms dotted the grass at her feet. She gasped and glanced up at the handsome silver-haired boy who grinned back at her in approval.

"There you go. Good job," he said. "Are you ready to try the circle again?"

"Absolutely."

They spread out again and held hands. Mia concentrated as hard as she could, remembering what she'd done before to produce those few flowers. Eventually, a handful of purple pansies appeared around the group, gradually forming a circle. Then they began to generate faster and faster. None of the group knew what to do.

The flowers continued to grow and multiply and were eventually joined by a tangle of vines. The magic was moving too fast for them to react. Soon, the entire protective dome was filled with the flowers and vines, forcing the five halflings against the walls of the dome.

"Vivi, stop it," Luna commanded.

"I'm not doing this," Vivi snarled, wrestling herself out of the grasp of a vine before letting out a howl when another blast of purple pansies formed beside her face, crushing her cheek against the dome.

"Somebody do something. I can barely breathe," Zander said from somewhere in the thick overgrowth.

"Carson, get rid of the dome," said Vivi.

"I can't." Carson's words were muffled by a vine around his neck and by the flowers filling his mouth.

Luna forced away some of the flowers long enough to make the dome disappear. They all fell to the ground and the explosion of flowers and vines spread out across the field, multiplying every second. The few halflings standing on the field and on the track around it screamed when the pansies began to move toward them. They ran, trying to escape them as fast as they could before they got sucked in too.

Luna, Zander, Carson, and Vivi tried to stop them. They blasted out their individual powers, then combined their magic in an effort to stop the flowers from growing and to kill the ones already spreading. They did everything they could to control the magic, but nothing they tried worked. No matter how hard they tried to stop the flowers and vines from spreading, they kept failing.

CHAPTER TWENTY-FIVE

Principal Elmhurst walked away from her work and returned to watching the group of five just in time to see the massive explosion of purple pansies take over the protective dome and nearly suffocate all five of them. How long should she wait before stepping in?

In all honesty, it should have terrified her. It would've been upsetting for any of her students to be taken over by a sudden and seemingly invincible garden of pansies. But it was different with the Scooby gang. Not only was it frightening to watch them be overwhelmed, their apparent inability to fight back was a bit of a concern.

These were her four strongest and most impressive students, plus a wild card who had quickly proved herself to be powerful and strong in her own right. It made sense that they'd done something as ridiculous as create an overwhelming flower garden that threatened to kill them all. It was a little more disconcerting that they didn't seem to be able to figure out how to keep it at bay. Yet, she hadn't panicked. There would be time for that later if it became absolutely necessary.

For now, they'd already progressed by making the protective

dome disappear so they weren't all killed right there in the middle of the practice field. Being out in the open gave them more space and made more opportunity for them to defeat what they had created. She would give it a little time. They would probably figure something out. The Scooby gang was nothing if not resourceful, and she had faith in them. They would eventually figure out a way to get the flowers and vines back under control and stop that from happening again soon. She just wanted to see how long it would take for it to happen, and what they would do to make it work.

It was fascinating to watch.

Down on the practice field, Mia was overwhelmed and terrified by what was happening around her. *She* had made it happen, but she didn't know how or what to do to stop it. She watched in horror as more and more purple pansies grew thicker and thicker, vines snaking around, winding their way through the grass of the practice field. Some of the vines were as thick as her leg now, and the pansies had grown until the blooms were as big as dinner plates. It was a fantastic idea for a surrealist painting, but in actual practice, it was not nearly as whimsical and fun.

She stared around frantically to try to find the four others. When they were stuck inside the practice dome, there were a few moments when she'd been afraid the plants had already taken Zander. He was crushed at the bottom, his face flat on the ground and the flowers and vines growing over him as though they were trying to smash him into the soil so they could use him as plant food. This was all getting to be a little bit too *Little Shop of Horrors* for Mia, but she didn't know what to do to make it go away.

Not that it seemed to matter to Vivi. The small Unseelie halfling seemed to be taking this entire experience as a personal insult directly from Mia. She flailed and kicked at the flowers, occasionally sending out a blast of magic to try to make them wither away. All the while, she glared at Mia as though Mia had made this all happen specifically for the purpose of causing trouble for Vivi.

"Make it go away," Vivi shouted at last.

"I can't!" Mia yelled.

"You made it, you can make it stop," Zander said. "Just concentrate."

"Carson made the dome shield thing around us, and he couldn't make it go away," Mia tossed back.

"That's because I was too busy being choked to death by these ridiculous flowers you made," said Carson. "Now, make them stop before they completely take over the field and head for the academy building. I don't think you want to have to explain to the headmistress why her corridors are now one big giant greenhouse."

"At this point, I really wouldn't care," Mia said.

She stared around again, horrified by the sheer extent of what was happening. They were only flowers and vines. Just plants. Yet they were some of the scariest things she'd ever seen in her life. In a lot of ways, she would rather face off against another boggart then be standing there being swallowed alive by a glorified flower bed. She let out a scream, then whipped around to face the wider part of the field.

"Go away! All of you, go away!"

In the next instant, all the flowers and vines were gone. They vanished just as suddenly and unexpectedly as they had appeared. The field went back to nothing but an expanse of green grass. The track was visible again without any of the blooms or vines to cover it up. Everything had gone right back to the way it was, as if she had never conjured any of it.

Inside the academy building, pride surged through Cassia. She stood in the corridor in front of the library, leaning against the wall next to Steve, the gargoyle. On the wall in front of them was a small temporary portal. She hadn't created it for any trans-portation purpose. There was no place she intended to go, and

Principal Elmhurst wouldn't be happy with her if she found out that Cassia had created a portal out in the corridor this way, available for anyone to use or accidentally fall into. However, the portal was just for her to look through.

The enchantments on the school made it impossible for her to create a portal leading outside the building. But for some reason, she had zero problems creating her mini viewscreen.

Almost like a tiny television, the portal swirled in front of her with shades of blue and purple around the edges of an image showing the five halflings on the field. She had watched nervously as the flowers continued to grow and expand, threatening not only the five but also all the other students outside and the buildings themselves if they hadn't regained control. Cassia had witnessed things like this before. It was all too easy for young fae who weren't trained and weren't familiar with their own skills and abilities to suddenly have spurts of power. Of course, they weren't usually this powerful.

Most of the time, when a young person of Cassia's kind—especially a halfling—experienced a sudden burst in the intensity of their power, it was only mild. Sometimes it might cause a little damage or a minor injury. But Mia wasn't just any fae. She was most definitely not just any halfling. Her abilities were incredibly strong already, which meant when she experienced the sudden surge in her skill, it was tremendously powerful. It was also almost impossible to get back under control because she didn't know how to handle it.

Cassia didn't get a whole lot of time to sit around and watch TV, but this was the most entertaining show she'd seen in a long time. It was a thrill when Mia finally found her own voice and took hold of the skills and abilities born into her and commanded them to do as she wanted. She didn't know what she was doing, of course. It wasn't an intentional act or a sign of any new abilities. Instead, it was an act of fear, desperation, and anger. But that was enough. It was enough to show her she had it in her.

"There you go," she said. "That's my girl."

"You were right in asking us to keep an eye on her," Steve said. "She's definitely special."

He sounded afraid, but Cassia wasn't sure what was causing that fear. It might have been watching the explosion of flowers, but she suspected it was much more likely a fear of Mia. The extent of her potential was clear to those who knew what to recognize. This frightened Steve, but excited Dan.

"Keep watching out for her," Cassia said. "It's only going to be more important from now on."

The gargoyles agreed. They knew just how special Mia was. And now that she had seen her powers come to life, she would be more open to developing them further. This was a changing point and opening that would allow her to grow and strengthen at a much more accelerated pace. It would be a lot for everyone in the academy to handle, but they had no choice.

The dichotomy of emotions experienced by the gargoyles outside the library was reflected on the practice field below. The Scooby gang stared at Mia in wonder, a slight hint of fear and worry flickering through them. This confirmed that *she* was the one who had brought about not only the extreme growth of the flowers, but also their instantaneous and inexplicable disappearance.

None of them were capable of doing it. Each of them had tried, all of them had done everything they could to harness the magic and bring it back under control. But they had been unsuccessful. It had taken Mia, the strange and untrained girl who they still didn't trust, to end it.

Witnessing her magic had stunned them, and the enormity of it was not lost. It had to have taken a lot of power to create that circle then make it vanish so quickly. They had clearly underestimated Mia. They had discounted her without a second thought, ready to see her get shipped off to one of the basic schools at the end of the semester. Now that had changed, and they were forced to see her in a different light. Forced to reevaluate what she might be capable of and what that meant for them as a group.

But it wasn't all excitement. Inside the building, Principal Elmhurst watched in shock and concern. Not for the first time, she worried about who Mia might actually be and what would happen if anyone discovered her there. It made her worry about the safety of this unusual but astonishing halfling, and she began considering various ways to protect the girl. Elmhurst had to guard Mia, to keep her safe from the creatures and bounty hunters pursuing her.

The principal had already added a few protections around the grounds before she spoke with a few of her most trusted staff members, ensuring they kept an eagle eye on anyone new, or any possible threats to the school or students.

But beyond that, Principal Elmhurst had to continue to help Mia remain safe from herself. Which meant learning to harness and control her powers. She was obviously gifted, and that gift could offer a tremendous range of benefits. But it could also be extremely risky. She was naturally very dangerous, the most important thing was to help Mia finally get control. That way she wouldn't hurt herself or others with what she could do.

Deeper in the academy, Cassia said goodbye to the gargoyles and strode to the portal room again. The fae guards moved out of the way when she approached, but she barely registered them. Her mind was elsewhere. She was thinking about Mia and the extraordinary gift it was to have found her.

All the moving parts and tiny choices which had led to her being in that night market in Shanghai at exactly the right time. If anything had gone differently, even one small misdirection, she may never have been there, and Mia would have disappeared into the market, never to be discovered.

But that didn't happen. They had found each other as perhaps they were meant to. Cassia was able to put the young girl on this path and guide her into what she could become. It was a long shot. From the beginning, when she recognized that Mia was special, she'd had no real expectation.

That was completely different now. A voice from long ago echoed in her mind and a slight smile came to her lips. She approached one of the smooth walls of the octagonal room and conjured her portal.

As she walked through it, she whispered, "My father might have been right after all."

The story continues with The Forbidden Portal, *coming soon to your favorite digital book store!*

THE FORBIDDEN PORTAL

The story continues with book two, *The Forbidden Portal*, available now at Amazon and Kindle Unlimited.

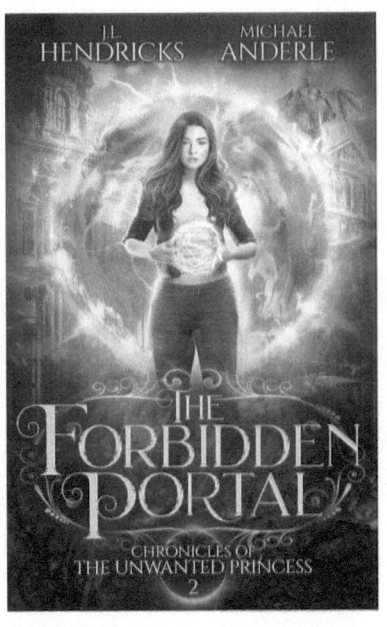

Get your copy today at Amazon or Kindle Unlimited.

WOW, first off, thank you so much for picking up this book and reading to the author's notes!

I am so excited that this series has finally launched! I approached Michael Anderle about doing this together back in October of 2018! He agreed right away, but it took me a little while to finish a project I had started and then once we began this one, it took longer to get right than I expected. The first book had three different iterations before we were finally happy. Then we sent it to the Beta Readers and had a lot of work to do. But I know it's a much richer story because of the fantastic people who volunteer to read LMBPN stories and offer their opinion on them.

So, I have to give a huge shout out to those on the LMBPN beta reading, editing, and JIT teams! And especially a huge thank you to Lynne and Kelly for managing the process on their ends.

But most importantly, I have to thank Mike. I wouldn't even be a writer if it weren't for him. Way back, during Christmas of 2015 I was out of work and wanted to read more before I went back to work in the corporate world. Turns out, I didn't have to thanks to a little-known indie author named Michael Anderle.

When I reached out to ask if he needed help with beta readers, something I had done before, he said yes. There were four of us who ended up being talked into writing books of our own and publishing. Three of us are still working in this industry today.

Along the way Michael has helped me to improve my skills at writing, and he's introduced me to other authors who've helped my career in ways I could have never done on my own. He's my mentor and friend. Now, after two shelved attempts at writing together, we are finally collaborators as well.

If you've read any of his books before, then you'll know this one was a little bit different from what he normally does. Did you notice there weren't any cusswords? That was something he and I discussed at length. And laugh over all the time. While I prefer making up my own expletives, like stink and crickets, he enjoys putting together long sentences that would make a sailor blush while laughing so hard they spit their beer out. LOL But he has no problems leaving them out of a book when a collaborator doesn't want them. Thank you, Mike!

I can't wait to see what we can come up with together next! I know it will be exciting and unique. Hopefully, it will also include a halfling, or a little faerie who sneezes magic.

All my best,

Jen

AUTHOR NOTES MICHAEL ANDERLE

MAY 13, 2020

THANK YOU for reading our story!

We have a few of these planned, but we don't know if we should continue writing and publishing without your input.

Options include leaving a review, reaching out on Facebook to let us know and smoke signals.

Frankly, smoke signals might get misconstrued as low hanging clouds so you might want to nix that idea...

Cursing

Jen and I met as she was reading the first set of stories I ever wrote called The Kurtherian Gambit where I would write these little notes to the fans I called Author Notes.

Now, doing author notes is a common practice.

In these author notes, or at the end of the book I would mention our Kurtherian Gambit Facebook page where the fans and I would socialize and chat. During one of these discussions I was answering questions about being a new Indie Author and what I liked about it.

Feeling I needed to get the conversation about writing off of a page about the stories, I created a Facebook group and named it

20Booksto50k® and she was one of the first fans to move to this page.

I continued to share my thoughts on this opportunity (writing) as a business on that page.

(Just a note we are about to celebrate the 40,000th member joining the 20Booksto50K® group. If you are considering taking up writing and working to sell your stories, come join us – it's free.)

It's about this time in talking with those first four that I learned Jen actually didn't find the main character's cursing to be nearly as hilarious as I did. While there is a group of readers who love literary fiction (and the turn of phrase associated with the prose) I'm not one of them.

Give me a good turn of phrase with cursing? I seem to admire it.

Having admitted all of that I will suggest that maybe I am not so quick to throw in cursing after writing so many books. Even the best turn of phrase can get old and stale after writing and editing it a few hundred times over the course of so many books released.

Jen's first story released as we all talked about being an author and it broke the top 10,000 on Amazon back in 2016. Her results with book 01 (along with the other three authors results) got the attention of many other struggling indie authors. She will forever be known as 'One of the Four'.

She did a …. *Great* Job!

(*No cursing...NO CURSING!*)

THE KURTHERIAN GAMBIT

On the Author side of things, I have great news for people who enjoy audiobooks. We signed a contract last week to publish the Kurtherian Gambit first twenty-one books and the four books from the *Dark Messiah* series with RB Media, a multi-cast audio publisher.

I remember driving back and forth to work, listening to a couple of my favorite stories on Audible with multi-cast narration. To this day, I still hear the sound effects in the ships when opening doors inside, or the blast of their engines as the spaceships rose out of the water, heading to the deep dark of space.

To know that my own *Kurtherian Gambit* series is heading for multi-cast is a really cool feeling.

I hope you have a fantastic week and weekend coming up!

Ad Aeternitatem,

Michael Anderle

Want more books by J.L. Hendricks?

Check out Miss Claus and Her Secret Santa for a fun and exciting new take on who Santa Claus really is! Did you know he was an Arctic Wolf shifter? You didn't? Then you gotta check out this completed series today!

Miss Claus and Her Secret Santa

ABOUT J.L. HENDRICKS

J.L. Hendricks is a USA Today Bestselling independent author who enjoys many genres, as evidenced by her catalogue of available books. She is currently focused on Clean & Wholesome Romance and Urban Fantasy, but has also written Space Opera, LitRPG, Paranormal, and Christmas books.

This past year has been spent researching the Clean & Wholesome genre for her new pen name, Jenna Hendricks. She also just finished writing an Academy Urban Fantasy series with a very exciting name in the Indie Publishing world.

One thing she learned early on is to accept help from others in the Indie world, and she is very grateful to those who have helped her along the way! The Indie publishing world is full of extremely nice and helpful authors, which is what makes this the best job she's ever had.

In early 2016 she decided to finally write, and finish a book, because of a few friends who encouraged her to do so. She hopes her stories entertain you and can bring a laugh on occasion.

Actually, it was her roommate's cat who talked her into staying at home to be her minion all day long! Pyper truly believes that J.L. is here to serve her alone.

Come and chat with J.L. on Facebook at:
https://www.facebook.com/JLHendricksAuthor/

And check out her Amazon author page at:
http://jlhendricksauthor.com/62fp

But don't forget her website and blog at:
https://jlhendricksauthor.com/

OTHER BOOKS BY J.L. HENDRICKS

New Orleans Magic

Book 0: Magic's Not Real
Book 1: New Orleans Magic
Book 2: Hurricane of Magic
Book 3: Council of Magic

Worlds Away Series

Book 0: Worlds Revealed (join my Newsletter to get this
exclusive freebie)
Book 1: Worlds Away
Book 2: Worlds Collide
Book 2.5: Worlds Explode
Book 3: Worlds Entwined

A Shifter Christmas Romance Series

Book 0: Santa Meets Mrs. Claus
Book 1: Miss Claus and the Secret Santa
Book 2: Miss Claus under the Mistletoe
Book 3: Miss Claus and the Christmas Wedding

Book 4: Miss Claus and Her Polar Opposite

The FBI Dragon Chronicles
Book 1: A Ritual of Fire
Book 2: A Ritual of Death
Book 3: A Ritual of Conquest

Chronicles Of The Unwanted Princess
(with Michael Anderle)
Book 1: The Portal of Chance
Book 2: The Forbidden Portal
Book 3: The Emerald Portal

See these titles and more at https://www.jlhendricksauthor.com/

CONNECT WITH THE AUTHORS

Connect with J.L. Hendricks

Facebook:
https://www.facebook.com/JLHendricksAuthor/

Amazon:
http://jlhendricksauthor.com/62fp

Website:
https://jlhendricksauthor.com/

Connect with Michael Anderle

Website: http://lmbpn.com

Email List: http://lmbpn.com/email/

Social Media:

https://www.facebook.com/LMBPNPublishing

https://twitter.com/lmbpn

https://www.instagram.com/lmbpn_publishing/

https://www.bookbub.com/authors/michael-anderle